Y0-DBU-827

Operation *Emigrant*

by

Niels Aage Skov

Copyright © 2009 Niels Aage Skov

ISBN 978-1-60910-003-2

All rights reserved. No part of this publication may be reproduced, stored in a retrieval system, or transmitted in any form or by any means, electronic, mechanical, recording or otherwise, without the prior written permission of the author.

Printed in the United States of America.

The characters and events in this book are fictitious. Any similarity to real persons, living or dead, is coincidental and not intended by the author.

BookLocker.com, Inc.
2009

I dedicate this book to Diane, my wife, muse, and superb critic, whose discerning eye and deft touch has enhanced the writing process and beneficially imprinted the narrative.

Table of Contents

To the Reader

As in my previous book, *Underground*, some small pieces of World War Two history are offered as accurate in the fictional narrative of *Operation Emigrant*; the dates and overall events, as reliable; the words and behavior of the actors as derived from accounts of participants in similar situations. I know, for I was there: one shadowy and anonymous resistance fighter.

The reliability of detail in the historical events—the bombing of Hamburg, the Peenemunde testing—will, it is hoped, be clear to the informed reader. The exploits of the main fictional characters—Lund, Lowell, Morian—were repeated many times over in the course of our resistance fight.

My purpose in both *Underground* and the present book is to bring the past to life in the perceptions and passions of a few people caught in peripheral eddies of the war's maelstrom. I feel this purpose is served best by fidelity to historical fact, letting the invented drama play against this backdrop. Readers of both books will recognize a few of the characters reappearing from previolus acquaintance.

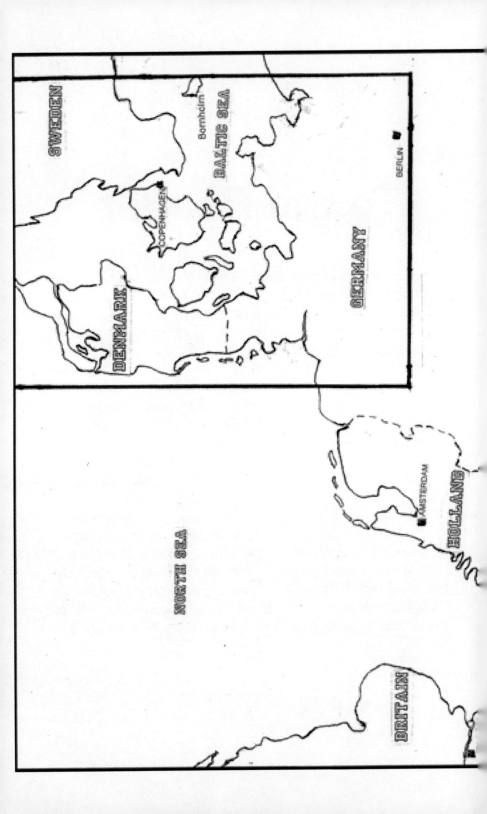

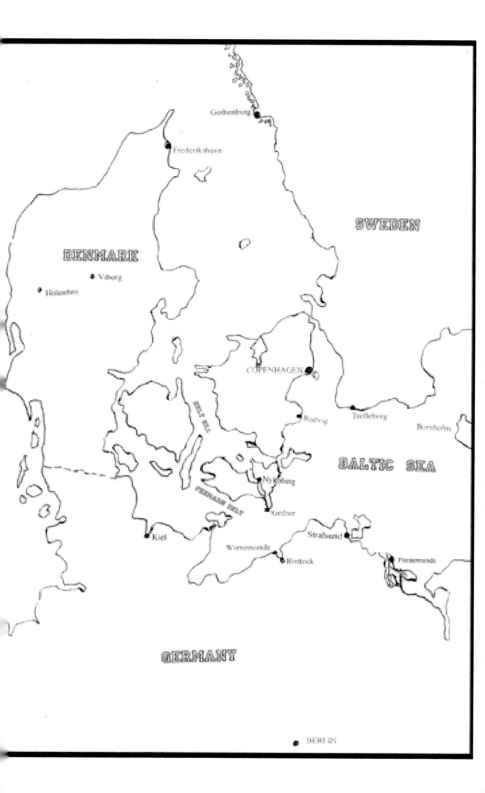

1

Lowell

Tom Lowell was hanging on to his bucket seat, when a sudden updraft made the plane jolt like a bucking horse. The Halifax bomber was not intended for transport of people, and the primitive seat installation had not included any provision to strap in the five passengers, who were all fighting the unpredictable motions of the low-level flight. Sergeant Nolan appeared from the cockpit and gave the heads-up signal with his flashlight: three minutes to go before they hit the silk. The five men left their seats, lined up at the Joe Hole and clipped their parachute chords onto the overhead slider. Nolan checked each of them to make sure; after all, they were not paras. Only Lowell had jumped for real, the others just a couple of times from the training tower. Lowell was last in line; the harness made him aware of the PPK under his left armpit, its presence as always reassuring. A gun could never be too close or too ready in the environment they were about to enter. Nolan slid open the Joe Hole, an opening in the floor where the lower gun turret had been removed, causing a blast of air to tear into the body of the plane. At the same time, the doors in the bomb bay started opening with a rumble audible even over the engine noise. Everybody stood transfixed watching the red light above the cargo door.

Lowell was one of a small group of Americans who had come to support Britain in the empire's life-and-death struggle with the Nazi monster. A native of Boston with an American father and a German mother, he had before the war undertaken graduate studies in history at the University of Gottingen, where he had painstakingly perfected the German his mother had taught him. While studying at Gottingen, he had fallen in love with a young Jewish woman, Rachel Cohn, whose father owned a small publishing house. When the Nazi government passed the "Nuremberg laws," a decree to deprive Germany's Jews of their property, Amos Cohn had been vociferous in criticizing the government. The result had been prosecution and conviction for anti-state activities, followed by immediate incarceration in the Dachau concentration camp. Cohn had been a widower, and with nobody else to take up his cause, Rachel had contacted several foreign newspaper correspondents and pleaded for exposure of her father's case. The further result had been the sudden disappearance of Rachel herself, and it had taken Lowell more than a month just to discover that she had been arrested and also sent to Dachau. Lowell's efforts to make contact or get information about her or her father had met with a wall of official silence, and an inquiry through the American embassy eventually brought only a curt message that Rachel had died "from illness." Lowell had returned to Boston, disconsolate and furious at the Nazi regime. He did not believe in presentiment, but his familiarity with German culture enabled him to predict the likely, almost inevitable, trajectory of Hitler's success in appealing to the nation's Teutonic instincts.

Four years later, at the outbreak of the war in Europe, Lowell was an assistant professor of history at Brown University, his anger against the Nazi state undimmed. When the opportunity arose in the fall of 1939, he interrupted his career without hesitation and joined the trickle of American volunteers taking flight training in Canada to qualify for the Royal Air Force. The following year the RAF took on Germany's air force, the Luftwaffe, in the Battle of Britain, and Lowell racked up a respectable record as a Hurricane pilot. He had three Messerschmitts to his credit by the time a bullet from a prospective number four plowed across his temple and reduced his left eye vision enough to disqualify him for further flight service.

When Lowell left America, his country had been at peace but with isolationists and interventionists in a screechy squabble. The Pearl Harbor attack had in one stroke united Americans in a bellicose patriotism driving for revenge, first of all against the Japanese. His RAF combat experience so far had given Lowell a different, more intimate take on the conflict. At the same time, his background in history allowed him to grasp the phenomenon in a far broader context. This was a war like none Thucydides could have imagined, a war so extensive as to ring the globe. Lowell's initial motivation to exact revenge for the crime against Rachel and her father had been gradually supplanted by the British attitude of quiet resignation to assume an unpalatable obligation that was compelled by civilization itself.

To continue, after his injury healed, what he viewed as an obligatory fight against the Nazis, he had turned to Britain's Special Operations Executive, a new branch established to nurture active resistance in countries under German occupation. On his first two assignments he had proven cool and effective under pressure; tonight's mission was an airdrop in Holland of five SOE instructors, of whom he was one, together with a cargo of

Sten guns, explosives, and triggering devices to the Dutch Underground. The drop was destined for a field in a farming area near the city of Meppel in northeastern Holland.

The ear-splitting rumble from the opening of the bomb bay ceased; the twelve containers loaded with material for the Underground dropped from their racks into the void, and the red light changed to green. As the first in line, Thomson dropped into the darkness, and the next in line followed. When Taylor, the man in front of Lowell, started to move, his foot got stuck behind one of the plane's structural ribs. Trying to pull loose, his foot slipped out of the shoe. With an oath he bent down, tore the shoe lose, and jumped into the darkness, shoe in hand. Without delay Lowell followed him. The infernal noise of the cargo hold was instantly replaced by near silence under the canopy of the parachute, as the drone of the four Rolls-Royce Merlin X engines drew distant. As he was swinging under the canopy of the 'chute, Lowell tried to discern ground features when his attention was diverted by the snarl of two different engines. He looked up as a Bf 110 night fighter flashed by, and he heard the tunk-tunk of its 20mm cannons as it bore down on the fleeing Halifax. He perceived a road below and hit the grassy shoulder, slid out of the parachute harness, and had his gun out and ready. Close on his right a voice excitedly called out, *"Hermann, hier ist ein Engländer!"* The exclamation clearly told that they were expected. They had landed in an ambush.

Lowell whirled and shot the dark figure who had spoken. He could make out a parked car in the darkness and ducked behind it, watching for the one called Hermann. Nearby he heard shots popping like firecrackers, and footsteps told him Hermann was running this way. Crouched behind the car, Lowell waited until the man was within six feet, then took him down with two shots, opened the car door, and found that the key was in the ignition. He started the engine, turned on the hooded lights, and drove slowly down the road, passed another car, probably Hermann's, and continued in low gear. Another parked car loomed up with someone standing next to it. Lowell stopped, rolled his window down, gave a low whistle, and said quietly in unaccented German, *"Hör 'mal zu,"* (Listen!). As the other fumbled to flick on a flashlight, Lowell shot him in the heart and drove on without hurrying, reached a main road and turned right, away from the landing area, and shifted into high gear.

He breathed deeply of the balmy night air streaming through the open car window. It carried scents of wet grass and flowers from the surrounding fields. He had been to Holland and knew it was beautiful. And it was good—actually wonderful—just to be alive.

Janiak

Konrad Janiak was standing far back in the queue of prisoners lining up for their one daily meal. It was being dispensed in the early afternoon from a large tub resting on the bed of an old Opel truck. Under the eyes of two SS guards, the group comprised almost a hundred concentration camp inmates, part of a larger consignment selected by the SS and contracted to work at the Peenemunde rocket test facility. Most of the inmates were fellow Poles of his, and today's work assignment involved cleaning up and removing debris after the last RAF raid.

Those who had received their soup were sitting on and around a large pile of concrete scraps, watched by two SS guards. Janiak was surveying the exact position of the truck as it was parked alongside the assembly building, trying to assess the chances of succeeding in his escape project. Sepp, the German prisoner who was ladling out the soup was near sixty, notably old in these surroundings and already worn down by the unremitting daily labor. To be sure, the German prisoners were favored by being assigned to kitchen duties, but even they were destined for short careers. The destiny of all concentration prisoners was death, inexpensively induced by the reliable means of starvation and overwork. The average life length on this project was just eight months. The Germans lasted a little longer than Poles or Frenchmen, but the eventual outcome was preordained. The high death rate necessitated regular infusions of manpower, but that was not a problem—there was plenty more to draw on.

It was not until he had become an inmate himself that Janiak had fully grasped the insidious idea behind the concentration camp system. Supplied by rebellious elements whose removal was desired by the Nazi government, the camps were a useful source of labor, organized and staffed by the SS, the elite guard Heinrich Himmler had built up to provide Adolf Hitler with the personal security every dictator needs to guarantee his survival. The black-uniformed corps, chosen from Germany's physically best specimens of young manhood, had quickly proven itself indispensable, and its area of responsibility had grown to include the concentration camps into which the Nazi state's opposition elements were being made to disappear without any telltale traces. Subminimal food rations combined with hard, brutally enforced physical labor would weaken and kill the inmates, in Janiak's estimate in an average of six to eight months. His decision to try to escape right away had been dictated by that compelling realization.

At long last Janiak was reaching the soup kettle, a 120-liter sheet metal tub from which Sepp was dipping out the soup, one ladleful for each prisoner as the receiver held out his bowl. With Sepp's metronomic precision Konrad got his soup and was nudged out of the way by the next man in line. He walked slowly along the side of the truck and stopped at the front bumper, looking around as if searching for a spot to sit down and eat. Pretending not to see any, he took the few steps to the building wall, away from the crowd, and sat down at the truck's front wheel, out of sight of the guards. If noticed, such irregular behavior might incur a good beating, but today that was a minor consideration. While quickly eating to still momentarily his ravenous hunger, he followed the events on the other side of the truck by listening to the sounds. Evidently neither of the guards had noticed Janiak's diversion, and Sepp was now resting his ladle. Janiak jammed his empty bowl under the left front tire, where it would be flattened into the ground when the truck started to move. Then he scooted sideways to the middle of the truck, detached from around his waist a sling made from a piece of electric wiring scavenged from another cleanup project, and slid under the truck. He knew this model, an old moving van, and deftly hooked the sling onto the frame, lifting his hips a few inches off the ground. Grasping the side channels of the frame, he could raise his upper body off the ground as well, a strenuous position but possible to hold for a short while. He had estimated he would be able to hang on for the trip ahead, but that remained yet to be seen. The alternative, to be dragged on the asphalt road, would quickly tear the thin prison uniform and then the flesh off his back.

Janiak let his upper body rest on the ground and breathed deeply, steeling himself for the coming effort. He could hear that Sepp was getting into the cab, and moments later Dieter, the driver, started the engine and shifted into gear. As the truck began to move, Janiak lifted his body just enough to clear the ground, and he heard the faint crunch as his bowl was obliterated. Rumbling away, he heard one of the guards shouting an order, and he saw the feet of the group moving, back to work.

After about a mile they stopped at the main gate in the perimeter fence, and he immediately let his body slump to the pavement, resting his arms. The truck would not return directly to the camp's kitchen, as it first had to pick up a load of potatoes and turnips in the village, a weekly routine on which his escape plan hinged. Here at the gate they were supposed to take on an SS guard for the trip outside. Some shouted conversation was causing a delay, which Janiak used to briefly close his eyes and rest. He knew this scheme was the sensible action to take, and to take now, before starvation could rob him of too much physical strength to carry it through. And then there was the information he had about Hitler's secret weapons program, critical data that must get into Allied hands fast, before the retaliation weapons could become operational.

The scraping sound of the main gate opening brought him back to the here and now. He could see black SS boots approaching and heard the truck's door open and close. The vehicle started with a jerk, as he hoisted himself off the ground once more. While they were gaining speed, he forced himself to think of the mission he was embarking on. Could it make a difference in the greater scheme of the war? Possibly, he decided. Ample foreknowledge of Hitler's plans might very well be of crucial value. A large pebble struck his neck when a pothole in the pavement made the vehicle bounce. He tried to hoist himself a little higher, but the muscles in his arms were numb and nearly out of strength.

The truck finally slowed, turned into a farmyard, came to a stop and backed up to a large barn door. Letting go his frantic grip on the frame channels, Janiak's body slumped to the barnyard dirt, and he felt the blood surging to his cramped muscles. He could see boots all around, some descending from the truck, others appearing from the house, and a brief babble of voices rose as the guard boots followed some work boots into the house. Now the prisoners opened the barn door and started shoveling potatoes into the truck from a pile on the barn floor.

So far, this was what he had expected to happen and what he had planned for. *From here on, I have to extemporize.* After a few minutes, the potato pile had been moved from barn floor to truck. Sepp brought a wheelbarrow from the barn, called to his partner to bring a hoe, and the two of them disappeared around the building, apparently going to the field for the turnips. So, the farmer saved himself work by using the prisoners to dig the turnips for him, while he placated the guard with ersatz coffee. Janiak waited until the sound of the wheelbarrow died away; then he slid out on the far side of the truck and silently moved farther into the barn, climbed a ladder to the loft and dug into a mound of fresh hay. Breathing the wholesome fragrance of the hay while relishing its softness, he closed his eyes and let his body relax completely.

He, Konrad Janiak, was actually free.

Esther and Ilse

It was late afternoon when Esther Lidman returned from downtown after this, her first shopping trip to buy food in Stralsund. Her shopping net held only some potatoes and a loaf of bread, as everything else had been sold out earlier in the day; her ration coupons were of no use, when the store shelves were bare, as was often the case when air raids disrupted the normal functioning of German society.

At twenty-two, Esther was an unusually attractive woman. Five foot five, with hazel eyes and dark hair, she was far from the Aryan female ideal the Nazis were always striving to promote, but regardless of their ideological convictions and preferences, men found it hard to take their eyes off her. The middle-aged butcher had sounded so genuinely sorry, when he told her that his cooler was empty, and he had hurried to assure her in a lowered voice that tomorrow he would reserve her a piece of *Speck* and some *Weisswurst*.

Esther was one of several new arrivals in town, people who had abandoned their homes in Hamburg during a weeklong, devastating British air raid. The city was still burning after the persistent onslaught of the bombers, while the exodus of refugees fleeing for their lives inundated surrounding towns and villages all the way to the Baltic coast. She had left her flaming apartment house and set out on her bicycle with only the clothes she was wearing; two days later she had reached her cousin, Ilse, in Stralsund.

The old harbor town of Stralsund had experienced its heyday when the Hanseatic League of merchants in the Middle Ages ruled both trade and politics within the cities of northern Germany and around the Baltic, the League's influence reaching as far as London in the west and the Norwegian town of Bergen in the north. By good luck, Stralsund held no military targets, and the war had left it unscathed, so far.

Esther and Ilse had known each other since childhood, having in common a partly Jewish ancestry. They were peripheral members of an extensive Jewish family, of which some had escaped their Nazi pursuers by fleeing to Britain, while others had been sent to forced resettlement in "the East." The latter were never heard from again.

Esther's deceased maternal grandfather, Oskar Meyer, had been an elder in Hamburg's large Jewish community and a prosperous merchant before the Nazi takeover. His wife Astrid was from a Holstein family of landed gentry by the name of Ruud. As a little girl Esther had spent summer vacations on their estate near Rendsburg, and she remembered the old couple with loving affection. Both of the grandparents had died shortly after Hitler came to power, and the synagogue with grandfather Oskar's personal records had been burned by Nazi hoodlums during the state-sanctioned *Kristallnacht* pogroms. It seemed to Esther like divine justice that the Nazis themselves had made it impossible for their own bureaucracy to establish her Jewish bloodline.

Ilse's paternal grandmother, also deceased, had been Oskar's half-sister, a thinner bloodline than Esther's but still a worrisome and potentially dangerous problem in the Third Reich, as the Nazis had christened their new Germany. Ilse was living alone, while her husband was working on a job assignment that had no provision for families. When Esther arrived they had decided as last survivors of the family to stay together for mutual support.

Esther carried her meager purchases up the stairs to Ilse's three-room apartment on the top floor. Her cousin greeted her and made a grimace when she saw the paltry result of the shopping trip.

"I'm not surprised," Ilse exclaimed, relieving Esther of the shopping net, "but fortunately I have a bit of bacon to go with the potatoes for dinner. Besides, Hans will be visiting next weekend, and he usually brings some potatoes. He knows a farmer on the Peenemunde peninsula."

Her husband, an aircraft engineer, was employed by the Fieseler Werken in Kassel but had been transferred to the Luftwaffe test grounds at Peenemunde. Ilse had moved to Stralsund to be nearer to him, and he was able to visit every other weekend. The city of Kassel had been a frequent target of Allied bombers, but the quiet old town of Stralsund was a delight, a haven of peace even under the trying circumstances of war, with air attacks raging all around. Older than Esther by six years, Ilse had been married for almost seven years to Hans Holzinger. They were childless, an unusual condition in this country where all potential parents were being exhorted to produce offspring who could strengthen the *Vaterland*, a fatherland which Hitler depicted as surrounded by hostile nations bent on its destruction.

While Ilse was preparing their dinner, Esther turned on the radio for the evening news. The announcer told about a daring action in Italy, where Colonel Otto Skorzeny, popularly known as "Hitler's Commando," and a handful of SS troops had contrived to snatch Mussolini from a mountain hotel high in the Abruzzi Apennines, where he had been confined after being caught by Allied forces. The commando group had taken *il Duce* to safety behind German lines in northern Italy, and the radio announcer went on to explain that this was another severe setback to the Americans, whose military incompetence was well known.

Esther turned off the radio and walked into the kitchen.

"When do you think we'll have a chance to meet some of these incompetent Americans?"

Ilse laughed. "It can't be too soon, as far as I'm concerned. When we do see them, this dreadful war will be over." Her face lost its mirth as she added, "I can't even imagine what must take place between now and then."

2

McKinnon and Hawes

Brigadier Ansley McKinnon was checking the schedule on his desk when WAAF Lieutenant Ann Curtis knocked on his office door and entered without waiting. She placed a mug of tea on the desk with a quiet "Good morning, sir. Minister Sandys called ten minutes ago. He'd like you to attend a meeting in his office at nine."

McKinnon nodded, eyeing the steaming hot tea. It was his favorite Bangalore variety, and Ann Curtis was well aware exactly how he liked it prepared.

"Thank you, Ann."

Ann Curtis turned and left. The office of Special Operations Executive in Baker Street was coming to life for another day of hectic, unpredictable activity. McKinnon's morning tea was the closest to what could be called routine in his busy day. Now, what could the minister want? He took the first sip of tea and looked out the window where a gray drizzle slightly veiled the London scene, making it appear inexact and fleeting. Handpicked two years ago by Hugh Dalton, Minister of Economic Warfare, McKinnon had left an established academic career as professor of Indo-European languages to head this newly created agency, the SOE. To his own unspoken but pleased surprise, he had shown a natural aptitude for the highly challenging work, which brought ever different problems, and his resourcefulness never failed. He possessed that intuition which is independent of skill or experience and in its essence borders on genius. McKinnon had been assigned the military rank of brigadier, a bureaucratic stratagem to give him some clout in discussions with military people. Of medium height with graying hair and a well-trimmed mustache, he was, at sixty-two, a bachelor, and in good physical shape. He walked with a springy step except when a piece of shrapnel in his left foot acted up, a memento of his service in Flanders in the Great War, now a quarter century in the past.

A knock on the door interrupted McKinnon's treasured tea time, as his aide, Major Jack Hawes, entered and placed a sheaf of papers on the desk before him.

"Good morning, sir. These decoded dispatches have just come in from Bletchley, but there is still no confirmation by radio on the drop in Holland. It appears that we must consider the drop in some manner compromised."

Hawes was a soft-spoken professional soldier, unmarried, a graduate of Sandhurst with an encyclopedic memory. He had been with Lord Gort's expeditionary force in France, when it made a fighting retreat to the beach at Dunkirk. On the beach, shrapnel from a Stuka bomb had removed Hawes' left arm at the elbow. No longer fit for field duty after his recovery, he had volunteered for SOE and had immediately proved well suited to meet the special needs of the new outfit under McKinnon's management.

"Indeed, Jack, we'll just have to be patient. There is nothing more we can do from here, although I do wish we could clarify the situation. It doesn't look good at all."

When Hawes had left, McKinnon leaned back in his chair and sipped his tea, looking through his calendar notes for the day and clearing from his mind any speculation about what might be Sandys' concern or what might delay the report from Holland. Speculation was a waste of time before all available information was at hand. And in SOE operations, "all available information" usually amounted to very little becoming very slowly available.

He filled and lit his pipe while letting his mind drift. A strange agency, this Special Operations Executive, in which the exigency of war had placed him. After the Germans had overrun Europe in the spring of 1940, Hitler and the rest of the world expected Britain to surrender, but Churchill refused to give up. Frustrated in his expectations of a British surrender, Hitler decided to conquer and vanquish the stubborn foe by invading England. To succeed, the invaders must have control of the air above southern England before embarking, and in early July the contest began, later referred to as the Battle of Britain. The German attempt to destroy the RAF fighters in the air failed, and the invasion threat faded. In the aftermath, Churchill and his staff took stock of the situation and calmly concluded that Britain, unaided, could never beat Germany. Simple demographics ruled it out: German manpower exceeded that of Britain by too large a margin.

Casting about for alternatives, Churchill and his staff came up with several ideas to undermine the brutal Nazi regime now ruling Europe. One of the ideas was to foment and kindle local resistance to the German oppressors by sending weapons, explosives and instructors to create Underground resistance, mostly by civilians, in the occupied countries. It was clearly a desperate move, a grasping at straws prompted by refusal to admit defeat in the struggle with the Nazi beast. The agency created to take on this task was named Special Operations Executive. It was now in McKinnon's charge, and in attempting to staff this martial oddity, he had started by specifying to his own satisfaction the ideal SOE volunteer. At the end of much effort and numerous changes, he had reduced his requirements to one-line specificity. The optimal SOE agent must be hard, isolate, and, should the need arise, a killer without hesitation or regret.

Although McKinnon had started with no illusions about being able to ferret out and enlist volunteers with this profile, he had in fact succeeded in a number of cases. Tom Lowell was one.

Theft

Lowell was crouching in the shrubbery a few feet from the fence with his attention riveted on the two-man patrol of Luftwaffe field gendarms approaching from the left, just inside the fence. He had the timing down now: twelve minutes between patrols, plenty of time for him to vault the fence and reach the aircraft parked on the grass by a low workshop building. He had checked during daylight and knew there was one Fieseler *Storch* sitting there between a couple of JU 52 transports. That plane was his aim; it constituted one precious chance to get himself out of this dilemma and back to England.

When the patrol's footsteps were no longer audible, he rose and walked over to the fence, a six-foot wire mesh crowned with two strands of barbed wire. He tested the wire; it was good and firm, easy to climb, no serious obstacle. He hoisted himself swiftly to the top of the mesh, and nimbly avoided the barbed wire when jumping down on the other side. He landed on all four in the grass, staying prone for a few seconds, listening. There was no sound in the darkness, only the whisper of wind, steady and still westerly, as when he had checked earlier. Then he got up and walked silently toward the place where he knew the planes were parked. Thank God for the deep darkness of August nights in these latitudes. Despite the darkness, the night was clear, just what he needed. The sea surface would be easy to see from the low altitude he was planning to use tonight.

Lowell almost walked into the corrugated aluminum side panel of a JU 52 before seeing it, groped his way around the tail end of the plane, and made out the dark silhouette of the smaller *Storch*. He ran his hands over the left side door, opened it quietly, and climbed into the pilot's seat. The smell inside was pleasantly familiar; this was certainly no Hurricane but it still smelled of airplane, and unmistakably so. Running his hands over everything within reach, he began a slow, methodical process of familiarizing himself with the controls: here was the fuel switch, the throttle, primer, flap handle, brakes. He had never been near any of the Fieselers before, but he knew their reputation for exceptional short-field performance. The stretchers in back told him that this one was the ambulance version; it would have a 270hp Argus V8 engine and a range of 240 miles, enough to get him to the English coast. He ran his fingers through the document pocket and felt what must be a record manual. He leaned back in the seat and closed his eyes. Time to think.

On the run and without safe contacts in the Netherlands, he was at maximum risk to be caught. He knew that would only be a matter of time, so he was in desperate need to find some way to return to England. The idea of stealing a German plane had come to him as he was dozing in a train station waiting room filled with refugees. At first dismissing the thought as harebrained, his mind kept returning to the idea. Slowly, he had warmed to the scheme and had cautiously surveyed

Schiphol, the main Amsterdam airport, which was serving the Luftwaffe as a forward fighter base. He had ignored an Me 109 squadron that was kept on standby alert—trying to abscond with an enemy fighter, now *that* would be harebrained—and any theft in daylight would certainly be impossible, but theft of a smaller craft under the cover of night, that just seemed doable, the more he thought about it.

Among the miscellaneous parked aircraft he had spied the Fieseler close by the workshops at the south end of the field.He opened his eyes and could dimly make out the two JU 52s flanking him, one on each side. The need now was to confirm visually what touching had told him. Partly screened by the transports, he would have to chance a quick look. Lowell checked his watch: the fence patrol would just have passed behind him. He dug a lighter from his pocket and clicked it on, screening the flame, as he confirmed what he had surmised: fuel valve, primer, throttle, flaps, the fuel gauge showing a full tank. He set the altimeter to minus three meters—situated below sea level, the Schiphol airfield was protected by dikes—and found the light switch to the instrument panel.

He snapped the lighter shut, got back on the ground, and stood motionless in the darkness. The silence told him that the brief flicker of light had not been noticed. He walked slowly around the transports to decide on a take-off path. A good thing the wind was too slight to matter. From the main hangar across the field a very thin light could just be made out where one of the tall hangar doors fit less than perfectly. A night shift must be at work there; with its German occupants the airfield was never without some activity. *I must aim to the right of that light to miss the hangar.* He knew the Messerschmitts were off to the left, about half a mile away, and glimpses of light could be perceived from the squadron's ready-shed.

Fixing the layout in his mind, he removed the Fieseler's wheel chocks and climbed back in the plane. While strapping himself in, he pondered what the reaction might be from the fence patrols. Well, he'd find out. He opened the throttle one quarter way, primed once, released the brakes and pushed the starter. There was an urr-urr, the prop moved just one turn and the engine belched once, then stopped. *A low battery!*

Lowell swore under his breath as he unbuckled, opened the door, and jumped out. There was no sign of the patrols, but from the workshop came the sound of a door opening and some fragments of conversation, ending with a voice saying in the Bavarian dialect, *"Karl, guck' mal nach."* Karl was being urged to check out something, no doubt the sound of his attempt to start the Argus engine. The workshop door closed, but a flashlight moved toward him, and he stepped behind the JU 52 on the left. The German swept the beam of his flashlight over the JU 52 on the right as he circled it, and the beam swept on to the Fieseler, when the man suddenly stumbled over one of the chocks Lowell had left in the grass. The German burst out with a guttural curse, getting up and shining the beam on the obstacle. Lowell removed a slim dagger with a four-inch, double edged blade from a sheath strapped to his left ankle and stepped up behind the German. In a swift motion he curled his right arm around the man's neck and with his left hand drove the dagger with an upward thrust into the man's heart. He felt a gush of blood on his hand as he withdrew the dagger and dropped the body. It was standard SOE procedure for a silent kill, effective but messy. Shooting was so much cleaner.

Wiping hand and dagger in the grass, he picked up the flash- light, turned it off, and replaced the dagger. The die was cast. He would try once again to start the Argus, this time propping it by hand. With swift and measured moves he climbed back in the plane, set the brakes, checked the switches, and thought for a moment. *Should I prime again? No, better not. If it floods, I'll never get it started.* He jumped to the ground, ran to the prop and swung it. The engine gulped but didn't fire. Once again. And again. On the fourth try, the engine sprang to life with a roar that sundered the night's quietude. Lowell dashed around the spinning propeller and the struts, jumped in, slammed the door, released the brakes, and felt the plane starting to move. The door to the workshop opened and provided a welcome beacon, with a German silhouetted and gesturing in Lowell's direction. He realized the man momentarily must be thinking that Karl was moving the plane. He taxied around the transport on his right, flipping on the panel lights and taking aim slightly to the right of the light leaking from the main hangar door. Then he firewalled the throttle, and the Fieseler with hardly any load lurched forward and was airborne almost instantly.

Watching the altimeter, he leveled out at 70 meters, throttled back to cruise speed, 90 mph, and turned to a course of 225 degrees. This altitude should keep him above obstacles, and the course would take him south of Haarlem. After four minutes he turned to 270 degrees, straight west. During the afternoon he had plotted and memorized his route on a map in a public library. Six minutes later, he passed over the coastline and descended to 20 meters, well below radar range. Now it would take a miracle for a night fighter to spot him.

As the darkness of night enveloped him, he felt exuberance at being airborne and in control again. The Fieseler was now on a course pointed toward Suffolk, somewhere near Lowestoft.

Wittmann

Luftwaffe Major Herbert Wittmann pondered the order just handed him by the subaltern from the code section. It was a terse reassignment to the Peenemunde test facility. Angrily, he flung the order on the desk. Why would the higher-up brass transfer him from his fighter group to something so dull, when his record with the fighter group, Kampfgeschwader 53, had been productive and very nearly flawless? At times military decisions made no sense at all. Well, you didn't argue or question an order signed by Goering's deputy. And it would afford a chance for a quick visit to his mother in Stralsund on the way. Reluctantly, he picked up the telephone and began making arrangements.

At thirty, Wittmann could by German standards be justly proud of his service record. Dispatched to Spain during the civil war, he had served in *Legion Condor*, Hitler's military contribution to General Franco's revolutionary forces. Flying early model Heinkel HE 111s, twin-engine bombers, his wing had taken part in the destruction of the Basque town of Guernica, trying out new, experimental bombing techniques against soft, undefended targets. The experiment had been a notable success that left sixty percent of the town in ruins. The resulting international uproar and condemnation had been a small price to pay for such valuable experience, which the Luftwaffe later put to good use in the London Blitz. Wittmann had never seen any reason to object to the Fuehrer's policies. War was not won by the softhearted.

Two days later, Wittmann got off the train in Stralsund. It was early afternoon when he left the railroad station and started walking toward the apartment house where his mother lived. The sun was pleasant, although it had lost the warmth of summer, and the coolness in the air augured an early fall this year. The street was empty except for a young woman just ahead of him who was carrying a bulging shopping net in one hand while clutching a paper bag to her chest with the other. As he was about to pass her, the paper bag broke and spilled its contents of potatoes on the sidewalk. As she put her net with the groceries on the sidewalk and bent down to gather up the potatoes, he noticed that she was attractive, in fact very attractive, so much so that he felt an instant surge of chivalrous helpfulness and kneeled beside her to help.

"If you will hold the net, Fraulein, I will put them in there for you" he said with a courteous bow. Esther looked up with a smile that made his heart skip a beat.

"That's kind of you. These are the summer crop, and I was lucky to get them."

As she bundled all her purchases into the net, he was studying her closely. She had not corrected him when he called her "Fraulein," so she might not be married. *Either way, this woman is worth going after.* He extemporized, casting about to prolong their meeting.

"Do you live close to here?" He asked casually.

"No, just across from the Altstadt."

"Really? That's where I am headed also. Allow me, then, to carry your net. It is now much too heavy for you."

"Oh, I can manage. It's only a few more steps."

He overrode her protest, gently took the net from her hand and started walking. She smiled again, as she went along, and his heart skipped another beat.

"This is no trouble at all." He'd better find out something about her. "Are you local or from out of town?"

"Refugee from Hamburg. The British have just about destroyed the city."

"Hmm...yes, I understand they did some damage. We'll have to beef up the air defenses."

"Do you think that will keep them away?" Although sounding innocent, she was asking a question that could well be interpreted as doubting the outcome of the war and Germany's superiority. She was on dangerous ground, but he laughed.

"I assure you, we have the situation well in hand. I know the Brits from personal experience."

She stopped at the entrance door, and he gave vent to some genuine surprise.

"This is where you live? This is also where I am going. Let me introduce myself: Major Herbert Wittmann. And you are?"

"Esther Lidman. So, Mrs. Wittmann on the second floor must be your mother?"

"Yes, and I am paying her a surprise visit on my way to Peenemunde."

"I'm sure she will be happy."

He insisted on carrying her bundle all the way to the top floor apartment, introduced himself to Ilse, clicking his heels with an ingratiating smile, and chatted for a few moments. When he had left and the door was closed, they both broke into subdued laughter like two schoolgirls.

"You made a fast friend," Ilse said, "I'll bet you that he'll be back before leaving for Peenemunde." She looked at the mound of groceries they were heaping on the kitchen table. "And I can see you have charmed the butcher as well. I haven't seen such Weisswurst for quite some time. It's a good thing men are such fools."

They both laughed again, as Ilse was putting the groceries away and began making preparations for dinner.

3

Escape

Janiak gave himself over to complete rest in the hayloft. He heard Sepp and Dieter return with a load of turnips in the wheelbarrow, unload, and repeat the task three more times. Then came the sound of the SS guard and the farmer emerging from the house, still chatting, and finally, after the barn door closed and the truck drove off, silence. He got up and made a cautious reconnaissance of the premises. The other end of the building held some empty stalls, separated from the storage part by a wall with two doors. A few small windows cast the interior of the building in a half-light, barely enough for someone to work but allowing a good view of the surrounding land. He saw that the turnip field bordered on the narrow strait between the mainland and Usedom, the island where the village of Peenemunde was located together with the test facility and a few scattered farms. The afternoon sunlight put a golden glow on the pastoral scene, turning it perfectly idyllic. Janiak knew that the test facility's attached concentration camp from which he had come was one of hundreds existing throughout Germany, furnishing slave labor—until the inmates died from hunger and overwork. It seemed as though the Nazis deliberately posed starvation, torture and death as adjacent counterpoints to picturesque villages and farmsteads. Take this beautiful island scene, a case in point. Strange people, these Germans.

The strait looked to be less than half a mile wide, an easy swim. Until dark it was time to rest and gather strength, but the hunger gnawing at his innards drove him to search the barn for something edible. He found a single potato the two prisoners had missed, but he recalled seeing a couple of chickens loose in the yard, and he knew they would sometimes lay their eggs in places other than the nests in their coop. A minute search rewarded him with two eggs. He ate the raw potato slowly, and the raw eggs followed. It was the first wholesome food he had consumed in six weeks, and it felt like his entire body reacted with approval. He climbed back to the loft, burrowed into the hay, and allowed himself to drift into a state of almost sleep.

When complete darkness had fallen over the countryside, Janiak left the barn and made his way to the beach. He rolled his shoes into his coat and tied the bundle around his neck with a shoelace. In the shallow strait the water was pleasantly warm, and he could not detect any current. Fortunately, the Baltic was an almost tideless sea. On the mainland shore he put his shoes and coat back on. Overhead, the sky was clear with thousands of stars, and when he found Orion in the northern realm he was able to orient himself, and he started walking, following the beach toward the northwest.

After an hour or so, a shack came into view beyond a pier to which two rowboats were moored. Evidently some of the local farm folks supplemented their food supply with fishing. A boat presented the possibility of a trackless escape, if he could find oars and oarlocks. The shack was closed and padlocked, but he got in by breaking a window. The place smelled of tar and fish and paint, and he hit his head on a lantern dangling from the ceiling. Further search led him to matches on a workbench, and when he struck one, the room was revealed in a flash:

fishnets, stakes, two pair of oars on one wall, a dirty coverall on a peg, cans of paint and kerosene, boards, tools...the match went out and he struck another. On the third match he saw the oarlocks. In the dark he pulled on the coveralls, hiding his wet prison uniform.

Ten minutes later he cast off and started rowing at an easy pace toward the northeast. Orion hung clear and reassuring in the northern sky, making for easy navigation. A gentle wind was blowing from the west, a good help to keep on course. He had a rough idea of the geography. This track should get him to Sweden, but he had no idea how far it was. He knew Sweden was neutral, which meant it beckoned with freedom, and he felt it was waiting for him. If he could only last that long.

Six hours later the dawn brightened like a pale pink wash on the eastern sky. The land had disappeared. The wind held steady, and he kept it on the right side of his face. A constant tug of self-preservation in the pit of his stomach kept him rowing without rest. The sea around him was blue on blue. The oarlocks gave off a squeak with each stroke. His motions had become mechanical as he rowed, and rowed...*strange how the voices could reach him across the silence of the sea so far from land...his mother was trying to tell him something about his hands dripping blood onto the floor boards of the boat....*

Throughout the turbulence of European history the Polish people have been located on soil forever coveted by two of the continent's most virile and aggressive people: to the west the Germanic tribes in the Teutonic heartland, to the east the Slavic hordes of nomadic Mongols inhabiting the Asian steppes. The Poles have for centuries been bred and raised while standing off these covetous conquerors from east and west. In more recent times, German kaisers and Russian czars have sent their armies with varying success to add to their realms the rich agricultural land and extensive beech forests of Poland. In the twentieth century Hitler and Stalin, equally rapacious dictators, have tried to succeed where their previous rulers failed in stamping out Polish identity. But over time the Poles developed enormous resilience and patience, coupled with an indomitable national spirit, that enabled them to prevail. As a result, Hitler and Stalin both hated the Poles and resolved simply to destroy in their different ways this stubbornly intrepid nation.

Janiak was born in Kraków, Poland's ancient royal capital and the fountainhead of Polish national identity. Kraków was the place where groups of school children would go on pilgrimages from other parts of the country to sense and imbibe the national spirit that has frustrated conquerors from the time of the Tartars. His father had been a prosperous merchant, an importer of select delicatessen foodstuffs from all parts of Europe and the Middle East until the arrival of German troops froze all such commerce. At twenty-two, Konrad Janiak had been close to graduating with a degree in chemistry when he was seized in a labor recruitment drive. It was one of those brutal affairs in which the SS closed off a randomly-chosen street section and screened out all able-bodied males, an operation akin to catching fish in a net with a mesh that yields the desired size of the catch. The captives were unceremoniously forced into a train of freight cars and taken to Germany, an ordeal without food or water that often substantially shrank the number of survivors, particularly when winter weather added yet more hardship. Janiak survived the transport and arrived in the city of Kassel, where he had been assigned to the Fieseler Werke. His chemistry background had taken him to the engineering department as assistant to one of the engineers, Hans Holzinger. Although the sixty-hour work week was excessive, Janiak's youth and energy had made the workload seem tolerable. Besides, Holzinger had turned out to be decent to work for. When the company transferred Holzinger to Peenemunde, Janiak had been transferred as well, and the full scope of their efforts had become clear to him, piece by piece. They were creating the V-2, a monster rocket intended to devastate London, a retaliation weapon dwarfing its forerunner, the two-ton V-1.

Must remember about the wind...it should be on my cheek, but which one...rowing is all that matters...I know I can't afford to stop...but now another voice is yelling...mustn't let that distract me from rowing...there is also the sound of the boat bumping...against something...must keep rowing....

Sweden

The Danish island of Zealand with Copenhagen is separated from Skåne, the southernmost Swedish province, by a strait called The Sound, which forms a liquid ribbon in the north-south direction. The two countries were not always divided along this line. In Viking times, a thousand years ago, Danish kings included all of southern Sweden in their domain; but since 1660 the Swedes have themselves ruled the area they possess today. It is the good fortune of the Swedes that their country—in pronounced contrast to Denmark—is blessed with the kind of borders that make for good neighborly relations. Toward the east and south the Baltic Sea, toward the west The Sound and the Kattegat draw natural maritime borders to the kingdom. In the northwest a long frontier with Norway follows mountain ridges that rule out borderland friction. The remaining piece enclosing the country is the border with Finland. That stretch is in the Lapland region, north of the Arctic Circle, an area coveted only by the nomadic Laps.

Being militarily lightly armed when Hitler in 1939 started his war with Poland and Britain, the Swedish government and industry circles chose a policy of accommodating German demands, which were numerous. The output of iron ore from Sweden's Gaellivare mines and the high-quality ball bearings produced at the SKF plants were urgently needed by German armament manufacturers, and as the war progressed, Sweden kept up a brisk pace of delivery while feverishly building up her own military establishment. For all the effort Sweden expended to please the Nazis, the German High Command in December of 1942 issued an order to draft an invasion plan to occupy the country. The operation was never implemented, as Hitler had his hands full fighting the Russians, and the Swedes had no inkling of the plan's existence until it came to light after the war.

Though yielding under German pressure to supply critical raw material to Hitler's war machine, the Swedes were helpful to Danes chafing under the yoke of German occupation forces. And when the SS attempted to arrest and murder Denmark's Jews, Sweden stepped in as a life saver and protector. In 1943 a Danish Underground resistance began to congeal against the German occupation forces, and Sweden became a refuge of last resort to Danish freedom fighters whose identities had been compromised. At the same time, Sweden yielded to

German pressure to produce and sell to Germany huge quantities of industrial products urgently needed to sustain the German war effort.

In 1943 an American aerial raid on Germany's ball bearing center at Schweinfurt sustained terrible losses: 60 Flying Fortresses were downed out of 220. Public opinion in the United States became enraged at the idea of Swedish supplies making up for German losses, which American fliers had given their lives to incur, and the American government aired the possibility of bombing the SKF ball bearing plants in Malmo. Under this pressure the Swedes at length agreed to cut their export by 60 percent, against economic compensation by the Allies. The Swedish actions were in part motivated by fear of Russia, her ancient enemy, and in part by influential circles friendly toward Germany.

Denmark

In the last centuries of the first millennium A.D. some notably virile tribal strains in Scandinavia spawned the Viking culture, a colorful phenomenon which, though short-lived, significantly shaped early European history. One Viking chieftain in the year 900 gathered the Kingdom of Denmark and ruled for sixty years as its first king, Gorm the Old. The Vikings were altogether a most interesting and accomplished lot. They were superb craftsmen and artists, creating gold jewelry of unsurpassed delicacy and beauty. Their society lived by a code of elaborate laws, which were restitutive toward victims of crime, a principle lost when Christianity replaced the Norse gods. For people who need supernatutal support, one god is as good as another, but the religious code brought by the followers of Christ dropped any concern for victims and chose instead to focus attention and energy on punishing sinners, often in gruesome ways. A regrettable retrogression.

The restitutive aspects of the Vikings' culture are largely forgotten today. Better remembered is their martial prowess that fired the eager crews of graceful longships spewing forth each spring from Scandinavian fjords and inlets, driven by population pressure and thirst for adventure, plunder, and women.

From Norway the longships steered west to invest Ireland and Iceland, plowing on to found outposts in Greenland, and eventually to reach all the way to North America. The Swedish Vikings went east and south, plying the rivers into the heartland of the Russ and founding cities such as Novgorod and Kiev along the way. Rowing their ships upriver, they at length found weirs with established portage and dragged the ships on rollers overland to relaunch in rivers running south toward the Black Sea. By this means they succeeded in reaching as far as Constantinople.

Vikings from Denmark struck west and south, conquering England and placing a Danish king on the English throne. In another thrust they wrested the dukedom of Normandy from the French king, Charles the Simple. Harrying farther south, they explored through the Bay of Biscay, around Gibraltar, through the Mediterranean and got all the way to Basrah, where the Tigris and Euphrates rivers have joined and issue into the Persian Gulf.

Whereas the Viking sentiment nicely combined acquisitive predilection with explorative curiosity, later generations oddly lost the natural drive to benefit from the experience of their elders. Clan societies are not empire builders. In Britain and in Normandy the Danish Viking roots faded into the mist of legend and saga, while only Danish sea power upheld a shred of former glory. And even that withered when Britain's Royal Navy and the Kaiser's High Seas Fleet swelled and joined battle for worldwide naval and military supremacy.

Denmark's regress from power and influence was gradual but irreversible. A succession of inept rulers with more ambition than ability contrived to squander the kingdom's wealth and—more importantly—large chunks of the kingdom itself, in some cases by unwise and unnecessary involvement in religious squabbles and wars. The provinces across The Sound were ceded to Sweden; the duchies Schleswig and Holstein were lost when the Danes failed to repel Bismarck's forces; and Norway gained independence.

Coming to terms with seeing one's influence wane and being in fact reduced to insignificance in the world at large is hard on a nation's self image. On balance, the Danes weathered the downgrade fairly well, opting to make a virtue of necessity by claiming that military endeavor really was beneath them, anyway. What to do when a Hitler or a Stalin or a Japanese military cabal rises to prominence somewhere in the world and poses a menace to other countries was left unanswered in the Danish formulation.

On the face of it, the German strategy in Hitler's war made sense: harness the conquered and occupied countries to work and produce what Germany needed to carry on and win the war, making up for the fact that the German population simply wasn't large enough to fulfill the Fuehrer's ambitions. At the beginning of the war, Germany had overrun Poland, Norway, Denmark,

Holland, Belgium and France. Organized and coordinated, these countries could provide sizeable work forces which were further expanded as the Wehrmacht swept huge areas of the Soviet Union to the German side of the equation.

The question now was, could German administrators convince the occupied countries to cooperate? This turned out to be a task for which Nazi ideology suited the administrators poorly, as it leaned almost exclusively on coercion rather than coaxing, and humans react positively only to the latter. The British had managed to rule India through minuscule echelons of well-trained administrators with a gentle touch, but under Hitler the German temperament proved unequal to such a challenge. Clumsy methods quickly raised local hackles, and thoughtful men and women began to refuse to aid the Nazi cause. Watching from the sidelines and savvy in matters of human relations, the British soon recognized the German shortcomings and missteps on the captive continent. Their reaction was to set up the Special Operations Executive to exploit this chink in the German armor.

The Danes were very slow to anger, but living under Nazi administration proved so galling that the ordeal slowly overcame their aversion to violence. Once the lines were drawn and firm, they began to rally to the Allied cause. Thousands of seamen in Danish ships, caught unexpectedly in foreign harbors by the outbreak of war, entered Allied service to supply transport for the armies gathering to retake Europe from the Nazi grip. A trickle of Danes volunteered for British military service to fight the German aggressors, some of them ending up serving in the Special Operations Executive.

Sandys

At one minute to nine McKinnon entered the office of Minister Duncan Sandys. Already present were Air Marshal Harris from Bomber Command with one of his aides, Captain Clarke, and Paul Cummings from SIS, the Secret Intelligence Service. Entering just behind McKinnon was Oliver Lansforth from Bletchley. Taking a seat, McKinnon looked around the circle trying to guess what topic would touch all of their sundry branches. *Probably some targeting information for Bomber Command.* When they were seated, Sandys cleared his throat.

"Good morning, Gentlemen. We are all short of time, so I will come straight to the point. In March last year we got the first confirmation that the Germans are at work on certain advanced weapons systems, and aerial reconnaissance showed a place called Peenemunde on the Baltic coast to be the testing ground. Bomber Command has initiated Operation *Crossbow*, so far with substantial damage to ground facilities and personnel losses at this test site. The actual production of whatever the other side is working on must be located elsewhere, but Cummings informs me that SIS so far has been unable to find out where."

Sandys stopped to let the information sink in. He was Churchill's son-in-law and had fought with the British Expeditionary Force in Norway. Wounded in action, he walked with a distinct limp. Sandys was no stranger to military service with its attendant dangers, but his exposure to military intelligence had been limited. Before he could continue, McKinnon spoke up.

"What was your first confirmation of the problem last year?"

Sandys hesitated just slightly. "Bletchley picked it up. Perhaps you would explain, Mr. Lansforth."

The representative from Britain's super-secret code-breaking agency looked uncomfortable.

"We, uh, were able to eavesdrop on an exchange between two Wehrmacht generals who alluded to some 'retaliation weapons.' Enough was said to point to aerial vehicles of some sort, maybe rockets, but we can't be sure. We simply don't have enough to go on."

Sandys nodded. "There was enough supplementary evidence to justify *Crossbow*, but Bomber Command wants to get to the actual production site."

At this, Harris nodded.

"Rail traffic photos indicate that the main source may be situated somewhere in the Harz Mountains."

There was a short pause before Sandys turned in his chair.

"This is where I thought of SOE. Your people, McKinnon, have just pulled off a fine piece of work in snatching that Dutch scientist before the Gestapo could do away with him. Do you think it possible to get us one of the people working at Peenemunde who would know where production is located?"

For an instant McKinnon looked incredulous before regaining his composure.

"Do you mean, we should kidnap a German and somehow spirit him out of Germany?"

In McKinnon's formulation the project sounded substantially different from Sandys' off-hand version.

"Well, yes, that was my thought. One of your teams did manage to get that Dutch scientist out from under the Gestapo's nose."

McKinnon thought for a moment.

"Isn't that rather more within the scope of SIS? I mean, if an SIS agent could convince a German to defect, the project would become far more manageable."

Sandys shook his head.

"Cummings tells me SIS has no assets that would be up to such a task at present."

McKinnon did not hesitate.

"We are talking about inserting a team on enemy territory to find at a heavily guarded secret test facility a person who is knowledgeable about their project, kidnap him, and transport him against his will out of his own country. Minister, I don't think either SIS or SOE will ever have any assets capable of such a feat."

Sandys frowned, and the atmosphere in the room seemed to get cool.

"Well, kindly think about my idea. Doesn't war at times compel us to tackle the impossible?"

The meeting broke up, and McKinnon started back toward his office. So, this was the reward for success: a request to arrange a suicidal mission. One lucky roll of the dice, and you were expected to perform the impossible! Under his unruffled exterior the SOE chief was reaching a slow boil by the time he sat down behind his desk and glowered angrily at the half-empty tea cup.

4

Huber

Heinz Huber, a clerk at the Stralsund Personalamt, the official registry of the city's residents, studied a list of the latest arrivals from Hamburg. The registry was one of several administrative agencies that enabled the state to keep tabs—close tabs—on every citizen in the Reich. At the age of fifty-nine, Huber was comfortably out of the draft range and could pursue his career in the bureaucracy, which he loved dearly. Backed by the unlimited power of the Nazi state, he was wielding a small fragment of that power, actually on behalf of the Fuehrer himself, as Huber saw it, and to what greater calling could a loyal German aspire? Contrary to the official expectations, Huber had never married, had instead devoted himself entirely to his career without the distractions of family obligations.

At the moment, his attention had been alerted by one name, Esther Lidman. He recalled seeing her when she registered yesterday, very attractive, but not the Aryan look desired in the new Germany. He remembered shipping one Lidman family off to resettlement a few months ago; there were some Jewish bloodlines among the Lidmans, enough to alert him to be ready to take action and perhaps to get rid of them. Himmler was certainly right, you had to stay ever vigilant to clear all the Jewish scum from the nation's bosom. And this one had taken up residence with a cousin, Ilse Holzinger. He had better look into her background as well. Huber dug into the files and extracted additional data. So, the husband was Hans Holzinger...aircraft engineer...had come from Kassel to work at Peenemunde...but the test facility could make no provision for families...so the wife had to live here...and she was a cousin to the Lidman woman. Yes, he would check on both of them. He dug into the files once more. Hmm...maiden name of Meyer...lots of Jews among the Meyers.

Huber nodded thoughtfully and polished his glasses while he pondered the situation. Could it be that the attractive Esther Lidman was nothing more than a stray Jewish sow? In fact, could there be two of them fouling the fatherland's Aryan body? They might well qualify for resettlement in the East. Nobody was sure

exactly where "the East" was, but the term carried an undertone of dread. He liked that. And he, Heinz Huber, would see to it that they were sent there, if at all possible. Better get both women in for some serious questioning. Separate interviews. He opened his desk drawer and took out two summonses.

Frandsen

The Baltic Sea was placid as late summer contended with early fall, unwilling to let warmth drain away entirely from the sheltered stretches of blue water. From the wheelhouse on *Rylen*, a twelve-meter fishing boat out of Rodvig on the Danish island of Zealand, the skipper, Egon Frandsen, looked toward the western horizon. Yes, he judged the weather was going to hold until they were home with their load of fish, a good one this time. The fish stocks were markedly improving, particularly herring and mackerel. It was all because of the large areas off the German coast that the Germans had closed to fishing in order to conceal their submarine exercises. Frandsen himself was never particular about respecting the closure lines. Those Nazi bastards were not going to deny *him* the fishing he had rightfully enjoyed for over two decades.

He had been introduced to fishing during the First World War, when as a boy he hired on as a helper during school vacations. When that war ended, he had found profitable work on the boats plying the North Sea, where stocks of herring and plaice had spiked during the war when mine fields had kept their breeding grounds off limits. To fishermen the post-war hiatus of huge catches on the North Sea grounds had lasted half a decade, enabling him to save enough to buy his first boat and return to his native town of Rodvig on Zealand's Baltic coast. The outdoor work and freedom of action inherent in the unpredictable, itinerant life of the sea-borne hunter magically suited Frandsen's temperament and aspirations. He was a man completely content in his chosen métier.

Now, what was that, far ahead and sligltly to port? Flotsam, maybe, though it looked more like a dinghy. His eyes became narrow slits in the weatherbeaten face, as he squinted, trying in vain to make out the details. He finally put his coffee cup in the holder to the right of the wheel, reached for his binoculars and focused on the object. Yes, it was a boat, all right, and somebody rowing, very slowly, and on a course toward Bornholm; but that was eighty or ninety miles away, for God's sake. Frandsen called down the companionway.

"Jens, come up here a minute."

A young man in a tattered sweater popped up from the cabin. Frandsen handed him the binoculars and pointed.

"What do you make of that?"

Jens took a long and careful look.

"I'd say somebody is trying to row to Bornholm, although that's going to take him quite a while."

Frandsen was shaking his head, while pointing *Rylen* toward the distant rower.

"We'd better find out what this is about."

They were almost upon him and Jens gave out a lusty hail but Janiak did not react. He had rowed without rest to put as much distance as possible between himself and the German coast. His hands were raw and bloody, and his arms and back ached unbearably. He had been hallucinating, sometimes hearing friendly voices, but at other times hearing the noise of SS guards in pursuit, while he continued mechanically, keeping the wind on his right cheek as the only means of staying on some semblance of a course. Jens finally caught the dinghy with a boat hook and hauled him alongside. Janiak stared, without seeing, into the friendly face of the grinning fisherman, realizing with relief that he was not a German. From the wheelhouse Frandsen called out.

"Get him aboard and below, and put a line on the dinghy."

Frandsen brought *Rylen* back on course, called Jens to take the wheel, and went below. Janiak was slumped on the starboard bunk with his eyes closed. When Frandsen shook him by the shoulder, he opened his eyes but had difficulty focusing. Then he summoned his strength and croaked in English, "Are you Swedish?"

Frandsen shook his head, "No, we're Danish."

Janiak stared at him dumbly and slumped sideways on the bunk. Frandsen went to a small cupboard and took out a bottle of aquavit. He poured some in a small tumbler, pulled Janiak back in upright position and held it under his nose.

"Drink this."

Janiak opened his mouth, swallowed the liquid and coughed. A fiery streak down his throat and into his stomach briefly cleared his mind. Frandsen recognized the effect and smiled.

"Now, tell me who you are and where you come from."

In a few halting sentences Janiak complied, while Frandsen observed him thoughtfully, the haggard look, the close-cropped hair with a bald strip shaved in the center to mark him as a prisoner. *So this is what a concentration camp does to people.* He turned to the companionway and called Jens. When the latter came bounding down, Frandsen had made up his mind.

"Give this man something to eat, if you can keep him awake long enough, and get those dirty rags off him. Just throw them overboard. Then bandage his hands and let him sleep. When he wakes up, we'll see if some of our clothes might fit him."

Back at the wheel, he pondered the situation. Taking Janiak back to Rodvig with them would only prolong his precarious situation. Denmark was occupied by the Germans, and keeping Janiak hidden would be a risky undertaking. The safest place for him would be Sweden, no doubt about that. Frandsen took a chart from the rack on the wheelhouse wall and studied it briefly. Then he laid a course for the town of Trelleborg on Sweden's south coast. It would take them out of their way, but not by much. He put his hands on the wheel, and turned *Rylen* two points to starboard, its bow now aiming at Trelleborg.

Report

McKinnon was still seething when he settled down in his own office after the meeting with Minister Sandys and the others. He took a tentative sip of the last of his tea, but it was cold. The pleasant ambiance of his morning ritual was gone. He picked up the phone and called Ann Curtis.

"Ann, I need another cup of tea."

"Yes, sir. And Major Hawes would like to speak with you."

McKinnon buzzed his aide on the intercom. "You wanted to talk with me, Jack?"

"Yes, sir. We just had a report from Coast Guard at Lowestoft. You will remember Alex Lowell, sir, he was in the group we dispatched to Holland four days ago. He landed in a field in Suffolk this morning at four o'clock in a stolen German plane. He is on his way here right now."

"Do bring him in as soon as he arrives. It's about time we find out what happened in Holland."

Five minutes later Ann placed a fresh mug of tea on McKinnon's desk.

"Here you are, sir, and Lt. Lowell just walked into Major Hawes' office."

"Thank you, Ann. Have them both come to my office, and you'd better bring some tea for them as well."

He tasted a tentative sip from the mug. Things were looking up, slightly. When the three of them were seated, McKinnon took a pack of Cremo tobacco from his desk drawer and started filling his pipe; while Ann was pouring the tea, he studied Lowell sharply. The American looked none the worse for wear, although it must be quite some time since he had slept. *Cool and durable, ideal SOE material.* Hawes offered Lowell a cigarette, Players Navy

Cut, and they all lit up. When Ann had left, McKinnon took a sip of tea and looked at Lowell.

"Well, Lowell, do fill us in on your adventure."

Lowell recounted the slight delay in exiting the plane when Taylor's shoe got caught, an event that most probably had saved his life by landing him slightly beyond the drop zone. He went on to recount his escape in one of the German cars after shooting his way clear. He had left the car, locked, outside a church in a small town, where he boarded an early morning train to Amsterdam. He mentioned conceiving the idea of stealing a plane, and finally described the events at Schiphol airfield. McKinnon listened in silence; Hawes was making notes on a clipboard strapped to the stump of his left arm. When Lowell had finished, McKinnon cleared his throat.

"The gun fire you heard from the drop zone, can you describe what it sounded like?"

"There were no automatic weapons. It sounded like pistols rather than rifle shots."

After a few more questions, McKinnon terminated the meeting.

"You have done exceptionally well under quite difficult circumstances, Lowell. I trust this mishap has not cooled your desire to work with SOE?"

A shadow of a smile came and went on Lowell's face.

"By no means, Brigadier."

"Very good, then. Go and get some sleep."

When he had left, McKinnon looked at Hawes.

"What do you think, Jack?"

"He is a good man. It sounds like the sort of ambush the SD would set up after having extracted prior information from one of the Dutch Underground people, probably under torture."

McKinnon concurred.

"And it is in essence what we were guessing when we received no confirmation." He was alluding to the fact that the SOE team had carried with them a portable radio transmitter to send a coded signal after arriving. When the signal failed to come, the mission had been assumed compromised. Lowell's report had confirmed that assumption.

"Alright, Jack," McKinnon tried to sound unperturbed at the loss of four valuable agents, "we will have to start over on the Dutch project."

"Yes, sir."

Hawes got up to leave, but McKinnon waved him to stay. Hawes sat down, and McKinnon blew a cloud of fragrant smoke before he spoke.

"Let me tell you what Minister Sandys would like to have us do." He outlined in a few words Sandys' suggested project. "What is your reaction, Jack?"

Hawes looked aghast as he spoke up.

"The logistics would be formidable, and I cannot imagine how a team would go about identifying a German with sufficient knowledge to be of value?" Momentarily he groped for words. "The project sounds, uh..."

McKinnon said dryly, "I believe the word you are searching for is 'suicidal.' Well, let us give it some thought. Perhaps we can come up with something."

Interrogation

Huber looked across his desk at Ilse, while trying to think how he might make her reveal some more about her background. He had started with the prescribed questions. *What was her place of birth, education, religious confession, places of work, when and where she met her husband, when and where were they married, why did she not have children, didn't she know the Fuehrer wanted all good Germans to have large families....*

Ilse held her anger, as Huber pried into her personal life; she just replied that there was no law demanding that families produce offspring like so many farm livestock. Oh, was she criticizing the Fuehrer's policies? Huber asked slyly, but she did not fall into that trap, merely replied that the Fuehrer no doubt had his reasons.

The questioning moved on to her siblings, only one brother and he was fighting in Russia, finally a satisfactory answer, then on to all the same questions about her parents, and their siblings, and then on to the grandparents, what could she tell about this grandmother, Elke Schulze...*Elke was a Jewish name, wasn't it...?*

In the end, nothing incriminating had been uncovered, although Huber did not concede such a conclusion, merely pointed out that the data on grandmother Elke Schulze and her half-brother, Oscar Meyer, were insufficient. He made it sound as though that in itself was ominous, possible evidence of skullduggery. Then he dismissed her and called in Esther, who had been waiting out of earshot. Going through the same routine, Huber's manner stiffened and he posed the questions with brusque impatience, having already made up his mind. At the end of their meeting, he looked at her with obvious distaste.

"Esther is a Jewish name, isn't it? We may have to resettle you in the East, unless you can come up with additional data to clear your grandfather, Oskar Meyer."

This was not entirely true; the normal practice called for evidence that Jewish blood could be convincingly shown to exist, but a great deal would always depend on the Sachbearbeiter, the particular bureaucrat handling the case. At length he dismissed her, and the two women left. On their way home, they compared their experiences and impressions and decided that Huber had been more aggressive toward Esther, enough so to cause worry.

Diplomats

Sir Victor Mallet, British envoy to Sweden, listened without comment to his secretary's report. Another volunteer wanting to join the British forces was nothing out of the ordinary these days, and God knows the Empire could use every man willing to serve. Moreover, this one might be of particular interest.

"Testing secret weapons at...where did you say?"

"Peenemunde, sir. It's on Germany's Baltic coast, east of Stralsund."

"Indeed, Miss Miller. And Stralsund is where King Karl XII boarded ship back to Sweden after riding there on horseback all the way from Constantinople."

Sir Victor was a history buff and didn't mind tossing off a few such comments.

"Yes, sir." Susan Miller was not up to verifying that bit of history, but there was no need to.

"Well, put him through the usual procedure, and notify Turnbull; he should be informed."

Sir Victor added the last comment without enthusiasm. He had provided office space for the SOE representative only reluctantly, and at the insistence of his superiors in His Majesty's diplomatic service. As far as Mallet was concerned, anything to do with clandestine operations was inimical to proper diplomacy.

In his office farther down the hall Lieutenant-Commander Ralph Turnbull was compiling a report to McKinnon on the budding resistance in Denmark under SOE tutelage, when the envoy's secretary told him about Janiak.

"A Polish chemist, escaped from a concentration camp, with information about secret weapons testing? Susan, be a sweetheart and bring him to me right now. I'll see to it that he gets through the routine."

Two minutes later Susan ushered Janiak into the office and left him with Turnbull. They shook hands, gently, as Janiak's hands were covered with bandages, while sizing each other up cautiously but with obvious interest. They were the same age, both liked what they saw, and in a matter of minutes Janiak was telling his story in halting English. Turnbull listened and did not interrupt, occasionally helping when the other was searching for words, and making notes as the story progressed. Janiak was a chemical engineer, had been caught on the street in Warsaw in a forced labor drive and put to work at Fieseler Werken in Kassel on the Fi 103, a flying bomb the Germans had designated V-1, powered by a pulse-jet engine. It was their first *Vergeltungswaffe*, a retaliation weapon intended to visit destruction upon Britain in payback for the RAF's bombing of German cities. Janiak was later transferred to the test ground at Peenemunde, where he worked with Holzinger, an aircraft engineer designing the fuel system for the V-2, a rocket-propelled bomb and a far greater threat. He had run afoul of his supervisor and had been summarily downgraded to inmate status in the concentration camp that supplied labor to the test facility. When he saw how starvation and overwork killed the inmates within a few months, he had concocted his plan to escape.

Janiak began to describe his escape, but Turnbull raised his hand to stop the flow of words.

"Wait. Let me get us some coffee. Here, have a cigarette, I'll be right back."

When they were comfortable with their coffee, Turnbull checked his notes.

"Before you tell me about your escape, let me ask a couple of questions. What was the nature of your work with this engineer, Holzinger?"

"He was worked on fuel system, they had problem with rocket blowing up when starting. Rocket fuel is ethanol and water to be mixed with liquid oxygen, hypergolic, you see, very easy to explode."

Turnbull looked baffled.

"No, I don't see. What do you mean by hypergolic?"

"When hypergolic, they ignite in contact. Rocket also holds hydrogen peroxide, mix with potassium permanganate to drive turbine pumps."

"I see." Actually, Turnbull didn't understand, although Janiak's halting English was clear enough, but no matter. In London they would interpret and understand his story. And what a story.

"Did you observe any explosions?"

"No, but Holzinger told me."

"You say the weapons were tested at Peenemunde. Where were they produced?"

"Some of parts for V-1 come from Kassel, Fieseler Werken is there. I don't know where V-2 parts come from."

While Janiak savored his cigarette and coffee, the latter with plenty of cream and sugar, Turnbull turned the information over in his mind. This was high priority; he would have to send it off right away.

"Alright, tell me about your escape."

Janiak put his cigarette down and took one last mouthful of coffee. Then he described the events leading up to his being picked up by the Danish fishermen, and Frandsen's decision to take him to Trelleborg. After entering Swedish territorial waters, they had encountered a patrol boat manned by Swedish naval personnel to whom the Danes had turned him over. The Swedes had been helpful, and kind as well; he showed Turnbull how his hands had been checked and bandaged by a Swedish doctor. The Swedes had asked many questions, but he had only told them about escaping from the concentration camp, not about the weapons testing at Peenemunde; that was information for the British, and he had insisted on getting to the British consulate to volunteer to fight on the side of the Allies.

After a few more questions, Turnbull handed Janiak over to his secretary.

"Alice, take this man through our volunteer process and make a reservation for him on the next plane."

He shook Janiak's hand, very gently.

"My secretary will take you through the formalities we require of all volunteers. I will see you again before you leave for England. And you were right not to mention this to anyone else. Say nothing to anybody else until you get to London."

When they had left, Turnbull sat down and began to compose his report, concise and in code. As he worked, he was smiling to himself. SIS and McKinnon at SOE would be interested, for sure.

5

Holzinger

Hans Holzinger checked the data for the third time. There was a bug of some kind somewhere in the fuel circuit, that much was certain. At yesterday's test the V-2 had blown up on the launch pad despite careful preparation. Dr. Braun had been furious and had excoriated the engineering staff. On paper the system looked good, but the ignition by hypergolic admixture was a touchy procedure, and furthermore in an area of technology where there was no prior experience to lean on by the Germans or anyone else. Casting about for a solution, he thought of discussing the problem with Albrecht at the home plant in Kassel. Albrecht was the chief V-2 designer and might see a way to get past this hurdle; at least, he was the most likely person.

Holzinger's real and more fundamental problem was that he would just as soon see the V-2 project fail. He felt certain that Germany was destined to lose the war, and a successful rocket weapon could only prolong the all-around misery; but the pressure was on, and he must give at least the appearance of making every effort. Besides, the Peenemunde engineering staff was under constant threat of being drafted to the Eastern Front unless they produced results, individually and collectively. He walked down the hall to the office of Heinrich Kessler, the chief of engineering at Peenemunde, and made his proposal. Kessler was at his wits end, willing to grasp at anything. He scowled at Holzinger.

"If you really think Albrecht can troubleshoot this one, get yourself on a train right away. You might also consult Lasser. After all, he's the one who hatched the idea of the V-2. I don't see how we can lose anything, but hurry!"

Holzinger laughed inwardly but kept a straight face.

"*Jawohl, Chef.* I'll hurry."

Late the next afternoon he got off the express train at the Kassel *Hauptbahnhof*, the main railroad station, which was operative again after being heavily damaged by another air raid. It would be too late by the time he could get to the plant, so he checked into a hotel across from the station. He spent an hour in his room going over his data on the latest problem, trying to anticipate what Albrecht would ask. Maybe the cooling of the wall of the ignition chamber was insufficient? Purely as a matter of guesswork they had settled on a three-millimeter diameter of the injection nozzles; maybe that was too large. There were all together too many possibilities. At length he put down his pencil; it was after six, better get something to eat.

Holzinger picked up *Kölnischer Zeitung* in the lobby and with the newspaper under his arm walked into the hotel restaurant. The place was only half full, and when he looked around for a table, he heard a familiar voice.

"Hans, over here!"

He turned and saw the speaker waving, Claus Henlein. They had been roommates as engineering students in Mittweida, but had lost contact in their subsequent careers. They shook hands with broad grins and during dinner caught up on events since then. Claus had served briefly in a panzer battalion on the initial drive toward Moscow but had returned to civilian life after losing his left leg, when his tank had come off second best in a skirmish with a Russian T-34. Holzinger had avoided military service so far, as his work carried a high priority classification. They ordered a bottle of Ruedesheimer with their meal, and as it emptied, their conversation turned to personal concerns. Henlein had been best man at the Holzinger wedding and was aware of the latent risk posed by Ilse's family background.

After the meal they ordered a Steinhager with their coffee, and under the influence of the liquor, Henlein was growing noticeably morose. He suddenly leaned over and became deadly serious, as he seized Holzinger's arm.

"Hans, I remember about Ilse's family background, and I tell you, you cannot be too careful!"

"I understand that only too well, Claus, believe me."

"No, Hans, you don't understand. Listen." Henlein squeezed Holzinger's arm and lowered his voice, looking around furtively before continuing.

"Two months ago my company sent me on an errand to clear up a technical problem with one of our products. It was a crematorium oven of a special design, and I traveled to Oswiezim in Poland. There is a concentration camp, a large one, and in German it is named Auschwitz. Going there became the worst experience of my life."

Henlein was pale and his voice was shaking, growing unsteady and faint in volume as he went on.

"While I was there, a train arrived from Berlin; the train track leads right into the camp. The passengers were all Jews, and they were being unloaded between two rows of SS with dogs, trained shepherds, and the people were ushered to a building to undress. They came out naked, men, women and children, and were hurried along to another building with a sign saying "Bathroom" where they were all crowded in together. The door was bolted, and from somewhere poison gas was inserted. There were muffled screams...."

Henlein's voice rose, and tears were streaming down his cheeks at the memory. In silent horror Holzinger looked at him while searching his pockets for a handkerchief and handing it to his friend.

"The SS were quite unconcerned that I was watching. I had no idea that our ovens were being used in this manner. My God, Hans, what are we doing? Have we gone completely mad? One of the little girls was holding her mother's hand, she was the age of my own Erika. What will the world think of Germany when this becomes known?"

The waitress had noticed Henlein's distress and came over to their table.

"Is there anything I can do?"

Holzinger shook his head.

"No, thank you. My friend has just received some bad news, but he'll be alright."

She left their table with a sympathetic smile. Bad news was not unusual.

Back in his room Holzinger reviewed in his mind the grisly revelations that had come into his possession during dinner. So, this was the truth about the "resettlement" of Jewish citizens taken east by the trainload to undisclosed destinations. An actual murder program on a scale to defy imagination. His mind reeled under the implications, present and future, that his country was calling down upon itself under the regime of the Nazis.

At length, Holzinger's thoughts turned to the problem at hand, dealing with the engineering difficulties of the V-2 rocket, soon to become Hitler's new super weapon. The information he had obtained during dinner cast the work at Peenemunde and his own role in an entirely different light. He brought out the plans and reviewed them methodically, making notes as he proceeded, in anticipation of the upcoming discussion.

Telegram

WAAF Lt. Ann Curtis placed the lengthy dispatch on McKinnon's desk.

"The Bletchley messenger just brought this, sir."

McKinnon scanned the message. As he was reading, Ann saw his attention level rising, and he leaned forward in his chair. At the end, he looked up at Ann.

"Would you ask Major Hawes to come."

He had just finished a second reading, when Hawes walked in, and he had regained his imperturbable normalcy. He handed the telegram to his aide.

"Say, Jack, take a look at this dispatch from Turnbull in Stockholm."

Hawes read the message carefully before commenting.

"Well, sir, perhaps we should be ready for this Janiak chap at the airport before SIS can muddy the waters."

"That was my thought too," McKinnon said leisurely, "because when Sandys hears about this, he will insist on implementing his idea of snatching a German. I would like to be prepared for that. Turnbull correctly addressed this report to SIS, but it is my guess that he will only notify us about Janiak's arrival time."

McKinnon's assumption was confirmed the next morning, when Ann brought a brief dispatch from Stockholm. She had read it and lingered until McKinnon had imbibed his first sip of tea.

"Oh, Ann, please be on hand at the airfield when the plane arrives in the afternoon, so you can pick up this Janiak chap and bring him here directly."

It was late afternoon, when Janiak retold his escape story to McKinnon and Hawes. This time, the ensuing questions from his listeners followed a different trajectory.

"Do you know where the parts for this V-2 rocket weapon are being manufactured?"

"No, I think maybe someplace in Harz area. Holzinger once asked about train from there had come in yet."

"Who would know?"

"Oh, engineers all know, of course."

"Who is this Holzinger?"

"Engineer I work with before I go to concentration camp. Good man. Tried to save me, but forced labor supervisor was angry, very bad, never listen."

"And you think Holzinger would know where the parts are being produced?"

"Oh, yes, yes."

"Hmm...Mr. Janiak, you say you wish to volunteer for our armed forces. Major Hawes and I serve in an outfit that is very much engaged in fighting the Germans. Do you think you might like to join and help us?"

"Oh, yes. Sure."

"Well, Mr. Janiak, I would like for you to go with Major Hawes. He will explain to you what we do, and he will handle the formalities, so that you can enlist with us."

When Hawes and Janiak had left, McKinnon picked up the telephone and called Sandys.

"Minister, I have been searching for a means to implement your proposal to obtain a German with knowledge about the secret weapons program they are pursuing at Peenemunde. I believe we have come up with something that might conceivably work...no, Minister, we don't have the details worked out yet, and I should like to say it will be a rather long shot...yes, Minister, as soon as we have details...yes, Minister, I thought you'd like to know...certainly, Minister."

McKinnon hung up and dialed Major Hawes.

"Jack, when you have signed Janiak up, please start composing a team to visit Peenemunde."

Sidetrack

Holzinger boarded the train for his return trip from Kassel and found a compartment with only two other passengers, a young nun who was sitting primly at the window watching the outside world go by, and an old farmer dozing in a corner. He settled with his briefcase in the corner across from the farmer. It was his intent to review and prepare a summary report of his discussion with Albrecht and his staff. They had made several suggestions that might well solve the problem with the explosions at the point of ignition. If they got past that difficulty, the V-2 should be ready for mass production and deployment. Would it be an effective weapon, perhaps even decisive in the war's outcome? He had never been enthusiastic about Hitler or the direction in which he had been taking Germany. What Henlein had revealed about Auschwitz was almost too horrible to contemplate. He knew that this was not what most German soldiers were fighting to achieve. He perused his notes and began to compose the report to Kessler. Interpretation of the notes and of his discussion with Albrecht and his staff at Fieseler Werken was a matter of personal judgment. It would direct the immediate steps to be taken, and he decided on a certain tenor in his intended report, an emphasis different from what he had first intended. Something that would take more time to pursue and might delay more promising steps.

He arrived back in Peenemunde late in the afternoon and went straight to the chief engineer's office with his high priority report. After a quick scan Kessler put the report down and sighed.

"So that's what they think back at headquarters. Well, it can't hurt to try what they suggest. Changing the nozzle sizes is a bit time consuming, but we'll try." He looked at Holzinger who was seated on the other side of his desk. "Is that your best judgment as well?"

Holzinger shrugged.

"I think the nozzles are one possible cause for the explosions, perhaps the most likely one, but the picture seems to me unclear."

Kessler agreed. "You are certainly right on that point. In any case, you have done a thorough job in Kassel. I wasn't keen on proceeding without drawing on their expertise. We can now pass the blame on to the home office, if the next test fizzles." Kessler had enough experience working under pressure to look out for himself and his staff.

Holzinger agreed, absentmindedly. He was looking forward to seeing Ilse the coming weekend. Their routine of a biweekly visit had been made possible by the comparative nearness of Stralsund. In the privacy of his room, however, he pondered whether to tell Ilse about Henlein's experience. The problem kept him awake for hours, and when sleep finally came, it brought harrowing dreams about women and children being herded by SS into gas chambers, Ilse among them calling to him for help. He woke exhausted and decided to keep the story from his wife. It could only cause worry to no constructive end.

Planning

It was half past eight in the morning when Major Hawes walked into McKinnon's office. As a good aide, Hawes was well aware that by this time, the director of SOE had enjoyed his tea in relative peace and would be ready to deal with the day's events.

"Good morning, sir. I have prepared a list of agents we might consider using for the Peenemunde excursion." He put a sheet of paper on McKinnon's desk.

"Thank you, Jack, and please sit down."

Hawes sat down across from McKinnon and extracted a cigarette from a pack of Players Navy Cut.

McKinnon glanced at the list, put it on the desk, and began to fill his pipe from a pack of fine-cut Cremo tobacco. For a few moments he sat, lost in thought, while the pleasant aroma of the fresh tobacco spread through the room. At length he fixed his gaze on Hawes and spoke.

"I agree with you that the team must comprise three agents, no more and no fewer. Janiak is an inescapable choice; Lowell and Lund are suited to this job, and they are two of a kind: fluent German speakers and proven resourceful. What I am pondering is the best method of insertion this time. What have you come up with, so far?"

"Well, sir, using a Lysander to drop them in Holland is risky at the moment." He was referring to SOE's frequent use of the Westland Lysander aircraft to land agents on fields prepared and secured by local resistance fighters. "But the long trip, presumably by train, from the landing point to Peenemunde would add substantial further risk." He stopped for a moment before continuing. "We have not so far tried aerial insertion or pickup in Germany itself, but in this case it just seems to offer the best alternative. The distance may be too great for the range of the Lysander, but I thought you might perhaps discuss the idea with Squadron Leader Wingate." Hawes was alluding to the commanding officer at Tempsford airfield, home to the Lysander aircraft of Number 138 Special Duty Squadron (SD), tasked with supporting SOE's clandestine operations with airlifts as needed.

Brigadier McKinnon stuffed one more wisp of Cremo into his pipe and proceeded to light it.

"Where do you propose they land, if we can get them that far?"

"I looked at some of the photographs RAF took of the area after the last raid on the Peenemunde installation, and there are some stretches of beach looking empty and remote from farms that might possibly serve. I am seeing Janiak this morning, and I will ask him about the surface condition of the beach where he set out in the rowboat. We could land them using a parachute drop and retrieve them by a pickup on the same beach."

"Hmm...without locals on the ground to provide at least a semblance of security and assistance, it seems like a very risky proposition, particularly when transporting someone of very high priority. But before I discuss it with Wingate, let me hear what you find out from Janiak. He might also come up with an idea about how to contact his engineering friend, once our team has landed."

"I have Janiak coming in for just that purpose at ten o'clock, sir."

McKinnon nodded. Hawes was always thinking ahead. The perfect aide.

"All right, Jack, let me know what you find out."

At ten o'clock Ann Curtis ushered Konrad Janiak into Hawes' office. A few days of rest and regular meals had removed some of the strain that had marked the face of the concentration camp escapee upon his arrival. Hawes observed him approvingly, as they shook hands.

"So, Janiak, how are you getting along with Sergeant McMillan?" Hawes was referring to the armorer at SOE's small shooting range, where Janiak was undergoing intensive weapons instruction and training in marksmanship.

"Oh, this morning I shot eighty-six percent, and Sergeant McMillan said it was far above average." Janiak spoke with the enthusiasm of a boy trying out his first toy gun.

"That's very good. We don't expect you'll need to resort to any shooting. In a pinch, there are other, uh...means...for our agents to use. You will shortly receive instruction about that as well." Hawes lit a Players before continuing leisurely, "Tell me what you know about the work schedule and habits of this Holzinger, the engineer you told us about."

Janiak described in considerable detail Holzinger's daily routines and work habits, while Hawes took notes and prodded with additional questions. Janiak's English was improving by leaps and bounds, and when he had finished, Hawes posed another question.

"Does he ever leave the enclosed area of the airfield and experimental installation?"

"Only when he visits with wife in Stralsund."

"Oh. And how often does that happen?"

"Every other weekend."

"And do you know, when was the last time he did so?"

"Let me see...today is Tuesday..." Janiak counted on his fingers, "he will visit her this next coming weekend."

"If we should wish to have one of our agents talk with him without arousing attention, would that be the best opportunity to do so?"

"It would be an only opportunity, I think. Nobody can enter enclosed...the enclosed area," he corrected himself, "without a special permit from the SS or from Luftwaffe office inside the enclosure."

Hawes asked a few more details before sending Janiak back to the shooting range. Then he jotted down an action schedule, picked up a map from his desk, and went to see McKinnon.

"I believe, sir, that we could land them close to the best point for making contact with the person we are after, and it even cuts some off the flight distance." Hawes summarized the information Janiak had provided and put the map before McKinnon. "This is the location, and it looks doable." He paused, letting his chief digest the information. Then he added, "But we'd have to move right away to catch this man, Holzinger, at the right time this coming weekend."

The two men discussed the plan further, probing the possible pitfalls and the chances of success before finally deciding to risk the lives of their agents in one of the gambles the war imposed on them.

6

Discovery

Huber took the telephone call and became instantly alert. It was from the registry in Rendsburg, and he recognized the voice of the woman clerk to whom he had made his inquiry the day before. Her message seized him with a rush of excitement, the kind a hunter feels when closing in on his prey.

"*Jah, Herr Huber,* you were quite right to be suspicious. Our records show that Astrid Meyer's maiden name was Ruud, a good Aryan name, to be sure, but her mother's maiden name was Cohn. I think this discovery will suffice to qualify your subject, Esther Lidman, for resettlement in the East."

Huber was elated at the news. This was what good public officials could and should accomplish, when they had their wits about them. He puffed out his chest just thinking about it. Of course, he had all along seen right through Esther Lidman's smoke screen, that was exactly what these filthy Jews produced to hide their tracks, but he was simply too astute to be taken in. He thanked the Rendsburg clerk profusely and hung up. What to do next? He could just notify the Stralsund police, and they could be trusted to handle it expeditiously, but first he would call her in again, have her sit down in that chair across from him, with her well-turned legs and pretty tits, and then he would tell her *his* decision, that she would be sent away, never to return. The Third Reich was not her fatherland, never had been, never could be; she was an alien element, a Jewish sow that would be removed—that *he* would remove—never to return. Would she squirm? He salivated at the thought. Maybe she would beg or try to bribe him. Or offer herself up for sex. He might consider just one encounter before shipping her off. He felt an erection coming on at the thought.

Huber opened his desk drawer and took out a summons.

Morian

The weather was overcast but dry at Tempsford airfield when Flight Lieutenant Henning Jensen brought the Lysander to a silky-smooth three-point touchdown, turned off from the runway at the midpoint intersection, and taxied to the main hangar. He shut down the engine and turned off switches and fuel, as Corporal Hannigan, his mechanic, materialized from the workshop and greeted him cheerfully.

"Hey, you got 'er back in one piece, no fuckup this time."

Hannigan was alluding to a near-accident the previous day, when the plane on landing after its test flight had suffered a frozen left wheel brake that nearly caused a ground loop.

The pilot grinned as he jumped from the boarding ladder to the ground, "Fuckin' straight! This baby's ready for service."

He handed the log book to the mechanic and started toward the base canteen, when Hannigan called after him, "And the squadron leader wants to see you."

Known around the base by the nickname of Morian, Jensen was a self-described Danish dirt-track bum with a richly obscene vocabulary. He had been competing in a major motorbike race at Whitworth in Lancashire, when the sudden outbreak of war in 1939 put such events on indefinite hold. Rather than returning to his native Denmark, Morian had volunteered to enlist in the RAF. At the age of thrity-three, he was judged far too old for the ranks of RAF pilots, where 22-year-olds were the preferred age group. He had instead trained as an air gunner and, in the rear turret of a Wellington bomber, scored his first kill on a German fighter. Morian survived his stint as air gunner despite the fact that the duration of tail gunner at the time averaged a mere three and a half sorties. With a devil-may-care approach to life and a natural affinity for engines, he managed eventually to transfer to pilot training and eventually racked up an impressive flying record, first during the Battle of Britain and later in Egypt. For a time he was assigned to testing and checking out reconditioned fighter planes, mostly Spitfires and Hurricanes patched up after aerial encounters with Luftwaffe opponents. His present assignment to the Number 138 Special Duty Squadron at Tempsford involved the dropping and retrieval of SOE agents in enemy territory, a type of service that took pride in making these harrowing and near-disastrous undertakings into daily routine.

Squadron Leader Dirk Wingate looked up from the pile of paper work on his desk as Morian entered his office and saluted.

"Sit down, Morian. We have received an interesting request from Baker Street. It involves a drop in an unusual location."

Wingate got up and turned to an RAF chart covering almost the entire wall behind his desk. The chart was in the scale of 1:500,000, standard RAF issue, and showed ground features in excellent detail. He ran his finger over a stretch of the Baltic coast.

"This is the drop zone, a strip of beach about a dozen miles from the city of Stralsund. Unfortunately, it is beyond the range even of our latest model Lysander. However, the SOE team being dispatched is only three people, and I thought you might do a partial refuel on the beach at the drop-off, if you brought along some jerrycans. Seven should get you back home. What do you think?"

With his eyes scanning the map Morian pondered the question at some length. Although he had justly earned a reputation as a daredevil, he had in reality managed to stay alive by careful planning coupled with consummate flying skill.

"That's a new wrinkle, sir, landing on Kraut soil, and I like it in principle. I believe it would also be a longer incursion than anyone has made before in a Lysander. But an enemy beach doesn't seem a healthy place for refueling. My passengers should get out of there without delay, and if I have to refuel myself from seven jerrycans, it'll take longer than I would like to stay around. I am thinking it would be preferable to do the refuel job in Denmark on the way back. Higgins has told me about a quiet little field on the west coast of Jutland where I might work undisturbed for long enough to take care of it. Besides, a dogleg across Denmark would be the best route."

Wingate nodded thoughtfully.

"True. And you would be keeping largely out of German air space, which should confuse the radars in their Himmelbett zones along the way about your destination. They will think it is one of our drops of explosives to the Underground. But if you don't refuel at the drop-off point, we could deposit the team much less conspicuously by parachute."

Morian shook his head.

"If we stake the retrieval on a beach pickup, I'd like to make sure beforehand about firmness and other beach features. A quick landing and drop-off will tell us all we need to know. Taking off alone will almost certainly be no problem; the plane will be so light that firmness hardly matters. But I'd sure like to know what to expect later, if I have to haul out of there fully loaded."

The two experienced pilots continued their planning a few more minutes, weighing and agreeing upon all pertinent details. At length Wingate terminated the meeting.

"Alright, Morian, make up a course plot both ways, and let's have a look at it first thing tomorrow morning."

"Yes, sir."

Morian saluted and left.

Lund

Svend Lund looked across the table as he raised his glass and looked into the gray-blue eyes of Elizabeth van Paassen.

"Cheers, lovely lady!"

Elizabeth lifted her glass but made an angry grimace.

"I still say McKinnon should have teamed us up again. He owes us that much."

Lund shook his head.

"McKinnon owes us nothing and you know that. He composes his teams without any thought to your and my preferences, as he should. Or rather, Major Hawes does, for it might very well be his choice in the first place."

Lund was secretly pleased that Elizabeth had not been included in the project SOE was wanting him to take on this time. During their first assignment together, she had performed brilliantly but had survived only by a hair's breadth, when he and another team member had pulled her, wounded and bleeding, from Gestapo's clutches. Elizabeth was the offspring of a Dutch planter and a British mother in South Africa. When her mother became a widow during the war, she had returned to Britain with Elizabeth to support the Empire in its struggle with Hitler's Germany. While her mother had picked up her former vocation of nursing, Elizabeth had volunteered to serve with SOE, where she met Svend Lund.

In the short time they had spent together on their first SOE assignment, he had fallen in love with this beautiful and courageous woman and did not want to see her risk her life again. She had arrived in London a virgin with only her mother's vague and incomplete instructions about sex, typical of the mixture of denial and ignorance conferred by the Victorian heritage. Lund, on the other hand dealt with the subject in the no-nonsense manner bequeathed by his Scandinavian upbringing. The upshot had been a hectic relationship after their return to London. Neither of them wanted to dwell on or even discuss the fact that under the pressure of wartime necessity and the service they had volunteered to perform, their relationship had to remain in the category of an "affair," however hectic. That they both fervently hoped to survive the war and afterward build their future together was a dream never articulated by either of them.

A graduate from Denmark's Polytechnic Institute, Lund had been among the very few who had prodded the placid and tolerant Danes to start an embryonic resistance against the occupation. He had received his own introduction to modern warfare fighting as a volunteer in Finland, when Stalin sent the Soviet army to crush that small country in the Winter War of 1939-40. It was an eye-opening experience, indeed a liberal education, to fight the Soviet troops with only the Suomi M31 machine pistol, a weapon of excellent precision and capacity, backed up by the traditional *Ahti*, a slightly curved dagger that for generations has served the Finns, both male and female, in self defense.

The ordeal in Finland had hardened him to expect and accept bloodshed at any time, when one operates in the murky realm of a so called "underground resistance movement." It had been an uphill effort to rouse his courteous countrymen against the Nazis, for the Danes looked upon war as uncivilized, an anachronism in the modern world. But with patience he had slowly recruited and trained a group of men his own age as saboteurs, disrupting export shipments of food and other products to the voracious German war machine and depriving the Nazi monster of some of the support it craved. The resistance in time began to approach a level at which the SOE could consider risking personnel and equipment to supply the saboteurs with explosives and weapons to magnify their capacity to fight the Germans. At this point his work had unexpectedly been cut short by one of those random incidents life brings when least expected. His identity had been compromised and he had chosen to leave his country and cast his lot with the British.

Even as Lund departed Denmark in a speedboat across The Sound to volunteer his services at the British consulate in Sweden, he had been waylaid by a German patrol boat. In the ensuing scrap he had succeeded in killing the crew and sinking the German boat. The feat had impressed the SOE agent in Stockholm and in turn McKinnon, who had recognized him as ideally suited to serve with SOE.

Elizabeth leaned across the edge of the table.

"Listen, Svend, I want you to promise not to engage in any more hare-brained schemes to rescue ladies in distress. You had unbelievable luck when you and Hansen did it for me, but don't try an encore."

Lund laughed, trying to turn their conversation to a lighter vein.

"I can predict with confidence that I'll never run into another lady remotely as attractive and deserving as you, so that's not a possibility. And as you know, the female sex is anyway rare in SOE ranks. For all I know, you may be the only one."

Elizabeth was still pouting but it was becoming difficult for her not to smile.

"All right, Svend Lund, but just remember that I want you back in one piece."

Engineering

To call it the engineering design office was actually a misnomer, Wittmann thought. "Redesign" would be a more appropriate label, for this was the fourth major change they were making to the propulsion system of that damn rocket. The talent tied up here could be more productively used to perfect the Luftwaffe's Düsenjäger, a new fighter, powered by jet propulsion. It was now rumored to be near the production stage at Heinkel, and it was believed actually to be a brain-child of Ernst Heinkel himself.

From the first day he arrived at Peenemunde, Wittmann had been bored. His assignment orders had been vaguely phrased, and Colonel Schwenke to whom he reported considered their presence here largely ceremonial, a reminder to the civilians that this was a Luftwaffe facility, despite the prominence of SS in the security aspect. The frantic activity at each prototype launch involved primarily the technical personnel, leaving him feeling like an outsider, which in fact he was.

He spied Holzinger at one of the drafting tables and strolled over to chat. He had been thinking about Esther ever since meeting her, and immediately after his arrival at the test facility he had made a point of searching out Holzinger, his best and most natural means of keeping or reestablishing his acquaintance with her. He had found out that Esther was single, and he had quizzed Holzinger with several questions about her. Still with Esther uppermost in his mind, he greeted the engineer jovially.

"*Wie geht's, Holzinger?*"

The engineer looked up from the drafting board and returned the greeting. Wittmann looked at the drawing.

"So, you are changing the fuel injection. Is that where the trouble lies?"

Holzinger nodded. "We cannot be sure, but it seems so. The mixing process is critical, and the cause of premature ignition may lie here. None of us actually has any experience with this hypergolic ignition."

Wittmann wondered vaguely what hypergolic meant but decided not to reveal his ignorance. He confined himself to a grunt and finally got to what was on his mind.

"So, you will be visiting in Stralsund this weekend?"

When Holzinger nodded, he continued, "I will be going there as well, a visit to my mother."

Holzinger was well aware that the other was angling for an opportunity to see Esther again, but he was totally preoccupied with the revelation about Auschwitz from his talk with Henlein. His discovery that "resettlement in the East" actually meant a sentence to death in a gas chamber had struck him like a thunderbolt. Any review of their personal information, any bit of stray gossip, could now present deadly danger to both Esther and Ilse. And Wittmann, this self-satisfied, swaggering minion of the Nazi state, would be the first to dispatch them to the death factory, should the truth become known. He kept his eyes on the drawing in front of him while nodding with feigned absentmindedness.

Wittmann finally gave up his attempts at chit-chat, seeing no way to pursue the topic further. Closing the one-way exchange with, "Well, maybe we will meet on the train," he turned and walked away.

Assignment

Major Hawes led Lund, Lowell and Janiak into McKinnon's office, where they all sat down in front of his desk. McKinnon looked around the little group, sensing the natural tension that always was present at the prospect of a field assignment. He started slowly to fill his pipe, and Hawes took the cue to offer cigarettes around. McKinnon knew that a person has difficulty concentrating when tense, whereas the mind is more retentive of information when the listener is moderately relaxed. After everyone had lit up, he remained silent for a few moments, enveloping himself in a pleasantly aromatic cloud of pipe smoke, before he began to speak.

"I have called you here to tell you that we have an urgent assignment for you. You have not worked together before, and it is essential that you become well acquainted before you embark on what will be a difficult and dangerous project. It will involve an incursion into Germany itself. I want you to think hard and fast whether you feel up to taking on an assignment of this kind. You would depart tomorrow, which means that your decision will have to be made today, now, during this meeting. Between now and your departure time, you need to discuss and take stock of your sundry skills, including your own assessment of your weak points, if any. You are all fluent German speakers; check out and compare your accents and decide in advance who should preferably be the one to talk, when the need arises. When you leave here, you will go to the shooting range and compare your proficiencies with the Walther pistol. From the range you will go to the gym where Dr. Markham will review methods other than shooting that may be preferable in dealing with opponents. Before leaving the gym, your appearance will be checked by Mrs. Hollingsworth, who will fit you as needed with clothes of authentically European, non-British origin." McKinnon leaned back in his chair and studied the three faces across the desk. "Do you have any questions so far?"

"When will you brief us on the details?" It was Svend Lund who wanted to know.

"The briefing will be here in my office tomorrow afternoon at 16:00. Any other questions?"

Lowell spoke up. "How long do you expect the project will take?"

"If all goes well, it will be a very quick operation. You will be gone for only a day and a half." McKinnon smiled when he saw the surprise in their faces. "Yes, as I said, the project is an unusual one." He looked at the half-circle across the desk. "If there are no other questions, are you all prepared to take on this assignment?"

Three affirmatives answered his question.

"Well, then, please report to McMillan at the shooting range. After your practice at the range and your instruction at the gym, please return here, and Major Hawes will have further instructions for you."

When they had left, Hawes finished jotting some notes on the pad strapped to the stump of his left arm and then got up to leave, but McKinnon motioned him to stay.

"What do you think, Jack? We have never had to dispatch a team in such a hurry before. Are these three agents mutually compatible enough and sufficiently complementary to pull off a project this difficult?"

McKinnon was voicing a concern endemic at the planning of every SOE operation. How well did the skills and attributes of the team members fit together? And were they sufficient to allow a reasonable expectation of success?

"Well, sir, Lund and Lowell are as good as any agent we have fielded. Young as he is, Janiak has already proven himself resourceful under pressure. I don't think the team could be any better. But in fairness, we are attempting something well beyond what any of our operatives has been dispatched to accomplish so far."

McKinnon emptied his pipe into a large ashtray on his desk.

"That's my feeling too. I hope we are not over-reaching, but we are committed now, and we will proceed. Let us use the code name *Emigrant*." The assignment of code names to SOE projects was standard procedure.

As their project was being christened, the trio was walking toward the shooting range, each man assuming an air of unconcern while pondering the unknowns ahead. Located in the basement of an old warehouse at the river, the range was managed by Sergeant McMillan, a canny Highlander and a very experienced instructor, who greeted them with as much enthusiasm as his dour disposition would permit him to display. McMillan was aware of the competitive inclination of his wards, and as there were no others at the range, he put them through a routine of his own design, subtly calculated to appear like a simple competition.

The first segment tested each man's marksmanship with the Walther PPK under unhurried conditions. Next came a series of eight shots fired within twelve seconds, with a point bonus for every second under the allotted twelve. Although his hands were still somewhat immobilized by being patched up with adhesive tape, Janiak demonstrated an unusually steady hand on the first test. In the second series where time was critical, Lund and Lowell were neck and neck, well ahead of him. As McMillan had foreseen, each man felt reassured by the impressive skill levels of his companions.

They left the practice range with the comforting knowledge that, should shooting become necessary, they could count on coming out ahead. Twenty minutes later they arrived at the gym, where David Markham, a middle-aged physician, was expecting them.

7

Summons

Esther and Ilse had been disappointed, when the day dawned with gray skies and showers, but by midmorning the weather had cleared for the two eager shoppers. It was almost noon when they returned from their excursion, loaded with hard-to-get groceries. As they climbed the stairs to the apartment, Ilse was recalling between fits of laughter how several stiff and churlish merchants had melted and turned compliant when Esther approached them with a few honeyed words of flattery.

"I can't believe how that obnoxious butcher was ready to trade his last piece of sausage for one of your smiles. What fools men will make of themselves at the sight of an attractive woman!"

Esther laughed merrily. "Oh, he is not so bad, really. Have you ever seen his wife? I have, and she is a fearful dragon. You can be sure his home life is no bed of roses."

As they entered the apartment, Ilse picked up an official- looking envelope below the letter slot in the front door.

"This is for you, from the Personalamt."

Esther tore the envelope open and glanced at the content. "It's another summons. I wonder what they want this time."

Ilse reached for the letter, and when she read it, her face abruptly lost its lighthearted expression. She sat down at the kitchen table and studied the form closely before looking at her cousin.

"This is from that snake, Huber. Apparently he is still on your case, and I don't like it at all. If that man can cause us trouble, he will. I'm sure of it."

"But what can he do?" Esther took the matter more lightly.

"I don't know, but it's always possible that he might find some scrap of information about our background that could be made to look incriminating, and I just feel he would lean over backward to give us trouble. You have to see him tomorrow morning, so we will know more about this before Hans comes. I would like to discuss our meetings at the Personalamt with him."

The two women reviewed once again what had transpired during their previous interviews. They tried to divine what Huber might have been looking into, but they could find no clue to justify another interview. They both realized that they were groping and at the mercy of the all-pervasive bureaucracy of the totalitarian state in which privacy and individual rights had years ago been snuffed out by the Nazis. Moreover, Huber could call them back for further questioning as much as he wanted. Recourse to higher authority, an actual complaint about bureaucratic misbehavior, was out of the question.

Markham

David Markham thoughtfully studied the faces of the three young men of the *Emigrant* team who were sitting crosslegged on a coir mat on the gym floor. Markham had known McKinnon since they had served together in Flanders during the Great War, and their friendship had developed into a lasting bond in the interwar years. While McKinnon had taken up language studies and an academic career, Markham had turned to medicine and had established himself as a highly respected London surgeon. When Hitler started this new, aggressive war, Markham's son Peter had been among the first to volunteer for the Royal Air Force. On one of RAF's earliest operational missions over Germany, his Blenheim Mk.I bomber was shot down and the entire crew lost, a minor event in the war's opening phases. It had taken place just two days after Peter's nineteenth birthday.

When McKinnon was working to assemble the remarkably diverse talent needed within the SOE organization, he had succeeded in enlisting the professional expertise of his friend to explore the murky area of unconventional warfare, which includes certain activities that are best kept out of the spotlight. The war these two old friends had fought in Flanders had still shown vestiges of chivalry, but in this new war against the Nazi scourge, means and methods had dropped to far lower levels. The struggle fought by SOE agents in far off places against German troops or police units called for something McKinnon had euphemistically labeled "survival skills." With the realism of a medical practitioner, Markham eschewed euphemism and prosaically referred to the contents of his brief instruction course as "killing skills."

In the course of their daily practice, physicians become intimately aware of the strengths as well as the weaknesses of the human body, normally using such knowledge to keep their patients alive and healthy. But the insights that are intended to be used beneficially for the survival of their patients can be applied also in other, very different pursuits: how to endure torture, and how to kill an enemy adversary swiftly and silently.

Lund and Lowell had been through all of the procedures before, but to Janiak they brought a sobering realization that their upcoming cat-and-mouse game in enemy territory could suddenly and unexpectedly turn deadly. With calm, clinical detachment, Markham began with a short lecture on human anatomy, using a life-size chart. He pointed out how life is a stubbornly tenacious phenomenon, yet can be terminated in seconds by someone with the requisite knowledge, knowledge he knew to have no purpose or place among civilized people. While speaking, Markham thought of his son, a life forfeited almost before it was begun. Had Peter's life ended painfully in the flaming inferno of a crippled plane? He hoped not. And he hoped he was preparing these three to survive whatever lay ahead for them.

At the end of his talk he brought out a small rubber-coated pill, which he passed around the group.

"You will each be supplied with an L-tablet like this one, which offers you an alternative to torture in case you are captured. It is potassium cyanide, and if you choose to use it, put it in your mouth and crush it between your teeth. I cannot tell you whether it is painless, but as the effect is lethal in fifteen seconds, that question is only of academic interest."

Each man observed solemnly the rubber-coated death pill, and Markham again studied their faces with interest. He finally asked, "Do you have any questions?"

There was none, and after an hour of instruction, the trio left the gym to return to Major Hawes' office at the SOE headquarters.

Outburst

When Esther was called into his office and sat down on the chair by his desk, Huber pretended to be preoccupied, leafing through a folder with feigned interest. He finally put it down and looked across his desk.

"Oh, our little Jewish visitor from Hamburg. Yes...we have managed to uncover your ancestry, of which you have claimed to be ignorant. Let me see now..." he opened a file on his desk and studied it leisurely. "Two of your grandparents turn out to be Jewish, pure Jewish, although that is a questionable term, I should say, perhaps rather an oxymoron, don't you agree?" He laughed mirthlessly before going on. "We now have conclusive proof of your Jewishness, and I must decide what to do with you."

Huber leered at her while laying demonstrative emphasis on "I" to make clear how her fate was totally in his hands. Esther met his eyes calmly. How different, this petty bureaucrat's salacious stare, from the merchants' cheerful acknowledgement of a pretty girl and their clumsy but harmless approbation. Ilse was right: this man was evil. It was simply a stroke of bad luck to have encountered him.

"What is this conclusive proof you are talking about?"

Huber glowered at her. This reaction was not at all what he had been expecting and looking forward to. The impudent bitch was not intimidated.

"I have undertaken certain inquiries, of which I have no obligation to inform you. I shall just say that it is up to me to decide what to do with you."

"Oh, really? And what choices do your regulations prescribe for you to follow?"

Huber stared at her, aghast at the impertinence of the woman. He had expected something quite different. Imagine this Jewish scum questioning his authority, and his procedures, all backed up by the overwhelming power and unquestionable discretion of the Nazi state, as represented by him, Heinz Huber, its *Behörde* and competent official.

White with suppressed fury he lost his composure, lost his carefully maintained air of superior and unruffled authority. He leaned across the desk toward her and snarled, "Get out of my office, you Jewish whore. You will hear from me soon enough."

Esther summoned all her courage, as she rose from the chair, trying to keep her knees from shaking. She turned, walked out into the street and, without looking right or left, mechanically continued walking to the Altstadt. Entering the apartment where Ilse greeted her, she broke down, sobbing uncontrollably.

At the Personalamt it took Huber several minutes to calm down sufficiently to decide on his next move. At the age of 56, Huber was no longer subject to the draft; he could devote himself to his career in the bureaucracy, which encompassed the regulation and control of the lives of ordinary citizens, activities he loved dearly. It was rare, almost unheard of, to have a citizen talk back, let alone question his actions. Germans were decent, law-abiding and compliant, and the Nazi *Gleichschaltung*, the orientation in one direction of the entire national body, had taken their obedience toward public authority to new heights. The logistics of the actual collection and resettlement of the Jews in Stralsund was Metzger's responsibility, and it had already been accomplished several months ago. He finally got up from his chair and walked down the hall to the office of his colleague, Frantz Metzger. Huber strolled through the office door and addressed Metzger jovially.

"Frantz, I have a little present for you, a Jewish woman who did not get included in your resettlement transports."

Metzger looked up with obvious surprise. At twenty-two he was at the opposite end of the military age scale from Huber. He had served on the Eastern Front in *Einsatzgruppe D*, an extermination squad, under Otto Ohlendorf, which had been responsible for the collection of Jewish men, women and children and summarily massacring them. Discharged after having lost his left leg to a land mine, Metzger had been assigned to the city registry, where he with glee had taken up the task of organizing resettlement of Stralsund's Jewish citizens.

"A Jewish woman I missed? Is that possible?"

He sounded so upset that Huber burst out laughing at the younger man's concern.

"Not to worry, Frantz, she came from Hamburg just recently and apparently missed our dragnet there. No fault of yours."

Metzger relaxed.

"I tell you, Heinz, we shouldn't bother with that resettlement stuff but deal with them the way we did in Ukraine."

"A good thought, Frantz, but we have to follow orders. When can we get this one shipped off?"

Metzger dug into his file and perused a list.

"There is actually a train passing through here at 7:30 on Sunday morning. I could arrange to put her on that."

"*Prima*, Frantz, let's take care of that right away."

Huber had regained his composure and felt things were getting back in hand. He walked back to his office in good spirits.

Wagner

In his office at RSHA, the state security headquarters in Berlin, Kiefer Wagner read his orders a second time. An assignment to the Copenhagen office! It sounded good by anyone's reckoning. He knew that living conditions in Denmark were highly rated by agents who had been there: excellent food and a population described as "politically indifferent" by people concerned with that aspect of the local people. Wagner worked in the Sicherheitsdienst, Amt VI. This was the foreign intelligence service of the SS, led by SS Brigadefuhrer Werner Best. It had taken Wagner some time to get a semblance of overview of the organization in which he was one very small cog. He had finally plotted a few salient data and learned some facts, laboriously adding details to fill out a picture that was still sketchy and fragmentary.

The RSHA was a subordinate organization of the SS. It was created by Heinrich Himmler in 1939 through the merger of the SD, (the security service), the Gestapo, (the secret state police), and the Kripo, (the criminal police).

The organization's stated duty was to fight all "enemies of the Reich" within and outside the borders of Nazi Germany. The list of designated "enemies" was long, reflecting both Nazi ideology and simple paranoia. Included were Jews, Romani people and other "racially undesirables," as well as communists and members of other secret organizations such as Freemasons. Thus the

RSHA in theory served to coordinate the activities among a number of different agencies with wide-ranging responsibilities including oversight of *Einsatzgruppen,* the death squads that followed the invasion forces of the German army into the eastern territories.

The first director of the agency, Reinhard Heydrich, had been assassinated in 1942 by Czech partisans. It had released a frenzy of revenge killings by the Germans in which some five thousand people had died.

This much Wagner had been able to piece together, no small feat, as the agency was anything but forthcoming about itself, in particular about internal matters, and employees were not encouraged to ask questions. Wagner had nevertheless been able to ferret out that his subdivision, Amt VI, was one of seven sections, among which he had also been able to identify Amt IV, Gestapo, which was headed by SS Brigadefuhrer Heinrich Erhardt and included a subsection in which Sturmbannfuehrer Adolf Eichmann was implementing the final solution, that of murdering the Jews. Small wonder that the acronym "Gestapo" carried an undertone of dread; it was justly earned. The label was widely used, particularly outside Germany, when referring to any of the Nazi security services.

Wagner was a good observer but lacked the experience and perspective needed to realize that RSHA was an immensely overblown bureaucracy. In fact, the complexity of RSHA was unequalled, with at least a hundred sub-sub sections huddling in a maze of offices, each fiercely fighting to defend and expand its turf.

The Team

It was four o'clock on Friday afternoon when Major Hawes led the team selected for Operation *Emigrant* into McKinnon's office. Hawes carried two suitcases, which he placed on a conference table opposite to McKinnon's desk. When they were all seated, McKinnon inquired leisurely about their progress at the range and at the gym. Then he turned to his aide.

"It sounds as though this team is about ready for the task at hand, Major Hawes. Would you lay out the operational plan?"

Hawes unrolled a chart and pinned it to the wall so that they all could see its features. Then he turned and faced the group.

"As I mentioned yesterday, your mission will not be an easy one, although it will in principle be straight forward. You will travel into Germany to locate and pick up a German national by the name of Hans Holzinger, probably against his will. Then you will bring him back with you. The specifics are as follows. Tonight you will proceed by aircraft along this route from the Tempsford airfield, across the North Sea and southern Denmark," he ran his finger along the penciled course line, "changing course here and going straight for the drop-off point on this beach about eleven miles from the city of Stralsund, here," he tapped the spot on the chart, "where you will land on the beach. The aircraft will depart without delay. From the drop-off point you will proceed on foot to Stralsund, where Holzinger, your target, is expected to arrive on an evening train. Janiak knows him, so there will be no problem of identification."

Hawes paused to let the information sink in.

"Any questions, so far?"

The question elicited one "No" and some headshaking. Hawes fished out a Players and lit it slowly before continuing.

"From the point of spotting Holzinger at the railroad station, you will have to improvise. The best idea may be to follow him to his wife's apartment and there attempt to convince him to come along voluntarily. You are authorized to offer his wife to come also. You may promise them safety and security in England until the end of the war, if that should appeal. Janiak tells us that there are no children involved, which immensely simplifies the situation. You will be carrying two syringes, each loaded with a medication that will render an average adult unconscious for a period of eight hours. If unforeseen problems arise, that could come in handy. It is imperative that you work fast, because your pickup is scheduled for the following night at two o'clock in the morning. Do you have any questions at this point?"

Lund spoke up. "What else can we tell them about the circumstances under which they would spend the rest of the war in England?"

McKinnon thought briefly before answering. "That is a good question that they may well pose and which may well influence their decision. Tell Holzinger that he will not be treated as a prisoner. After debriefing in London, he and his wife will be settled in a village in southern England, probably in Sussex."

Lund spoke up again. "Eleven miles from Stralsund to the point of pickup, that will take a minimum of three hours walking. And that's assuming this Holzinger comes voluntarily. The schedule seems awfully tight. And if we give him an injection so that we would have to carry him...." He let the statement trail off, but his point was clear.

McKinnon concurred. "Your pilot will make one low pass. In the case of necessity, that is, if there is no signal from you, he will return twenty-four hours later. If there is still no signal, he will depart and not come back. You will then have to improvise your own return."

The ramifications of being left in enemy territory were stark and perfectly clear; when the prospect elicited no comment from any of the trio, Hawes opened one of his briefcases, brought out a wallet, handed it to Lund, and addressed the group.

"These are Lund's identity papers. He will be traveling under the name of Martin Hagen, a late member of the SD. He is already familiar with this ID, as he has used it before, but the photograph has been changed and is now up to date."

Lund nodded, and Hawes brought out a wallet for Lowell.

"And this is a similar ID for Mr. Lowell. The name is Erich Wolff, also a late SD agent."

Hawes extracted a third set of papers.

"And this is the ID together with a travel order for Janiak, who will simply keep his identity as a Polish chemist but with the name of Konrad Dawiec, traveling from the Fieseler Werke in Kassel to the Peenemunde test facility. Be aware that Janiak's papers are easily checked by telephone and therefore not as solid as the others. The chance of someone checking on an SD agent is slight. Take a good look at your respective IDs, and before you board the plane tonight, be sure to memorize each others' ID names."

Hawes handed each man a small map.

"As you can see, the map covers only Stralsund and the area toward the northwest, taking in the beach where you will be dropped and picked up. I suggest you try to memorize the map." He opened a second briefcase and placed its contents on the conference table.

"Here we have three Walthers in shoulder holsters, the PPK model, each with a full magazine and one spare clip. These are the syringes, loaded and ready, and these are the L-tablets that Dr. Markham will have told you about. Here are three German flashlights, one for each of you, and three envelopes with German currency, four hundred marks in each, enough for some train travel, should that become necessary. Please put on the guns now and help each other adjust the harnesses."

While the team was busy arming itself, McKinnon had Ann Curtis bring tea for everyone. Lowell and Lund were old hands at carrying shoulder holsters and helped Janiak with the necessary adjustments until his jacket covered the gun and harness without any telltale bulging. After fifteen minutes, Hawes approved the results, and when they were settled down with the tea, McKinnon spoke up.

"This is rather faster than we usually prepare a team. I am not entirely happy about being so rushed, but in this case circumstances are compelling. Lund has had the most Underground experience. He will be the leader of the team. It is necessary to designate one person as leader. His word will be final when it comes to tactical field decisions. Are you all comfortable with this arrangement?"

There was some nodding and mumbled affirmation from the three men, whom circumstances had unexpectedly thrown together in a mutual life-or-death dependency. The team designated to carry out Operation *Emigrant* was ready.

8

Beached

The Westland Lysander III was no airliner, Lowell thought, but for personnel transport it was vastly more comfortable than the Blenheim. He was occupying the copilot's seat next to Morian, while Lund and Janiak sat behind them. Janiak was dozing, but Lund was going over the mission in his mind, trying to anticipate what lay ahead. The project on which they were setting out was similar to one he had just completed. It had involved the liberating of a scientist from Gestapo's clutches and taking him to England. Their SOE team had succeeded, but he was well aware that they had been favored by luck in several respects. The present operation was a far deeper incursion into enemy territory. How would his teammates hold up? He had no reservations about Lowell; Janiak had proven himself determined and resourceful, but he was still a novice. If they had to deal with two people to be persuaded, protected and guided, they would surely have their hands full. Lund closed his eyes and tried to relax, but his mind refused to let go of the problems looming ahead.

In the seat next to Morian, Lowell kept track of ground features, an easy enough task, as Morian kept the plane at an altitude of only two hundred feet, and they had encountered no fog. So far, they had crossed nine coastlines, which he had duly noted on the course line drawn on the chart in his lap, intermittently making use of a hooded flashlight. They were now bearing down on the destination beach, right on course. Having timed the last contact point, he had calculated their estimated arrival time, and he turned to his two companions in the back, shaking them awake with his left hand. Then he leaned toward Morian and shouted, "ETA in one minute."

Morian grinned while shouting back, "Hey, it's pretty handy to have a real copilot onboard. Yes, I can just make out the beach. Watch what this baby can do." He swung the plane slightly to the right, throttled back and made a steep left turn to line up perfectly with the flat stretch along the water's edge. With the engine idling he side-slipped the Lysander in a shuddering descent right down to the beach, leveled out ten feet above the sand, and let the plane run out of flying speed to settle gently onto the sand in a perfect touchdown. While Lowell was watching with silent approval, Morian omitted using flaps or brakes, testing a long stretch of beach for firmness by simply letting the plane run out of momentum.

Poland is one of the countries in Europe most endowed with tree cover, and in the spring, when the snow melt swells its rivers, they carry all manner and weights of forest debris from far inland all the way to be floated into the Baltic Sea. A stout beech tree, one of the winter's windfalls, had been discharged in April by the river's overflow into the sea, drifting to land by late summer on the stretch of waterfront northwest of Stralsund, which Wingate and Morian had thoughtfully selected. Local farmers had quickly cut up the log and spirited the sections away, leaving only the roots with a very short stump attached, not much of an obstacle, but enough. The Lysander's left wheel struck the stump, and the strut tore off with a sickening sound of metal rending, as the plane came to a stop in vertical position with its nose and propeller buried in the sand.

The four men were thrown violently forward but restrained by their seat belts. Morian let go a heartfelt obscenity in his native Danish before asking, "Anybody hurt?" Without waiting for an answer he kicked his door open and crawled out onto the sand. Moments later, when they were all out, Lund ascertained that no one was injured, and he immediately turned to practical matters.

"We've got to get away from here quickly. Let's make sure we each have our stuff. Morian, you won't get far in that uniform; do you have any civilian clothes for this kind of situation?"

Morian nodded, "I always carry an outfit in my haversack." He was already doffing his uniform and changing. "One of you, get one of the jerrycans out here. We'll have to burn the plane, and it'll make a nice bonfire when the jerrycans blow."

"Morian," Lund cut in, "do you carry any false ID for this kind of situation?"

"No, but I've memorized in German a request for help from anyone the RAF describes as a 'friendly-looking' local."

They all burst out laughing, and Morian continued, "On the other hand, if there should be a shortage of friendly-looking locals, I brought a small .25-caliber Browning, not much of a weapon, but easy to hide."

Lowell crawled back into the plane, and a moment later emerged with a jerrycan. Morian pried it open, threw his uniform back into the plane, and looked at Lund. "Ready?"

Lund nodded. "We'll wait for you a couple of hundred feet inland."

The team plodded across the beach, climbed a low sand berm and came to a stubble field, where they stopped to wait, while checking their map and compass. Behind them Morian had poured a trail of gasoline across fifty feet of beach, leaving the open, half-full can in the plane's door opening. Then he ran to the inland end of the gasoline trail, lit it with a match, and ran on to join the waiting team. The fire flared as it reached the open jerrycan, Lund snapped a short, "Let's go," and they started on a brisk walk inland. They shortly hit a dirt road, clearly marked on the map, and at the same moment the sky behind them lit up as the first of the jerrycans still strapped in the plane exploded. Lund broke into a slow jog. They passed half a dozen farms, all of them dark, while the fire kept building behind them.

Conundrum

Feldwebel Ernst Gerber of Marine Coast Police Detachment 1251 in Stralsund was always pleased to be on night duty. The city's small unit of coast police was located in Feldstrasse, a quiet street, and Detachment 1251 had little to do during the day; night duty could be counted on to allow a peaceful doze in the comfortable armchair in the office of Sonderfuehrer Wilhelm Springer, the unit's commanding officer. The persistent ringing of the telephone finally roused Gerber enough to make him pick up the receiver, but the gravelly voice of Josh Engelhart, the city police chief, carried just enough urgency to get him fully awake.

"A plane crashed on the beach, uh, is it British?...you have no particulars?...so, be over here in fifteen minutes, and I'll have the Kubel ready. You can guide us to the site." He swore as he put the telephone back and rang the direct line to Springer.

"We have a report, Herr Sonderfuehrer, from the city police, of a plane crash on the beach about eighteen kilometers out of town...*jawohl*, I told them to drive here directly and lead the way for us...Lehman and Albrecht, *jawohl*, I'll get them here right away." As he was dialing his next call, he swore once again. Why did this have to come up on *his* watch?

Half an hour later the police chief's Opel led the Kubel, a small military scout car, with Springer and two soldiers of the coast police to the sizzling remnants of the Lysander. The fire had left only a few ribs, the wingtips and the wheel hubs. The rest formed a small, glowing mound atop the engine block. Two local farmers were also at the site, one of whom had alerted the city police from a neighbor's telephone. The other farmer was the neighbor whose phone had been used. Springer had immediately ascertained that all footprints in the sand by the plane's occupants had been obliterated by later arrivals on the beach. He was an experienced officer, and he immediately sent one of his men in each direction to search the beach for anything unusual. He was standing by the remnants of the wreck, poking into the hot debris and extracting some exploded jerrycans. He turned to the police chief.

"Engelhart, what do you make of these?"

"They must have been loaded with spare fuel, but how would they make use of it? Where could they land and refill their tanks? And where could they have been headed?"

"Good questions," Springer said, "and this is the kind of conundrum war seems to provide in abundance." He absentmindedly kept poking at the embers, before he spoke again. "Engelhart, you'd better have your men check the nearest farms to see if there is anything to learn from the locals, and at daybreak have your men sweep the beach about one kilometer in both directions for clues, although I doubt there will be much to find. I will get in touch with our headquarters in Lubeck, and they will in turn report this to RSHA in Berlin. Then you can expect some GFP *Kopfjäger* to come poking around in your peaceful town." Springer was referring to the Wehrmacht's secret field police, which had earned for themselves the nickname of *Kopfjäger*, or headhunters.

Engelhart nodded his agreement. "And I'll have my people keep an eye on our railroad station and bus station, although I can't imagine the plane's occupants venturing into Stralsund."

Springer grunted, then added irritably, "And I can't imagine what the hell they were doing, or planning to do, in the first place."

Deliberation

By Lund's watch they had been underway for nearly an hour when the road ahead was lit up by car lights. The team retreated far enough into a field to be out of the headlights, as an Opel followed by a military Kubel tore by at high speed. When the cars had passed, they continued until a few lights ahead announced the outskirts of Stralsund. Lund led the group into an empty field and said, "Before we go on, this is a good time to discuss our situation. I'm sure we have all been thinking about how to get out of this pickle." He spoke without betraying any emotion, as he continued in a level voice.

"Here is my thinking. With our German ID papers we do have the means to get ourselves out of Germany and attempt a return to England. I am leaning toward trying to get to Denmark, where I have some connections, and from there I know how to get us to Sweden. We will have to come up with some way to bring Morian along without papers, but as we will be traveling under SD identities, we could take him along in the role of a prisoner. As I see it, the more pressing question is whether we should try to complete our mission by contacting Holzinger. When the Germans realize that there are no human remains in the burned-out plane, police will be combing the town, maybe reinforced by soldiers of the secret military police, and the railroad station will certainly be watched. Our situation is now far more complicated than we expected, but I know you have all been thinking about what to do, and I want to hear your ideas."

There was a short silence. Lund tried to read their faces, but the darkness was too intense. Then Lowell spoke up, the cadence of his Boston English in marked contrast to Lund's Danish accent.

"To take your last question first, I would like to carry on and convince Holzinger to join the party. I realize it will complicate matters if he refuses, but I think it's worth a try, when we've come this far."

"I think he will go with us," Janiak broke in, "and I think, maybe it is good idea to look for boat to get to Sweden. I did so alone, and this time we have more rowers."

Lund made a mental note of his excitement and enthusiasm that made him stumble over the English syntax.

"Are you saying that you actually rowed a boat to Sweden?" The question came from Morian, and he continued as if thinking out loud, "You know, it just might be possible to get our hands on something better than a rowboat in Stralsund. After all, it's a harbor town, so there must be all kinds of craft, including fishing boats. It seems to me that might offer some real possibilities."

Morian's suggestion released a sudden animated discussion in the group, revealing that they all wanted to make contact with Holzinger and let the outcome of that encounter shape their further course of action. At length Lund brought the discussion to an end with a short summary.

"All right, our plan will be for Janiak to wait alone at the railroad station for Holzinger and follow him to his apartment without Holzinger noticing him. The rest of us will wait near the station and discreetly follow Janiak. Until then I think we'd better divide the team to attract less attention. Lowell, you and Janiak can reconnoiter the town, locate the police station, find out about military barracks or installations, if any, and find out where that Kubel came from that we saw rushing by a while back. There is bound to be some naval police in town, what they call coast police, and the Kubel may be theirs. Try to locate it, in case we want to borrow it." He paused before going on. "Morian and I will check out the harbor. Morian has no ID, but if we get cornered and questioned, I'll pull rank as an SD agent and tell them Morian is my prisoner, perhaps explain that he is an escaped Royal Air Force POW. I'll have to think of something. We'll see if the harbor offers anything we might use to get ourselves out of this place." He paused again, briefly. "And finally, let's all stick to crowded areas to make ourselves inconspicuous."

Wingate

A few minutes after arriving at his office on Saturday morning, Major Hawes took a phone call from Tempsford. On the line was Squadron Leader Wingate, who was brief and to the point.

"The Lysander we dispatched with the SOE team last night has not returned and is now overdue. We must assume it is lost. I will keep you informed, if we hear anything."

Hawes thought for a moment.

"Could it be delayed in Denmark, where the pilot was planning to refuel? How do you assess the situation?"

Wingate hesitated only slightly before replying.

"I can think of a dozen possible reasons for the Lysander being overdue, by far most of them in some way fatal. Still, Jensen is one of the best pilots I have had in my squadron, his skills almost unsurpassed, and for all we know, he and your people may at this moment simply be refugees in enemy territory. All we can do is wait and hope."

Their conversation ended on that unsatisfactory note. After replacing the telephone in its cradle, Hawes walked down the hall to McKinnon's office and found his chief working his way through the morning's dispatches. SOE's far-flung network in Europe, North Africa, and the Middle East produced a steady stream of reports and requests on their primitive portable radios, their feeble and only means of keeping in touch through Bletchley with SOE headquarters in London.

McKinnon motioned Hawes to sit down and proceeded pensively to stuff and light his pipe, while Hawes reported on the telephone call from Wingate, including his own speculation about the fate of the SOE people. McKinnon blew a cloud of fragrant blue smoke. He habitually reacted to problems and bad news with an air of positive but detached calmness, scrutinizing each situation and trying to ferret out any promising line of action.

"So, our *Emigrant* team may be in serious trouble, or worse? We must assume the former, and frankly, Jack, I cannot remember fielding a team more qualified to take care of itself under the most trying circumstances. On the face of the few facts in our possession they are now on the loose in enemy territory, and they may yet do all right. We'll just have to wait and see."

McKinnon paused, then added under another cloud of blue smoke, "And I think it is premature to involve Minister Sandys at this time."

Hawes nodded and rose from his chair.

"Very good, sir."

Consultation

It was almost noon on Saturday, when secretary Gieselinde Thoene at the Reichsicherheitshauptamt in Berlin brought a teletype message from the office of the security police in Lubeck to her boss, SS Brigadefuhrer Werner Best. After perusing the message, Best took time to ponder its implications. Depending on his assumptions, it was a borderline case of jurisdiction between the SD and the Gestapo, not unusual in the mammoth security system Hitler's Reich had fostered under the grip of Heinrich Himmler. An enemy plane had crashed, no doubt in the process of inserting agents. It would surely involve personnel from several RSHA departments and could become a headache. Best decided to consult his colleague Heinrich Erhardt, the Brigadefuhrer in charge of the Gestapo section. The two of them had recently experienced some quite unpleasant difficulties and failures in their attempts to block an SOE operation, thereby incurring Himmler's wrath, which was still simmering. In the aftermath of that debacle, a modicum of operational cooperation had been established between their sectors, a rare occurrence in the upper echelons of the Nazi bureaucracy, which fought its turf wars tooth and nail. The present situation called for caution. As they were of equal rank, Best strolled over to Erhardt's office and walked through the open door with a familiar, "*Wie geht's*, Heinrich? Take a look at this." He handed over the message and sat down.

When Erhardt had finished reading the message, Best continued, "You are from East Prussia, and you know the Baltic region intimately. What do you make of a small British plane snooping around that far from home? What could they be after? What kind of mission could they have?"

Erhardt leaned back in his chair, picturing in his mind the Baltic coast and its significance to the current war effort.

"As you know, Werner, we do have quite a number of military installations in the region. There are U-boat flotillas stationed all along the coast, at Wilhelmshaven, Pillau, Gotenhafen and Danzig. And we have a training base at Hela. So, take your pick. And let's not forget the goings-on at Peenemunde. Our office there has been supplying von Braun's project with workers for quite a while and in large numbers."

He paused and lit a cigarette.

"Now, as to what the English are doing flying around in that area in a small plane, I suppose it can only be with the intent of inserting some of their people. What else could it be? Look, Werner, no bodies were found, so apparently they have already succeeded in landing some agents, and you'll have to comb the area and try to catch one of them to find out what they're up to."

"Hmm...yes, of course...I have already taken steps to do that," Best lied smoothly, "but I thought you might have some further insight."

Erhardt shook his head.

"I will alert my own people at Peenemunde, and when you catch one of the agents, let's see if we have some common ground on which to proceed." Erhardt had come from a humble background and liked to sound formal; he felt it emphasized the high level at which the two Brigadefuhrer functioned.

9

Messenger

Esther wiped her eyes. Her explosive crying had come as the release of a safety valve after she had walked home, looking straight ahead and keeping her emotions bottled up. She looked at Ilse.

"You were absolutely right about Huber. I didn't realize how evil he is."

She told her cousin the details of their meeting, how he had smirked and savored his possession of unchecked power on behalf of the Nazi state.

"I cannot fathom what drove him to spend such time and effort on my case."

"Oh, I can quite well imagine what goes on in his little mind," Ilse said drily, "it is a dirty version of the cheerful response you get from our local merchants, when they react to you as an attractive woman brightening their day. I'm glad Hans is coming tonight. I want to ask him what we can expect from that bureaucratic snake. In the meantime, let's not lose heart. You can give me a hand with the potatoes, and turn on the radio, so we can hear some music until the news reports, then we can again try to estimate how soon this war will be over."

Taking up the dinner preparations, she tried to give her comment an upbeat lilt she didn't feel. The forcible removal of the country's Jews to an alleged but unspecified resettlement in the East had been indelibly etched in the minds of both women, ever since the exodus to the East had started. Esther did what Ilse asked and tuned the radio to a broadcast of light operettic music from Toulouse. They worked in silence, while the music filled the apartment, temporarily banishing the sense of foreboding they both felt. When dinner was ready to go in the oven, Ilse made some herb tea, and they sat down together in the living room. Esther perused the newspaper, reading aloud a few items of interest, and they discussed the news while sipping the tea.

It was almost five o'clock, when the doorbell rang, and Ilse went to the entryway to open the door.

"Does Esther Lidman live here?"

Coming from an elderly city messenger, it sounded more like a statement than a question.

"Yes," Ilse replied calmly.

"Then call her out here."

Momentarily aghast at the man's deliberate rudeness, Ilse havered her fury, turned toward the living room, and called in a demonstratively soft and polite manner, "Esther, if you can spare a moment, would you please come out here."

The messenger snorted contemptuously, when Esther appeared.

"Here is a travel order for you. As you will see, you have to be at the railroad station Sunday morning at nine fifteen for transport to resettlement in the East. And you'd better be there on time!" He thrust the document at her and with a sneer stalked down the stairs.

Jorgensen

By noon on Saturday, Lund and Morian had been combing a sizeable slice of the harbor area, which was dominated by Stralsund's fleet of fishing vessels, mostly small and medium size boats. The fishermen themselves were men too old for military service, and the crews were supplemented with teenage boys still too young for the draft. Walking purposefully to blend into the bustling scene, the two SOE agents were making a thorough survey of the area, including a pier belonging to a shipyard, where two MTBs were undergoing repairs. These fast, torpedo-equipped craft were designed for patrolling and harassment but had by default become the unlikely backbone of Germany's surface fleet. When the war started, Germany had counted on great achievements by its new "pocket battleships," but Britain's Royal Navy had with a vengeance pursued and sunk or neutralized all of the heavier units, down to and including destroyers.

One of the vessels in the commercial harbor section attracted the attention of Lund and Morian; it was a small Danish freighter by the name of *Rita* that was in the process of unloading agricultural products.

Morian looked at Lund.

"Maybe this little ship deserves some close attention. Let's find out if she's scheduled to return to Denmark, and if so, how soon. They just might have room for a few passengers."

Lund nodded, walked across the gangplank, and addressed the sailor who was directing the unloading.

"Security police. Where is your skipper?"

"He's below, in his cabin."

"Tell him to get up here, and I'll see him on the bridge."

The captain's name turned out to be Aage Jorgensen, a ferry captain temporarily laid off from Danish government service due to reduced travel. At the age of fifty-two he had found idleness disagreeable and had signed on as captain of the *Rita* to serve in extended longshore traffic in the Baltic. Lund checked his personal papers as well as the freight manifest and posed a few supplementary questions. The responses revealed that *Rita* was scheduled for a quick turnaround, going back to Copenhagen on the following day, Sunday, for another load of foodstuff, mainly bacon, rye grain, and powdered milk.

"How are the Danes adjusting to being occupied by the German Wehrmacht?"

Lund posed the question as a non sequitur, shifting without any prior warning from routine questioning of humdrum detail to a highly charged topic on which comments were fraught with political implications and called for a careful choice of words. Captain Jorgensen was startled but kept a perfectly unruffled expression as his eyes met Lund's.

"Oh, I would say daily life in Denmark has evolved an acceptable routine to get through the current situation with the least amount of friction and upheaval."

Lund smiled inwardly, as he spoke again.

"I understand that British agents have been fomenting trouble in your country. Do you think it will escalate?"

Jorgensen shrugged with a show of perfect indifference, as if the matter being discussed pertained to the weather outlook.

"I doubt it. Your Wehrmacht seems to be keeping substantial forces in the country. No doubt they will be able to handle any unruly elements. At least that appears to have been the situation to date."

For a moment Lund stood in deep thought, absentmindedly gazing at the scene of peaceful activity on the pier. Seeing Morian standing close by, leaning on a light post and smoking a cigarette, gave him a sudden flash of inspiration. This sailor with whom he was verbally sparring, a quiet-spoken countryman of his, definitely had his wits about him. Lund felt instinctively that he could be trusted and, if put to the test, he might be willing to help the SOE team in their present predicament. The problem would be to convince him of their true identity. Up to this point their conversation had been in German. Without change in pace or tenor or facial expression, Lund abruptly switched to Danish.

"Actually, it will be interesting to observe the behavior of the occupation troops—and of the Danish resistance— as it becomes obvious to everyone that Germany is rapidly losing the war. What desperate measures do you suppose the Nazis will try?"

Captain Jorgensen had been following Lund's glance, taking in the harbor scene. Now he turned toward Lund and paused only briefly before calmly answering in Danish.

"You are surely in a better position than I to predict German behavior. Perhaps *you* should tell *me*."

Lund laughed.

"I think we'll both have to wait and watch. In the meantime we have to make the best of the situation, which means to try to limit the damage the Hitler regime can inflict on the rest of the world. Are you willing to do your part?"

Jorgensen dodged the question.

"What do you have in mind?"

"At the moment I have on my hands a German engineer who has been working on a German superweapon that is almost ready to be put into service. He wishes to defect and tell the British what he knows. If we can get him to Sweden or Denmark, it would be of great value for the Allies. Your ship presents us with one possible means of transport."

Jorgensen sidestepped the question and changed the subject.

"And since when is your security police engaged in helping German defectors to escape to the other side? I thought your job was rather the opposite."

Lund smiled.

"As you may guess, my SD identity is false. I am Danish, as you can tell: My name is Svend Lund. I serve in the British Special Operations Executive, and I'm engaged in this rather important mission which has run into some unforeseen difficulties."

"And what kind of proof do you have to support this interesting story," Jorgensen asked. "Surely you will agree that it is badly in need of corroboration."

Lund had anticipated the question and phrased his answer with care.

"As you will realize, I am traveling with proof of my assumed, false identity, not with any proof of being an undercover agent. But let me demonstrate some supportive proof. Notice the man standing over there, leaning on the light post and smoking?"

Jorgensen gave a confirming grunt.

"His name is Henning Jensen, nickname of Morian, a motorcycle racer before the war. He is now a decorated pilot in the Royal Air Force. I'll call him."

Lund stepped out on the open balcony and whistled to Morian, who unhurriedly crossed the gangplank and climbed to the bridge. After a brief introduction in Danish, Lund came to the point.

"Morian, tell Captain Jorgensen how we got into our present awkward situation."

Morian put the explanation succinctly.

"Well, the Krauts don't keep their beaches clean, so when I landed at night, we hit a fucking tree stump that tore off my left landing gear."

Jorgensen pursued further information.

"When and where did that happen?"

"Last night, on the beach just northwest of here."

Jorgensen turned to Lund and picked up the thread of their conversation.

"And what exactly are you asking me to do?"

Lund hesitated.

"To be honest, I'm not sure. The engineer I mentioned is the most important part of our present problem, but I also have several other agents on my hands. As you are already leaving in the morning, we have no time for elaborate arrangements. For now, let me just say that I and a number of other people will be extremely grateful for your help. Several lives may depend on it."

Jorgensen smiled, for the first time during their conversation. He was well aware that Lund was smoothly, step by step, enlisting his cooperation, proceeding by treating it as having been agreed to.

"All right, I will help you out. Within reason. As you might guess, the fact that this ship and crew are non-German is enough to attract the attention of the local police. I have noticed that we are being watched from time to time. It is good that the two of you didn't come together, and when you leave, you had better go one at a time. I trust we are all aware that in helping you, I'm putting myself and my ship on the line."

Morian spoke up.

"Perhaps it will comfort you to know that there are some six thousand Danish sailors plying the Atlantic in

Danish ships, all of them volunteers serving the Allied cause. You and *Rita* are in good company."

Dragnet

SS-Brigadefuhrer Werner Best leaned back in his chair while studying a map of the Baltic coast. He had requested the field gendarms from Rostock and Stettin to set up highway checkpoints in depth, respectively west and east of the city of Stralsund. The railroad police had been ordered to check all trains leaving Stralsund, and to do so with two-man patrols rather than the customary single policeman. The Gestapo offices in Rostock and Peenemunde had been alerted as well, and the Stralsund city police had been directed to screen all passengers boarding trains out of the city.

Best was satisfied that this dragnet would catch at least some of the inserted agents, whoever and wherever they were. Just as important, it was proof positive to demonstrate that his SD was vigilant and thoroughly professional. He had also taken the step to request from Erhardt the backup by Gestapo's Department E-1, which had far larger personnel resources available than the SD. Besides, if anything should go wrong, the Gestapo would have to share the blame.

The case at hand was out of the ordinary, presenting potential difficulty as well as opportunity to get back in Himmler's good graces, if indeed such a term could ever be suitable in that context. At the moment there was no need to bring the matter to the attention of the Reichsfuhrer. That would have to wait until preliminary results, hopefully favorable, could be reported.

Best put the map away and turned to the day's routine tasks.

The Barge

By late afternoon on Saturday, Lund and Morian had finished their harbor reconnaissance and were eating a meal in a small restaurant near the railroad station. The last item they had scrutinized was a motorized canal barge taking on a load of bricks. The loading had been carried out by hand, and in the course of the day a large stack of building bricks had been slowly transferred from the pier to the barge's ample hold. The task was performed by two columns of Russian forced laborers, brought in for the day from farms in the nearby villages.

When the two observers took a last look at the scene just before leaving the area, Lund stepped from the pier onto the barge's small aft deck and addressed the skipper, a man in his sixties, who had been directing the physical labor of loading. Flashing his ID with a curt "security police," Lund demanded the skipper's ID, checking it carefully while subjecting the man to a close scrutiny. The skipper's name was Anton Scherer, age 67, a native of Stettin in Western Pommerania. In the course of the ensuing conversation Lund had established that Scherer was the owner of the barge and was about to take the brick load to Kiel. He would be making a stopover at Warnemuende for the night, as longshore barge traffic was limited to daylight hours. Further questioning revealed that the barge was scheduled to depart with the fishing fleet at seven on Monday morning, and that local regulations compelled Scherer to use a harbor pilot if the barge was loaded. Lund checked the barge's delivery manifest and left after having admonished Scherer to keep their conversation to himself.

In the course of their meal, Lund related to Morian what he had found out from the barge skipper and how he had left the latter with instructions not to discuss their visit. Morian pondered the information before speaking quietly in his native Danish.

"You know, Kiel is in the direction we want to go, but Warnemuende would be even better; that's the German end of the ferry connection from Gedser in Denmark."

"I know," Lund said, "and I checked the location on his chart; it's on the coast a dozen miles north of Rostock, about half-way to Kiel from here and only some twenty-three miles from Gedser on the Danish coast."

The two Danes grinned at each other, as Lund added, "and that is definitely in the direction we want to go. From Gedser we can hop a train to Copenhagen, and there we'd be nearly out of trouble."

Watching

Lowell and Janiak were having a beer and some *Brotchen,* hard rolls, in the station restaurant. In the course of a quick reconnaissance they had located the city police station and the office of the coast police with the Kubel parked in front, as Lund had guessed. They had spent the rest of the day in the waiting room at the city hall, watching the throngs of people applying for permits, registering as refugees or arrivals, seeking shelter, or bringing their innumerable other problems for the vastly overloaded bureaucracy to deal with.

When the city hall closed at five in the afternoon, the two SOE agents went to the railroad station, where Holzinger's train was scheduled to arrive at 19:21 in the evening. The station and the restaurant were sufficiently crowded to provide a measure of the same security afforded at the city hall: a large enough pool of humanity in which one could submerge and disappear. A two-man patrol of city police had appeared but only to withdraw after a quick survey, seemingly discouraged at the prospect of attempting any close scrutiny of the crowded scene.

Five minutes before the train's arrival Lowell parted from Janiak, purchased a newspaper at the kiosk and walked out of the station. He sat down on a park bench with a good view to the station and lit a cigarette. On another bench about a hundred feet distant Morian was smoking and observing the passing pedestrians. Next to him Lund was holding a newspaper up before his face, watching the street over the edge of the paper. The team was in place.

While pretending to read, Lund pondered their situation. So far, things had been manageable, but would Holzinger cooperate? And if so, would he want to take his wife to England with him? The prospect of having the team expand to six persons was daunting. Leading a group that size through enemy territory, dodging enemy security organs, now on high alert by the plane crash.... He counted in his mind the agencies that would be involved. The city police, of course, and the coast police. The plane crash would probably also attract the attention of the security police, the infamous SD. They in turn could be expected to notify the railroad police, and also to bring in the Wehrmacht's secret field gendarmes, the GFP. The Nazi state had no end of agencies to call upon. The prospect of taking such an unwieldy group through the dragnet that must be in the process of unfolding did not appear to have any reasonable chance to succeed.

Lund looked at his watch. The train was ten minutes late so far, but just then he heard its whistle in the distance, and by listening he could follow its progress into the station, where a gasp of steam released from the locomotive announced the end of movement. In a matter of moments a thin stream of arriving passengers began to pour onto the sidewalks, and he saw Janiak emerge. Lund unhurriedly folded the newspaper and got up from the bench. When Janiak was almost out of sight on the sidewalk leading to the Altstadt, Lund started following. Behind him Lowell and Morian set out in the same direction. The stream of arrivals quickly thinned out, and it became apparent that Janiak was trailing a civilian accompanied by a Luftwaffe officer. Lund swore under his breath at the unexpected complication this implied. In the Altstadt their quarry disappeared with the officer into an apartment house, while Janiak continued and turned onto a side street that took him out of sight from the apartment building. Lowell and Morian hung back, pretended to meet and engage in conversation, whereas Lund proceeded, caught up with Janiak and gave immediate vent to his question.

"Who is the officer?"

Janiak was ready with his answer.

"There are some Luftwaffe officers assigned to test project in Peenemunde. The test project," he corrected himself. "He is one of them, and his mother lives here."

Lund drew a breath of relief. What luck to have Janiak on hand with such background information. He made a quick decision, motioned Janiak to come along, and walked toward Lowell and Morian who were still pursuing a feigned conversation at the next corner. When they passed, he said quietly, "In three minutes, follow us to the Holzingers."

On a large tablet in the building entrance Lund and Janiak checked the names of the residents: Hans Holzinger was on the fourth floor. They ascended quietly.

10

Insight

In the Copenhagen office of the Sicherheitsdienst agent Kiefer Wagner was perusing recent files, trying to catch up on the local scene. A comparative newcomer to intelligence work, he had recently arrived from RSHA in Berlin to join SD's Copenhagen branch, his main qualifications being a background in Schleswig where he had acquired a fair grasp of the Danish language. At length he turned his chair to face Luther Schmitz, the agent in charge of SD's branch in Denmark.

"Luther, why is it that the Danes give us trouble in so many ways, minor items mostly, but annoying? It seems to me that they have gotten the best of all possible worlds: plenty to eat, no military service, no air raids to disturb them at night. Why is it that they persist to support the so called resistance, which can never amount to much in the first place?"

Luther Schmitz put down the report he was working on and lit a cigarette before answering. He was an old hand at intelligence work, having served since the SD had been established as an independent section of the RSHA headquarters in Berlin's Prinz Albrecht Strasse at the outbreak of the war.

"Kiefer, you have only been in this country for two weeks. You haven't had time to find out much about the situation here, which looks to you quite simple. Well, it isn't as simple as it appears at first blush. We took charge of this country and Norway three years ago. We had to fight the Norwegians for a few weeks—their mountains were an obstacle that required some time to overcome—but the Danes knuckled under with almost no show of force. It was only later on that they began to have some second thoughts, encouraged by the English, as one could expect. So, they started resisting our administration in various ways: Refused to hand over some torpedo boats from their small navy, actually scuttling these perfectly good vessels instead; refused to send the communist members of their parliament to safekeeping in one of our concentration camps, instead built a comfortable camp of their own for them; refused to hand over their Jews for resettlement. Just one damn thing after another. That's the actual background. And, as you may know, you are replacing a fine agent who was shot dead right here, in this office."

Kiefer nodded.

"I've heard mumblings about that. The guy died with his pants down, getting ready to fuck a pretty female SOE operative. Hard to believe that we had to let the killers get away."

"Hmm...well, yes, Kiefer, they were lucky, but keep that to yourself when you talk with new arrivals from Berlin."

Schmitz smoked in silence for a while before continuing.

"I can't exactly put my finger on the reasons why, but people in this country won't go along with the least bit of *Gleichschaltung*, of orienting themselves with us toward a common goal, as we sensibly did among ourselves right away when the Fuehrer took over. But the facts are that English agents have succeeded in fomenting some unrest and in fanning resentment toward our troops who are simply carrying out their duties here."

Kiefer Wagner had also lit a cigarette and was pondering how much additional information he could fish out of his superior without sounding either too inquisitive or lacking in confidence about the firmness of Germany's hold on its occupied countries, or about the certainty of eventual victory. He decided to venture another question to gain as much insight as possible.

"What actually happened to the Danish Jews?"

Schmitz took another drag on his cigarette.

"They seem to have disappeared. We did get hold of a handful, but I'd say the rest of them, at least five or six thousand, probably managed to get to Sweden. Somebody on our side may have leaked the information about Eichmann's plan to round them up. In any event, they vanished overnight. Just like that. Hard to understand, but there was apparently plenty of local help to hide them and transport them across The Sound to one of the harbors on the Swedish side."

Wagner sat motionless, trying to view from the vantage point of these local people the situation into which he, a complete outsider had been injected to help carry out the policies of his government. The cigarette burned his fingers, making him stub it out in the ashtray. He met the gaze of his superior, aware that questions, and even harmless sounding comments, always could be interpreted as being critical of his own side, his government, or the policies he was charged with carrying out. He decided to make one last comment.

"But at least we seem to have the cooperation of the Danish government, as far as I can tell. The local authorities are condemning sabotage and other resistance acts, right?"

Schmitz snorted derisively.

"Look, Kiefer, it's an odd phenomenon, I know. On the one hand the Danes are of prime Aryan stock, but on the other, democracy has made them undisciplined and cowardly. You simply can't trust them. We have to keep alert all the time. Bear that in mind on every assignment you get."

The Offer

Before Hans Holzinger had time to hang his coat in the entrance hall to their apartment, Ilse was blurting the story about Huber and the city messenger's visit. At the point where she mentioned the messenger, Holzinger was reaching for a coat hanger, but his hand faltered in midair, as he turned toward his wife, fumbling for the hanger without looking.

"An order to Esther for resettlement?"

He sounded as if he hoped his wife would qualify the statement, that she would somehow downgrade its certainty or reality. Mechanically, he simply hung his coat on the wall bracket, stepped into the living room, and sat down heavily.

"Tell me the whole story again from the beginning."

When Ilse had finished, Esther broke in. She had regained her composure and was able to face the prospect of resettlement with resignation, accepting the inevitable while searching for some positive aspects.

"Maybe the conditions where they're sending us aren't all that bad. When I take the train, it could even mean a positive change. Remember how many of our friends and acquaintances are already there, wherever that is."

Holzinger shook his head and almost shouted, "No, no you can't do that, it's out of the question!"

Startled, the two women looked at him, and with a slight hesitation Esther said, "Why?"

Holzinger started to speak but was cut off by the sound of the doorbell. Ilse went to the door, and they heard a male voice; after a short exchange, Ilse returned, ushering Janiak into the room and addressing her husband.

"Hans, this gentleman has come to see you."

"Janiak!" Holzinger rose from his chair, staring at his former assistant as if seeing a ghost. "Where...what happened?"

Janiak smiled at his confusion.

"It is a long story, and I have much to tell and much to explain. But first, allow me to introduce myself." He bowed to Ilse who had closed the front door and followed him into the living room. "Am I correct in thinking that you must be Mrs. Holzinger?"

Ilse nodded.

"And my name is Konrad Janiak. I used to work as your husband's assistant at Peenemunde."

He looked at Esther.

"And you are?"

Holzinger had gathered his wits enough to take over the introduction.

"This is my wife's cousin, Esther Lidman. But tell us what happened to you."

"I would rather have my companions tell you. They will be here any minute, and they have come from far away to meet you and to make you and your wife a proposal."

As if on cue, the doorbell rang again. This time Esther was the one to respond; she went to the entrance, opened the door, and looked into the steel-blue eyes of Alex Lowell. Surprised, Lowell thought for a fleeting moment that he was looking at Rachel. The same eyes, similar lovely features that seemed to reflect a beauty from within. But Esther was slightly taller than Rachel had been. She stood momentarily transfixed, as the newcomer with a smile said, "Good evening, lovely *Fräulein*, may we come in?" Without waiting for her reply, Lowell gently swept her aside to let his two companions walk quickly past them into the living room. His smile widened as he quietly closed the door with his arm still around her.

"Now, lovely *Fräulein*, shall we join the others?"

His arm tightened in a hardly perceptible squeeze, and with a nod of consent Esther returned his smile. Giving in to a sudden impulse she let her body yield to his, and they lingered for a moment, mutually entranced, while sounds from the living room indicated the newcomers were being seated. Then she gently detached herself and motioned for Lowell to enter the living room. He took the last seat at the table, while Esther remained standing at the door, leaning against the wall.

The delay in getting everybody seated had given Lund a welcome few seconds to consider the complication presented by Esther's presence. With perfect timing he now took charge of the situation, speaking quietly but with clear articulation.

I presume that you are Mr. and Mrs. Holzinger, and this lady," he looked at Esther and Janiak spoke up.

"She is Mrs. Holzinger's cousin, Esther Lidman."

Lund nodded and turned to the Holzingers.

"Very good. Let me explain to you why we are here. Our names are not important, Mr. Holzinger. What is important is that we have been sent here by the British authorities in London to present a proposal to you and your wife." He paused, but not long enough to invite interruption.

"You may or may not be aware that Germany is rapidly losing the war. The Anglo-American alliance in the West and the Soviet Union in the East each possess resources in manpower and material that are immensely superior to those available to Germany. In this situation Hitler is apparently grasping for super weapons to stave off Germany's defeat as long as possible, and we are aware that you, Mr. Holzinger, are working on one such weapon at Peenemunde."

He paused briefly and looked around the circle. Seeing that his listeners were paying rapt attention, he continued.

"No new or additional weapons can change the war's outcome, but they may conceivably create additional suffering and perhaps extend the hostilities by a few months. The British government is therefore seeking critical information about the German weapons program and urges you, Mr. Holzinger, to do what you can to help shorten the war, for everyone's sake. I have been authorized to offer you, in return for your cooperation, passage to London and secure living for you and your wife until the end of the war. If you elect to accept our offer and come with us, you will, after debriefing in London, be settled in southern England. The two of you will be able to spend the rest of the war in safety, studying or otherwise occupying yourselves, as you may choose.... What is your answer?"

Jantz

Horst Jantz was searching through the day's incoming messages on the RSHA teletype. As Himmler's special assistant, Jantz had unlimited access to all information flowing into and out of the RSHA headquarters in Prinz Albrecht Strasse. His long career as a case analyst with Kripo, the national criminal police, had caught the eye of Himmler, who had transferred him to RSHA to serve as the Reichsfuhrer's eyes and ears in the central organization itself. Jantz' duties in effect amounted to silent, discreet oversight of the organization's top people, reflecting Himmler's need to know of any mistakes committed by his underlings, and to cater to the Reichsfuhrer's personal paranoia.

Having scanned the incoming teletype tray, Jantz checked wireless messages from sundry sources not served by teletype. A message from the SD in Lubeck caught his attention. It had been decoded by the Enigma system, and the SD Abschnit Lubeck must have been forced to fall back on the telegraph as a result of the raid on the city by American B-17s a few days ago. The message was terse and brief: *Small enemy plane crashed on beach near Stralsund, its occupants are believed survived and on the loose in German territory.* Jantz turned his attention to the outgoing messages and quickly ferreted from relevant outgoing traffic a complete picture of the situation. So, the SD and Gestapo's E-I department jointly were casting a dragnet.

Jantz returned to his office in deep thought. What could be the mission of the enemy agents now at large on German soil? The answer to that question might well be the key to catching up with the intruders. What could attract British attention enough to dispatch agents to investigate or take action in the area of the Baltic coast? Jantz lit a cigarette and focused his mind on the question. In his work with the Kripo he had found it useful to analyze the motivations that underlay the commission of crimes. Applying this procedure to a war situation seemed logical as well as much simpler than in the criminal case. Criminals were aberrations from the norm, their actions inherently difficult to predict, whereas military strategic thinking ran along simpler, common-sense lines.

So, what could motivate the British to dispatch agents to some target in the eastern Baltic? Jantz was well aware of the U-boat facilities and the training of crews in the Baltic Sea, but the British and Americans had already gained the upper hand in the Atlantic. He was not taken in by Goebbels' propaganda; Germany's navy, the *Kriegsmarine*, was never a match for the enormous sea power of the Allies. What else lay to the east of Stralsund? Peenemunde, of course. He was well aware of the secret experimentation going on there under von Braun's management, which had already produced the V-1, a flying bomb powered by a pulse-jet engine that was harassing London and inflicting thousands of civilian casualties. The British had demonstrated their interest in Peenemunde by conducting a major raid on the test facility. That facility had to be what the enemy agents had been destined for. Jantz felt sure about it. He took a long drag on his cigarette. But what was the mission of the inserted agents? What could they possibly hope to accomplish at Peenemunde? An attempt at sabotage? He dismissed that as unrealistic. Stealing plans or information? Extremely difficult. Bribing someone among the personnel to leak data or information? That would carry enormous risk, but it could not be dismissed as a long-shot possibility.

Jantz didn't feel he had correctly guessed their mission so far, but he felt certain about the agents being destined for the Peenemunde test facility. He would wait and see what the dragnet might bring in. He looked at both the SD and the Gestapo as bumbling amateurs, when it came to investigative police work, relying mostly on coercion and torture to extract information, but they were perfectly capable of setting up check points and sending out roving patrols. In this case that might well net them an enemy agent or two. In the meantime, he could only ponder and watch from the sidelines, a frustrating prospect.

Assessment

Brigadier Ansley McKinnon took a yellow pack of Cremo pipe tobacco from his desk drawer and began absentmindedly to stuff his pipe while assessing the likelihood that the team he had sent to carry out Operation *Emigrant* might still be viable and functioning. The possible factors to prevent the return of the Lysander were numerous. That it might have been spotted and shot down by a night fighter was unlikely but possible. In case that had taken place on the trip out, they would all have perished, but if it had happened on the return trip after making the drop, the team might be all right. The Lysander could also have been ambushed on the way back, when Morian was refilling his tanks in Denmark, a more likely scenario in which the team also would be intact and operative. Finally, landing at night on an unknown beach was fraught with risk. The plane could have encountered soft sand or mud to prevent a takeoff.

McKinnon decided that the odds were favoring his team being alive and functioning.

As he was lighting his pipe, he answered a knock on the door; Hawes entered and put a Bletchley dispatch on his desk.

"Sir, I believe we can consider this to be good news."

McKinnon read the message, a translation of a dispatch from a security police office in Lubeck to the RSHA in Berlin. *An enemy light plane crashed and burned on the beach at Stralsund. The plane's occupants probably alive and in the area.* McKinnon looked up at Hawes, and they both broke into smiles.

"Well, Jack, our optimism is proving justified."

"Indeed, sir. We may now have a four-man team operative in Stralsund. Fitting in the pilot without any ID will present a minor problem, but with Lund and Lowell both equipped to pose as SD agents, they will be able to overcome that."

McKinnon nodded.

"Assuming that this chap, Holzinger, will cooperate, the question now becomes one of accomplishing the return trip. How Lund and Lowell will attempt that is not easy to forecast. What do you think, Jack?"

"Just hazarding a guess, sir, I'd say they're most likely to try to reach Sweden or Denmark."

McKinnon blew a fragrant cloud of blue smoke.

"That would seem the most likely scenario. We can only wait and see. By the way, what caused the SD to communicate by radio?"

"Bletchley says an American raid on Lubeck with B-17s may have knocked out their teletype connections."

McKinnon nodded thoughtfully. "Let's hope their repair crews are slow."

11

Decision

Holzinger hesitated, gathering his thoughts. What Lund had articulated was what Holzinger had been thinking but not been able to put into words. It made perfect sense, although saying so in public would incur immediate reprisals. Of course Germany was losing the war, but as things now stood, just venting the possibility of a defeat was enough to cause the speaker to disappear. He thought of Henlein's story and its ramifications for his own family, caught up in the Nazi state's relentless pursuit of "racial cleansing" of the national body, a pathologic whim of Hitler's deranged mind and now a deadly threat to the people closest to him. Holzinger straightened up in his chair and calmly met Lund's gaze.

"Does your offer extend to Esther, my wife's cousin?"

Lund had expected the question.

"Mr. Holzinger, I am only authorized to make this offer to you and your wife. The logistics of bringing the two of you to England already presents a considerable challenge. Perhaps we might be able to arrange a pickup for Esther at some future date. That would be something to negotiate once we are back in London."

Holzinger shook his head.

"That is not a possibility."

Unruffled Lund replied.

"I quite understand your concern, but I give you my word that I will do everything in my power to have her cousin taken care of later, so that she might join you in England."

"No! You don't understand!" Holzinger almost shouted the words, startling the little group. "I will tell you why!"

He fought to control his emotions and gather his thoughts before continuing. Then he described his trip to Kassel, his chance meeting with Henlein, and finally Henlein's experience in Auschwitz. When he finished, his listeners sat in frozen silence until Lund spoke up, his voice and intonation conveying more than a little skepticism.

"Are you saying that Germany's Jews—men women and children—are being shipped by the trainload to Poland to be murdered and cremated?"

Put this way, the project sounded outrageous, incredible, and far fetched, so much so as to be unbelievable, but Holzinger stood his ground.

"Yes, that is precisely what I am saying, and my wife tells me that Esther has just received a summons to be picked up for the so-called 'resettlement'."

Holzinger's story had affected Lowell with a rush of emotion. He grasped the edge of the table and leaned forward, staring at Holzinger but not seeing him. His reaction was different from Lund's. He accepted without hesitation what Holzinger had said. This must be the explanation of the official notice that Rachel years ago had "died from illness." She had been young and healthy, a highly unlikely victim of any sudden, fatal illness. The official notice had almost certainly been a cover, perhaps the standard bureaucratic explanation to conceal the simple fact that she had been routinely murdered.

Lund thought quickly. The situation had come to an impasse. He sensed that whether or not the claim about the Nazi resettlement policy was true, this was not the time or place for a lengthy debate about the probability. If the Holzingers' cooperation could be purchased only at the price of Esther's inclusion in the evacuation group, so be it. He looked slowly from Holzinger to Ilse and to Esther, and his voice betrayed no impatience, when he spoke.

"Very well, Mr. and Mrs. Holzinger and Miss Lidman, if you all choose to come with us, are you willing and prepared to follow exactly our instructions?"

He looked at each of them in turn and received confirmation from each before he continued. Speaking English, he addressed Janiak, whose identity was already known.

"Janiak, are you prepared to accept this added complication to our task?"

"Oh, yes, I think it is necessary."

Janiak sounded unfazed and positive, actually cheerful. Lund looked at Lowell and, omitting his name, asked, "How about you?"

Lowell nodded, "I'm in agreement." His voice was hoarse with emotion.

Lund looked at Morian, who exclaimed a hearty, "Hell, yes!" before Lund could pose the question.

Speaking quickly in English Lund said, "I believe our best bet to get out of Germany may be by sea. Morian and I reconnoitered the harbor today, and we found two vessels, each of which may offer possibilities for transport. One is a small Danish freighter that will be returning to Copenhagen already tomorrow, Sunday. Until then it is being watched, as all foreign vessels are. The other is a canal barge that has been drafted into longshore traffic. It will be leaving Monday morning for Kiel with a load of brick, but it will make a stopover for the night in Warnemuende, where we can take it over. I have looked at the train departures westbound from here, and there is one tonight at 3:20 a.m., a slow milk run, which will arrive in Rostock at 5:42. I am guessing that Morian is right about various security agencies getting ready to screen the trains out of here, but they may not have gotten their people deployed yet. Either way, we can have the Holzingers simply take the train to Rostock, where we will meet them and go on to Warnemuende, hijack the barge during the night, and try to reach Denmark."

Lowell asked, "Why not take over the barge here in Stralsund?"

Lund had expected the question.

"Because the barge will be using a pilot to get out of Stralsund harbor, and the problem of getting rid of him would almost certainly sink our scheme."

Morian spoke up.

"We are bound to encounter heavy security, both at the railroad station and on the train. They will be very suspicious, and it's going to be impossible to try to get Janiak and me through. We may stand a better chance by just letting our three German wards go by train, while the rest of us grab the Kubel, go by road, and we reunite with the train group at the train station in Rostock."

Lowell started a comment, "I think...." but the sound of the doorbell stifled their discussion. Esther stepped into the hall, closed the door behind her, opened the front door, and looked into the smiling face of Major Wittmann.

"Good evening, *Fräulein* Lidman." Wittmann clearly expected to be invited in.

Esther thought fast but spoke slowly. "How nice to see you again, Herr Major." She hesitated before continuing, "I would like to invite you in, but I am embarrassed to say my cousin and her husband already are making ready for bed...surely you understand?" She smiled mischievously and blushed, delighting Wittmann who immediately became solicitous and returned her smile with a conspiratorial expression.

"But of course, *Fräulein*. I just wanted to invite you for a morning stroll, ending with lunch at Hotel König Friedrich."

"Oh, that would be lovely. Shall we say at ten o'clock?"

Her smile held just enough promise to captivate Wittmann. He could see that this was going to be an easy conquest. He clicked his heels and confirmed, "Until ten tomorrow," before heading back downstairs.

Esther closed the door quietly, returned to the group in the living room and reported.

"It was Major Wittmann making a date with me for a stroll in the morning and lunch in town. I could not think of any other way to get rid of him, so I told him to come at ten."

Lowell had regained his calm. He forced his mind to let go of the distant memory of Rachel and picked up their previous discussion.

"I think Morian is right. Trying for all of us to go by train is too risky. It might well end with our having to force our way through which could be disastrous. It seems unavoidable to divide our forces until we reach Denmark. One possibility would be for me and the two women to go on the freighter, while the other four can try to make the trip to Rostock in the Kubel." He looked at Lund, "Do you want me on the ship or in the Kubel?"

Lund smiled. He liked Lowell's offhand manner in dealing with crucial operational decisions.

"You'd better take the cruise. I'll go by road."

In order to obtain everybody's consent to the final plan, he switched to speaking German, and the discussion became somewhat lengthy, as Ilse pleaded not to be separated from her husband. In the final outcome, the two Holzingers were to take the train to Rostock. Lund, Janiak and Morian would go by road in the Kubel, while Lowell and Esther would go by ship with Captain Jorgensen.

Janiak had stayed silent during this part of the planning. Now he spoke, striking a lighter note.

"I think Major Wittmann will be greatly disappointed tomorrow at ten."

Roadblock

Dusk was enveloping the Stralsund-Rostock highway on Saturday evening, when Scharfuehrer Johann Schmauser of field gendarmerie Abt. 581 arrived to set up his checkpoint. He had been on duty when the message came from division headquarters, and he had studied it carefully before taking action. It was an order to set up a checkpoint to monitor traffic on the highway between Rostock and Stralsund. All westbound traffic was to be screened to find and apprehend enemy agents fleeing from the crash scene of a small plane on the beach near Stralsund. They were now believed to be attempting an escape westward.

Schmauser had been serving for less than a year, but his prior training in Hitlerjugend had been thorough in preparing him for this kind of assignment. After his draft notice arrived just before his birthday last April, he had been introduced to the special duties of the military police, Germany's field gendarmerie (FG), in his opinion the backbone of the Wehrmacht. Now that he was himself one of the feared *Kettenhunde*, the "chain dogs" that kept the sundry other branches of the Wehrmacht on their toes, he took pride in filling an important function. Aside from the intra-Wehrmacht function, his outfit was occasionally called upon to search for enemy pilots who had bailed out when their planes were crippled by German flak guns. He had personally captured one British airman, a casualty from the recent bombing of Hamburg. His prisoner had been easy enough to deal with, as he had suffered a broken leg when his parachute deposited him in a hard landing on the tile roof of a factory. But enemy agents... now, that was quite different. They would be armed and dangerous. Here was a chance for him to see some action and apply what he had learned. Maybe gain favorable attention. He had deftly contrived to be put in charge of the assignment, with Erich Weiss as Kubel driver and Otto Hecht as gunner manning the Kubel's mounted MG 34 machine gun.

Schmauser chose his location on a stretch of road flanked by ditches on both sides, deep enough to stop anything but a tank. They parked the Kubel at a curve in the road, so that westbound travelers would not see it until close, and they placed it athwart the middle of the road, leaving just enough room for a car to pass on either side. Then the three settled down to wait. By seven in the evening only one vehicle had passed, a small truck carrying farm produce to Rostock. As it was going westward, the three young gendarmes checked it thoroughly, much to the annoyance of the old farmer driving it.

When the truck had left, they broke out their rations and ate while discussing the possibility of any enemy agent coming their way. Erich Weiss scoffed at the idea. "If I were trying to get out of Germany, I sure wouldn't choose to drive on a public highway. It would be safer to walk or steal a bicycle." The others agreed.

"You may be right," Schmauser allowed, "but perhaps the Englishmen are not so clever."

They all laughed.

Night Drive

Janiak stopped at the corner of Feldstrasse and pointed down the street, where the Kubel was dimly visible in the middle of the block. Lund whispered, "Well, let's see if we can get it started," but Morian interrupted him. "Listen, let's not all crowd around. Engines are my specialty, so why don't you guys stay here, and I'll see what I can do."

Lund and Janiak watched as Morian walked silently toward the Kubel and almost disappeared in the darkness. Several minutes went by until the quiet of the night was shattered by the sound of the Kubel's engine springing to life. The hooded headlights simultaneously lit up a small section of the street, and the vehicle surged toward the two figures waiting at the corner.

"Hop in," Morian yelled, slowing just enough for Lund and Janiak to jump aboard, and he headed out of town toward Rostock. In moments they had left Stralsund behind with the empty road stretching before them, surrounded by the dark and silent countryside.

Lund felt certain that they would encounter a checkpoint before they could reach Rostock. There had by now been more than sufficient time for the Wehrmacht's secret field police, or for the regular military police, to set up traffic control in depth around Stralsund by encircling the city with enough checkpoints to screen out any intruders trying to escape by road. He could not come up with an alternative to shooting their way through, and their little group was too lightly armed to challenge a GFP patrol. The other side would have at least one Schmeisser submachine gun plus some nine millimeter handguns, P38s or Lugers, formidable firepower compared with his and Janiak's two PPKs. He put his hand on Morian's arm and signaled him to stop.

When the little car came to a stop in the darkness of the empty and silent highway, Lund spoke up.

"I have a feeling we will run into a checkpoint before reaching Rostock. If we do, I'll try to talk us through on my ID as an SD agent. They will probably insist on seeing papers from all of us, and at that point, we'll have to fall back on shooting our way through. Besides, my explanation for driving a Kubel with the markings of the coast police probably won't sound convincing. In other words, we will have to force our way through against their heavier firepower. I think we can expect a three-man patrol, two of them armed with P38s and rifles, the third with a Schmeisser. The worst scenario would be to encounter a patrol with a Kubel carrying a mounted machine gun. If that should be the case, we'll have to improvise. Morian, drive up as close to the road block as possible. I will get out, walk to the one in charge, and say my piece. If the one with the Schmeisser walks to the car to inspect it, he will probably go to the driver's side.

Morian, you will take him down when he is within arm's reach, so you can't possibly miss with the little Browning. I will deal with the others as the situation may call for. Janiak is our backup and will go for the nearest one of the others, whatever the situation may call for. Remember, Morian, to drive as close as possible before you come to a stop. They will have the advantage of being better armed. We will have the advantage of surprise." Lund paused a moment before asking, "Do you agree to this plan?"

No one spoke, as the ramifications of challenging with only two .32-caliber pistols a well-armed and alert military patrol sank in.

Then Morian laughed. "I hope they haven't gotten their patrols in place yet, but if they have, I hope you guys have practiced your marksmanship recently."

Janiak just said, "OK."

They could think of nothing more to discuss. Morian started the engine, and they continued in a sober mood into the darkness of the empty highway.

Frustration

In Berlin, evening quiet had settled over the RSHA security headquarters. Horst Jantz, Himmler's special assistant, was still sitting at the desk in his office, smoking and thinking, although it was long past his regular office hours. The message from the SD office in Lubeck about the crash of the small British plane had awakened his professional instincts from the days when he was a Kripo investigator, and the puzzle about the plane's destination and purpose was still prodding his curiosity. He had dug out a map of the Baltic region and had minutely perused it, finally concluding that only Peenemunde could be a logical destination for the British agents, confirming his initial guess, but he was unable to visualize any possible scenario from which enemy agents could reasonably hope to benefit.

Jantz finally stubbed out his last cigarette and walked down the long corridor to the communications room, where two operators were handling the night traffic. He pawed through the tray of outgoing mail. So, Brigadefuhrer Best was encircling Stralsund with SS checkpoints and beefing up the railroad police with SS roving patrols. Well, that might yield an agent or two and answer what he most wanted to know, the destination of the British intruders now at large. Experience, intuition, and just plain common sense told him that an operation meriting the risky and cumbersome insertion of possibly several agents so far from home must have a purpose deserving very high priority. Peenemunde was the only answer he could come up with, and that merely raised additional questions, equally tantalizing and obscure. All very frustrating.

Jantz left the teletype room and returned to his office where he picked up his coat and hat. A widower and childless, he walked to his usual restaurant and ordered a late dinner. The evening paper carried interesting news from the Eastern Front, but his mind kept returning to the problem from Stralsund. It was almost midnight when he entered his bachelor apartment and went to bed.

Ram

They came upon the checkpoint quite suddenly as they rounded a curve in the road. Another Kubel was parked sideways across the middle of the road, leaving only a narrow passage on each side. The black silhouette of a mounted MG 34 machine gun loomed above the rear of the parked vehicle, and three soldiers of the field gendarmerie could be perceived in the near-darkness, one in the driver's seat, two standing on the ground smoking. Of the latter, one stubbed out his cigarette and signaled them to stop, while the other turned and started to climb in behind the machine gun.

Morian said between his teeth, "I'm going to ram this fucker! Hang on, and then shoot." He slowed their car in a good imitation of coming to a stop, but at a distance of some twenty-five feet he stomped on the accelerator. The little car surged forward, causing the two soldiers on the ground to jump in desperate attempts to get out of the way. One of them made it by diving into the ditch by the side of the road. The other tried to follow him but was pinned and crushed as the vehicles came together in the crash. The soldier in the driver's seat tried his utmost to get in behind the mounted machine gun. He vaulted over his hapless comrade pinned between the vehicles, succeeded in reaching and sliding into the gunner's seat, and struggled to swing the gun into position.

Lund dove after the soldier in the ditch, gun at the ready, while Morian and Janiak jumped after the would-be machinegunner. Lund fired one shot, killing the soldier in the ditch. As he turned, he heard two shots from Janiak's PPK and saw the machine-gunner slump down onto his weapon. With the beam of his flashlight Lund examined the soldier who was wedged between the two vehicles and determined that he had been killed by the impact. He turned the flashlight on the gunner and made sure he was dead as well.

Morian was struggling with the safe on the Browning, cursing the small gun. He finally gave up and hurled the little gun into the darkness with a hearty obscenity in his native Danish.

"And to think that I've carried this piece of shit around, in the hope that it would get me out of trouble some day. Well, I'm glad you two did better."

"I'd say you are the one who saved the day, gun or no gun," Lund replied. "That maneuver of ramming the Krauts taught them quite a lesson; just too bad for them that they didn't live to benefit from it!"

"Yes, and let's try to keep one step ahead of them, as we did this time," Morian agreed, "and I'll help myself to better fire power right now, seeing that this guy won't need his any more." He fished the P38 out of the holster on the belt of Janiak's victim in the machine-gunner's seat and put the spare clip in his pocket.

Janiak leaned against the car, trying to stop his knees from shaking. The realization that he had just killed a man was momentarily forcing all other thought from his mind. Lund turned toward him, instantly sensing the other's mental state.

"Janiak, thanks for taking down the gunner. I'd say that was the most crucial move, the one that everything else hinged on. I hate to think what he could have accomplished, if he had gotten that machine gun working."

Morian also turned toward Janiak, realizing Lund's intent. He laughed leisurely. "Yes, I'm sure sorry that I couldn't squish that guy, too. A good thing that you took care of him, Janiak."

He poked at the two vehicles, trying to assess the damage.

"I hope we can make one of these two piles of junk function enough to take us to Rostock. I don't feel much like hiking tonight."

With some effort they managed to pry the two Kubels apart. The one with the machine gun mounting had suffered most from the collision, and the frame had been twisted beyond repair. On the one belonging to the coast police, the front fenders had been bent onto the front tires, blocking the front wheels from turning. Morian found a rifle among the scattered equipment and used it as a crowbar to force the fenders sufficiently back to release the wheels. Then he climbed in, started the engine, backed clear of the wreck, and turned the engine off.

"This baby needs some body work, but aside from that it should be good enough for the rest of the trip to Rostock," he announced.

Lund said, "Listen, we've got to get out of here before any other traffic comes this way. Let's put the bodies into the wreck and set it on fire. That may confuse the field gendarmerie enough to cause some delay. Morian, drive our Kubel over here before we torch the wreck."

Ten minutes later Morian poured gasoline from a spare jerrycan over the three Germans and in a twenty-foot trail down the road. "This fire routine is getting rather boring," he said, as he struck a match to light the gasoline trail. The fire leaped to the wreck and a few moments later flared when the Kubel's fuel tank exploded.

12

Planning

It was nearly four o'clock on Sunday morning and still dark when Morian dropped Lund and Janiak in the outskirts of Rostock and continued in the damaged Kubel on the highway toward Lubeck; the others started on foot toward the railroad station. The three had discussed the most inconspicuous way for them to reach Warnemuende, and they were now implementing their simple plan. Morian would try to leave the Kubel with an empty gas tank a couple of kilometers on the other side of town on the Lubeck road, leading pursuers to believe they were taking this route, attempting to travel by road to Denmark. He would double back on foot and rejoin the others at the railroad station. In case of a checkpoint, he would make a run for it and improvise.

The town of Rostock was dark and silent when Morian drove through. Two kilometers out into the countryside he stopped, made a small puncture in the gas tank and drove on a short distance until the Kubel stuttered to a halt. Leaving it at the side of the road, he started back toward town on foot.

The Rostock railroad station was quiet but not entirely empty when Lund and Janiak arrived. Movement of the large number of refugees, a growing segment of the population overwhelmingly dependent on rail transportation, made this component of Germany's infrastructure stressed around the clock. Lund checked on the scheduled arrival time of the train from Stralsund, and the two SOE agents found a quiet corner in the third class waiting room. It was just after five when Morian arrived to join them, and when he was seated, Lund started a whispered conversation in Danish.

"Obviously, our various movements have not caused any general alarm or intensive search so far, but that can't last very long. They will start coming after us shortly, and we will be sitting ducks traveling this way. The ferry route to Denmark will certainly cause Warnemuende to be combed and keenly watched, and I don't know how we would be able to keep a low enough profile in a small town like that."

Morian kept his voice very low when he replied.

"Listen, as you know, I'm definitely a newcomer to this branch of the war, and the way we have to knock off Krauts right and left tends to give me pause. I mean, our luck can't possibly hold much longer, and when all hell breaks loose, as I think it must be about to do, we'll be in real trouble. How about finding a quiet hotel room to hide in both today and tomorrow? Tomorrow night we could get ourselves to Warnemuende, maybe by simply walking, and see what the situation looks like when we get that far."

Lund thought for a while before commenting.

"I like the idea of a hotel room, if we can get everybody in there discreetly. I think a large hotel would be best, and a location on the side of town toward Warnemuende would be preferable, but we'd better wait until after breakfast time to arouse less notice."

Their planning was interrupted by the sound of the incoming train from Stralsund. Lund sent Janiak to find the Holzingers, and he shortly appeared with them in the trickle of arriving travelers. They all sat down together, and Lund relayed Morian's suggestion about a hotel room. The Holzingers agreed, and Lund turned to Janiak and told him to locate a place to meet their needs, specifying the preferred location and features. When Janiak had left, Lund turned toward Morian.

"I thought the situation in Stralsund would stay quiet until that Luftwaffe major arrives at ten to pick up Esther, but taking out an entire patrol of field gendarmerie—the effects will surely be immediate. I can't even imagine how they will react. We'd better find that hotel quickly and get ourselves out of sight."

Rita

Lowell and Esther stayed well behind as the Holzingers entered the Stralsund railroad station and purchased tickets to Rostock. Ilse and Hans were each carrying a small suitcase with a few clothes—it would look unusual to travel without any baggage. The night train was on time, only half full, and the couple found a compartment to themselves. Trailing behind them, Lowell made sure that they got into the empty compartment. The choice of one of the SOE team to travel along with Esther had been limited to Lund and Lowell as the only ones with sufficient ID papers to brush off possible checks until she could reach Denmark, and there to organize their further progress toward the Swedish haven. Lund had chosen for himself the riskier task of taking the Kubel to Rostock and from there to shepherd the Holzingers to Warnemuende and to their further escape on the barge.

When the train left with the Holzingers, Lowell told Esther to follow him to the harbor, keeping him just within sight. When she saw him boarding the ship, she was to wait a few minutes and then follow him, if all seemed quiet.

Lowell entered the harbor and found the *Rita* where Lund's minute directions had placed her. Silent as a shadow he crossed the gangplank, roused Captain Jorgensen, and introduced himself in English and by his own name. Then he explained Lund's plan. Jorgensen was dubious.

"Without speaking Danish, and never having been to Denmark, do you really think that you can manage to get yourself and the young woman to Sweden without being detected by the Germans? Copenhagen has been crawling with Gestapo recently, after some of your fellow agents shot up their headquarters and got away."

Lowell smiled.

"Lund will be going by a different conveyance, and we plan to meet in Copenhagen, where he will organize our trip to Sweden."

Jorgensen still looked doubtful.

"It seems to me your plan depends on luck to a considerable extent."

Lowell concurred.

"You are right, but there is a saying that luck favors the best prepared actors on the stage of reality."

Their discussion was taking place on the unlit bridge, where he could observe the pier as well as the darkness allowed. He tensed as he saw the outline of Esther as she materialized near the end of the gangplank. Moments later he introduced her to Jorgensen, who guided them below to his cabin. After they were seated, he laid out the plan he visualized for their departure and transport.

"We had better not turn on any lights, that might just attract attention. I have not mentioned your presence to any of my crew—there are five of them—but I will do so after we are underway. They can be depended on to keep their mouths shut at our arrival in Copenhagen. The harbor pilot will show up at eight o'clock to get us underway. There is an equipment locker aft of the main hold, which can serve as a hiding place while the pilot is aboard, say, from daybreak until an hour or so after we leave the harbor. From now until daybreak we will stay here in my cabin, and Miss Lidman can take a nap on my bunk, if she would like."

When Jorgensen made the offer to her in German, Esther declined, but she sat down on the bunk and leaned against a pillow, while Lowell quizzed Jorgensen about current conditions in Denmark, the growing resistance, and public attitudes. After a few minutes their quiet conversation in English appeared to her as a distant drone, and it combined with the excitement of the night to take its toll. Her eyes closed, and she was instantly asleep.

At seven o'clock Lowell gently shook Esther awake, and Jorgensen led them to the equipment locker, a three-by-six foot steel cabinet holding some tarpaulins, rope and slings, all neatly stacked and with sufficient space for the temporary occupants. Jorgensen assured them that their stay would be brief, and that he would return when it seemed safe. They seated themselves side by side on a coiled hawser, and there was just enough room in the steel box for the two bodies to co-exist. When the door clanged shut, Lowell gently put his arm around Esther; she relaxed and leaned against him, closing her eyes in their temporary enclosure, supremely content to be by his side, and warmed by his physical presence. Total relaxation overcame her again, and in the quiet darkness she sank back into sound sleep.

Sleeping in his arms, Esther's presence sent sweet fire shooting through Lowell. Already when they met a few hours earlier, he had felt enormously drawn to her, so much so that he found it difficult to focus his mind on their mission and the immediate problems it presented. He recalled the feel of her body when she had briefly leaned against him in the Holzingers' entry hall. It had been a test of his will to resist an immediate impulse to embrace her, just as he now had to force himself to refrain from doing so.

As the sounds of the crew beginning another day became faintly audible to them, Lowell was further overcome by a feeling that fate had directed their paths to cross at the crucial juncture when the venomous evil of the Nazi state was reaching out to destroy her, as it had destroyed Rachel. He swore to himself that she would not suffer that fate. He would get her to England, no matter how many Nazis he would have to kill along the way. And he foresaw that there would be several scrapes coming up. He assessed their shipboard situation as fairly safe, whereas Lund's dash in the Kubel with what amounted to two novices was a far riskier undertaking. If they were held up or killed, he would have a demanding task on his hands, taking Esther to Denmark and on to England via Sweden. He had a slip of paper Lund had given him before they parted, asking him to memorize the information it contained and then destroy the slip. He closed his eyes in the darkness and recalled what it contained. *The captain's name was Aage Jorgensen; the best contact person in Copenhagen was Anna Hansen, owner of a bar named "Bodega" in the street*

Vesterbrogade near the main railroad station; a backup was Helge Lindbergh, a physician at the Bispebjerg hospital.

Lowell had come to the realization that Lund was a real pro at this kind of warfare. The paper's information "would be useful," Lund had said, "in case they were separated," or if Lowell for some reason had to take charge of completing their mission and getting them to England. Lowell went over the details of the message once more to make sure the information was firmly fixed in his mind. When he got out of this box, he would destroy the paper slip.

Of the four non-Germans now comprising the SOE team, Lowell was the one with the most profound understanding of the typical German mind-set. He respected the intelligence and logic that predominate among the Teutonic tribal features, and he was well aware of the pride that frequently competed with these features to influence collective action. Adding yet another factor, the security agencies that confronted the SOE agents at this moment would be under strong pressure to show result.

Assuming intelligence, logic, and pride on the part of their adversaries, and adding heavy pressure to show results in the cat-and-mouse chase that was getting underway, what could the SOE agents and their German wards expect to have to overcome? And, more specifically, when and to what extent would their adversaries have divined the purpose and general scheme of the SOE's project? The disappearance of Hans Holzinger would be a key element in explaining the presence of the SOE agents. That would not have become obvious until Holzinger would have been missed at the Peenemunde test facility on Monday morning, but unfortunately, intervention by Colonel Wittmann would unveil this aspect already on Sunday morning—in just a couple of hours. At that point the disappearance of the entire Holzinger family would certainly stir up a general alarm. The two security agencies primarily responsible for taking counter measures in this matter were the Gestapo and SD. What steps would they be likely to take?

He bent his head and gently kissed Esther's hair. *Yes, I swear I'll get you to London, no matter how many Nazi murderers try to stop us.*

Foiled

Heinz Huber was an early riser, even on Sundays. And this was a special Sunday, the day when he would be serving the German state a worthy offering, Esther Lidman, a miserable piece of Jewish filth who had dared to question his authority and was now destined to regret it. Huber decided to brighten his morning by going to the train and seeing her off, enjoying to watch her being swept away, never to return. The railroad station was empty when he strolled through. It was still a few minutes before the scheduled arrival of the special train, but it bothered Huber that the one passenger who should be waiting was nowhere to be seen. Would she ignore the order Metzger had sent by special messenger? That sounded hardly possible. He paced the platform impatiently while keeping an eye on the station entrance, but no one appeared. In the distance he heard the train approaching, and he saw Metzger at the station entrance, quickly scanning the scene and waving when he recognized Huber. Metzger walked toward Huber as quickly as his limp allowed.

"Herr Huber, I don't see the woman here, and I am certain she was put on notice by special messenger." The young servant of the state sounded both disappointed and incredulous.

"Yes Frantz, and this is outrageous." Huber was red in the face and sputtering. "We have never before had a single case of a Jew not showing up for resettlement after being summoned. We cannot hold the train, but we must immediately enlist the city police to arrest and jail her until you can arrange another transport opportunity."

Ten minutes later the two diligent bureaucrats broke the Sunday morning quiet at the city police station, where Gerhard Ackers, the assistant chief, was enjoying a cup of ersatz coffee with his morning paper. He listened politely to the two officials as they excitedly relayed their story. When they had finished, he looked thoughtful.

"Tomorrow, I will send a man to investigate, and we will find out why Fraulein Lidman did not appear."

"No, no," Huber was shouting, "the matter is urgent. We must not allow more time to pass. She may be absconding, and we may never find her."

"Have you any reason to believe that she would do so? Or does this Fraulein have any special importance?"

The excitement demonstrated by his visitors clearly failed to infect Ackers.

Huber pulled himself together and delivered his reply with the utmost formality.

"She is a Jew, and the decision to resettle all Jews has been made at the highest level. I believe the circumstances speak for themselves."

Reluctantly, Ackers opened the door to the next room and motioned for someone to come. A policeman in his early sixties appeared, and Ackers explained the situation to him in a few words before turning to Huber.

"This is Wachtmeister Max Haff, he will go with you and make the necessary inquiries."

Ten minutes later the three men mounted the stairs to the Holzinger apartment, and Haff rang the doorbell. When no one answered, Huber rushed off to find the building superintendent. This turned out to be an elderly woman, Frau Hofer, who reluctantly climbed the stairs while protesting that she had insufficient authority to enter the apartment just on Huber's say-so. She was greatly relieved at the sight of the policeman and willingly produced her pass key to allow the group to enter. After looking through the rooms, Max Haff shook his head and made ready to leave, returning the pass key.

"So the family is not at home. They may have gone for a walk or they may be away on some legitimate errand. We may return later, Frau Hofer."

She looked relieved and allowed that the Holzingers were a fine and respectable family. Huber snorted derisively, but Haff ignored him. As they were about to leave, Major Wittmann entered through the open front door. He took in the situation in a quick glance and addressed Max Haff.

"What is going on here?"

Yielding to the persuasive power of an immaculate uniform, Haff came to attention.

"It appears that a Jewish woman, Esther Lidman, has failed to comply with a summons to leave for resettlement this morning, and I am here to look into the matter."

Wittmann was momentarily speechless, as the full implications of this piece of information dawned on him. Esther's racial background was of secondary importance to him as was the fact that she apparently had foiled an attempt to resettle her. What was striking him forcefully and deeply hurting his pride was the fact that she must have been stringing him along, pretending to accept his invitation to lunch without any intent to keep their agreement. Wittmann's male ego and his considerable vanity had never been injured like this before. As the full scope of her deceit became clear, he concluded that he had been made to look ridiculous. He, Major Herbert Wittmann, had been somehow taken advantage of, maybe even made to look foolish by a pretty girl. He felt his anger rising.

Hotel Neptun

The two-room suite in the large and elegant Hotel Neptun was listed as occupied by Lund in his identity of Martin Hagen (an SD agent whose career had been terminated a few weeks earlier by SOE agents on a different assignment). Some discreet reconnais-sance had revealed a backdoor entrance through which the rest of the party had entered unobserved. They now enjoyed a handsome water view only two blocks from the Warnemuende road. Neither of the train travelers had been able to sleep while underway, but exhaustion, physical as well as mental, had caught up with both of the Holzingers, who were resting in the bedroom. Lund and Morian were starting to formulate their further plans, until Lund broke it off.

"I don't think my mind is clear enough to make any sensible plans just now. I know we all need sleep, and I think we are safe enough for a little while to allow ourselves a bit of rest. How do you guys feel?"

Morian spoke up.

"Without rest we're for sure not going to carry out any plans. I'll volunteer for the first watch, while you two get some shuteye."

A few minutes later, all were asleep except Morian. He pulled a chair up to the window, lit a cigarette, and sat down to contemplate their situation. Taking part in a different aspect of the titanic struggle this war had developed into, Morian was attuned to the highly individual one-on-one confrontation the fighter pilot was trained to encounter. He often functioned with a wingman, but his preference of roaming the limitless reaches of the atmosphere alone had made him eminently suited to seeking out and destroying other lonely hunters who differed from him only by the swastika painted on their fuselage. By comparison, his present involvement as an impromptu SOE operative was one of being submerged in a sea of enemies, where he could survive only by reliance on other agents, fellow combatants, whose courage and abilities he would never know in advance but had to accept simply on faith. It was not his preferred way to fight.

As with fighting men in general, Morian was preoccupied with the here and now of the struggle that occupied him. The larger setting in which the warring nations contended rarely received his attention, but the present situation had forcibly brought him face to face with factors and circumstances that until now had been blurry and indistinct background. Born and reared in Denmark, he knew only the Danish scene intimately, and even that had in his absence changed profoundly under the impact of experiencing occupation by foreign troops, an unheard-of condition in the kingdom's thousand year history.

He stubbed out the half-smoked cigarette and let himself sink dreamily into pleasant reverie. Now, what about the other countries in Europe's northern fringe? He knew that Iceland was occupied by Allied troops to keep the tiny nation from falling into Hitler's grasp. Finland had been forced nominally into the German embrace, when Stalin had tried to extend his grasp to dominate the areas of Petsamo and the Karelian Isthmus. Norway and Denmark had been strategically essential to Germany, key pieces in the chess game of military operations, but Sweden was in a different category. Why had the Swedes been spared German domination? He knew that they possessed iron ore deposits essential to Hitler's armaments production. Were they supplying what Hitler wanted in order to stay out of trouble...? He didn't know.

The sound of regular breathing by his resting comrades had a mesmerizing effect as it combined with physical exhaustion and mental fatigue to paralyze his capacity to think. The hotel seemed a safe refuge. The chair was comfortable. His eyes slowly closed, against his will.

13

Pursuit

In the Holzinger apartment Wachtmeister Haff interpreted Wittmann's silence as indifference, and he spoke up to bring the matter to a close.

"Well, I shall report the Lidman woman as an escapee, and we should be able to pick her up shortly."

"No, no," Huber stormed, "her cousin, Ilse Holzinger is also Jewish, so we may have a conspiracy here that needs to be unraveled. This is most serious and deserves the highest priority."

The Holzinger name roused Wittmann from his momentary inertness. He turned to Huber.

"What do you know about the Holzingers?"

Huber puffed himself up. Now, finally, they were listening to *him*, the official who had single-handedly uncovered a plot, or something like it, he wasn't quite sure, but no doubt some Jewish skullduggery.

"I have an instinct when it comes to personnel matters, and it led me to dig into this case. I followed this Jewish trail from Hamburg to Rendsburg to Stralsund and finally uncovered enough evidence to send the Lidman woman to resettlement in the East. I was working on the particulars of the Holzinger woman's case, when this happened, and it appears quite obvious that the family is implementing some scheme to avoid the resettlement that the law ordains for all Jews."

Wittmann's vanity made him vulnerable to flattery, but he was not a fool. He realized that Holzinger's prospect of seeing his wife and Esther banished to God knows what in the East might very well have unhinged the man to the point of reacting rashly. Wittmann couldn't imagine what Holzinger could or might do, but he was deeply involved in the Luftwaffe's very secret and sensitive experimental work. Having him missing and at loose ends could not be countenanced.

Addressing Haff, Wittmann took charge of the situation. "I want you immediately to put the city police on high alert. You will have to assume that the Holzingers will try to leave the area, perhaps try to disappear among refugees in the general confusion. Hans Holzinger is involved in sensitive military work and must be found and apprehended without delay. Hurry back to your office and get this started. I will go with you and do some telephoning to take other steps."

Huber beamed with pleasure. Finally someone acknowledged that this case was urgent. He started to speak, but Wittmann cut him off. "You and your colleague will say nothing about this to anybody." He turned toward the stairway with a brief "Come!" over his shoulder to Haff.

Ten minutes later he was reporting the situation and his action by telephone from the police station to Colonel Schwenke at Peenemunde. This just might enhance his career, he decided. For good measure, he made a call to Gestapo's office in Lubeck. After these accomplishments Wittmann leaned back in police chief Engelhart's chair and contemplated what to do next. Being unable to think of anything else, he tried to assess the chances that Esther and the Holzingers would be caught. Good, he decided. Perhaps he would see Esther one more time. He would like that.

Revelation

Horst Jantz had finished lunch in his usual restaurant. It was a small place, conveniently located in the same block as his apartment building, and he enjoyed the extra attention accorded him as being one of their repeat customers. The Stralsund incident was still tantalizing him as he lit a cigarette and, once again, went over the details in his mind. The known facts were few and fit into no operational scheme he could visualize. He did not like problems that made no sense in any combination of logical enemy pursuits. And yet, his instincts and experience as an investigator told him that the dispatch of a plane and perhaps several agents this far—a high-risk undertaking in the best of circumstances—all testified to the scheme's high priority. He finally decided to go back to the RSHA headquarters and check the message traffic for further clues. It wasn't unusual for him to drop in at odd hours, a benefit, if one could call it that, of having no family or other distractions.

The Sunday quiet did not extend to the communications section. There were only four operators on duty, but they were busy, two handling the teletypes, the others working on decoding incoming wireless traffic from the far-flung battle fronts and from some of the German-occupied countries. Jantz quickly scanned both the incoming and outgoing teletype trays of interest as well as the incoming wireless traffic. There were several messages pertaining to the Stralsund incident, and he sat down and began to take notes. One wireless message from Rostock reported that a field gendarmerie patrol had actually been wiped out on the Stralsund-Rostock highway. Jantz read it a second time, for it seemed hardly believable. He knew the Wehrmacht's "chain dogs" to be as tough as one could expect from an elite outfit; they rarely came off second best in any scrape. Did the enemy agents travel with automatic weapons? And the location indicated that the inserted agents must have abandoned their plan about going farther east, probably to Peenemunde. They must now be fleeing and so desperate to get away that they had simply blown a hole in the dragnet. Well, that would certainly stir up a maximum effort of intensified search. The entire region must be going on alert status right now.

Jantz pawed through the rest of the messages. *Checkpoints set up both west and east of Stralsund...railroad police checking trains leaving Stralsund...and with two-man patrols.* This one was from Gestapo in Lubeck and he suddenly came to attention. *An engineer from Peenemunde missing...with a Jewish wife and a Jewish sister-in-law.* And here was one from a Colonel Schwenke, apparently Luftwaffe liason officer at Peenemunde...but wait....

The whole picture suddenly came together in a flash, and it made perfect sense! He sat, momentarily stunned, contemplating the scope, the simplicity, and the audacity of the total scheme. British Intelligence was at this moment well advanced on a project of snatching an engineer from the Peenemunde staff, someone who would know the essential current information about the V-2 experimentation that the English planners badly wanted. The Jewish wife must be the explanation for the man's defection. How could British Intelligence know about that? There were multiple possibilities, of course. Jews had their own network, no doubt. Coordinating the necessary moves would have been quite a challenge, but the British were smart, capable, when it came to this kind of operation, he'd give them that. The crash on the beach had been an accident, unexpected but not impossible to overcome. It now depended on the quality of Germany's counter intelligence effort—basically simple police work by the various agencies involved—whether the British plan were to succeed or be thwarted.

Clearly neither the Gestapo nor the SD had divined the full implications of the British insertion, nor for that matter was that Luftwaffe Colonel at Peenemunde aware of what was afoot. Evidently he, Horst Jantz, was so far the only one with the insight and experience and brains to piece together the sundry scraps of information to bring the total picture into focus. This was an opportunity to call favorable attention to his good work, and he knew exactly how to do that. His face broke into a thin smile, as he went to his office and called Himmler at home.

"I apologize for disturbing you on Sunday, Herr Reichsfuhrer, but I thought you might wish to be immediately informed about a matter of some urgency and importance."

Before Jantz had fully explained the situation, Himmler cut him short.

"I shall be in my office shortly. Tell Brigadefuhrer Erhardt and Best to report to my office immediately."

Himmler hung up without waiting for an answer.

Rylen

A squall passing over the Fehmarn Belt momentarily churned the surface water and blotted out the horizon. Aboard *Rylen* Egon Frandsen and his helper Jens Olsen stepped into the wheelhouse, where Frandsen throttled the engine back to idling speed and took in the slack on his midwater trawl, while assessing the pelting rain before turning to his helper.

"Jens, pour us a cup of coffee. We may just have time for one while waiting for this to clear."

They had made a quick turnaround at home after unloading their last catch—a good one, Frandsen had to admit—and had hurried back to sea because the sprat was choosing to make a late-season run. It was one of mother nature's quirks of which fishermen eagerly take advantage whenever they occur. The fat little fish was very unpredictable, but its food value was substantial, no small matter in wartime, and enough to make a fisherman scramble to seek out the immense shoals that could contain sprat by the millions.

Frandsen was fishing along the line of the Fehmarn Belt's *Sperrgebiet*, an area closed to fishing "for military reasons." Well, they were actually far *inside* the forbidden area, for the fishing was better here. Frandsen didn't give a damn about those "military reasons," and they could shove their *Sperrgebiet*. This was where he had been fishing all his life, and he had a far better right to be here than those Nazi bastards. Besides, Hitler's troops had their hands full elsewhere these days. On the Eastern Front near Kursk they were locked with the Russians in what might be the largest armored battle in history. And in the west the Royal Air Force bombers were systematically leveling the cities of the Third Reich.

The Fehmarn Belt formed a narrow strait between the Danish islands of Lolland and Falster to the north, and the island of Fehmarn and the German mainland to the south. At the moment, the sprat seemed very fond of this body of water, and Frandsen was scooping them up by the hundredweight. The squall moved on and Frandsen put his coffee cup in the holder.

"Come on, Jens, we've got more work to do."

Himmler

In his office Himmler looked coldly at his two underlings standing at attention before his desk, at length fixing his gaze on Brigadefuhrer Werner Best.

"I see that we have enemy agents on the loose in the Stralsund area. What has SD done to apprehend them? After all, enemy agents on the loose on our fatherland's soil are very much a concern for this branch of our security apparatus, is it not?"

Best cleared his throat. "Certainly, Herr Reichsfuhrer. I have requested field gendarmerie to set up checkpoints around Stralsund and I have alerted the railroad police on the Stralsund line to increase their patrols. And I have asked Brigadefuhrer Erhardt to notify Gestapo in Lubeck and Peenemunde to bring their resources to bear."

"In that case," Himmler continued evenly, "you are aware, I assume, that one of your checkpoints has been destroyed, no doubt by the agents you are trying to catch?"

Brigadefuhrer Best had not had time to check the incoming messages. He swallowed hard. "No, Herr Reichsfuhrer, I was not aware of that."

"So, I gather that you did not think the matter of sufficient importance for you to keep up to the minute about developments."

Best gulped, but before he could formulate a suitable reply, Himmler turned his attention toward Erhardt, who seemed to shrink under his gaze. "As for you, Heinrich, tell me what our Gestapo has accomplished under your management in this urgent matter?"

"Herr Reichsfuhrer, my people in Rostock and Peenemunde are working on this case, and with the field police we have been casting a dragnet over the area. I expect we will be able to apprehend one or more enemy agents any moment."

Himmler looked unimpressed.

"So far, these intruders have been costing us dearly and have gotten away with it. So let me ask both of you, what exactly is the mission of this team of agents? In order to catch them, it would be helpful to know what they are after. I presume you have both been analyzing the situation, so tell me your conclusions or at least your guesses."

After a moment's silence, Best spoke up, his voice tentative, as he decided to proffer Erhardt's earlier suggestion as his own.

"Herr Reichsfuhrer, it occurred to me that our submarine bases along the Baltic coast may be the object these snooping agents are interested in."

Himmler snorted derisively and turned to Erhardt.

"What about you, Heinrich is that also your opinion?"

Having seen Himmler's reaction, Erhardt quickly disowned the idea.

"Herr Reichsfuhrer, I think their probable destination was our testing ground in Peenemunde, although their precise purpose appears obscure to me."

"Well then, let me tell you that I see no obscurity. On the contrary, the picture appears perfectly clear, in fact simple and straight forward. The British have lured an engineer from Peenemunde to defect, and they are in the process of extracting him under our noses...under *your* noses, I should say."

The Reichsfuhrer leaned back in his chair and glowered at his two subordinates, savoring their discomfort before driving his point home.

"I must tell you both that I do not wish to be doing simple analytical work for you. That British Intelligence arranged a Peenemunde defection, and that the British are now trying to take the defector to London are simple facts you should have figured out—information *you* should have brought to *me*, not the other way around. How can I with confidence look the fuehrer in the eye and tell him that we have the fatherland's security in hand, when I must personally watch that you draw the proper conclusions from data in front of you? Now that I have set you on the right track, is it too much to expect you to take it from here and apprehend the agents and the defector? If you cannot do that much, perhaps I should look for more capable talent to head up your departments."

Himmler dismissed the two Brigadefuhrer and leaned back in his chair, thoroughly pleased with his own performance and with the role he had assigned himself in this matter of high importance. Jantz was proving to be the perfect choice for internal overseer, *his* perfect choice.

Countermove

Brigadier Ansley McKinnon had finished his morning tea ritual when WAAF Lieutenant Ann Curtis placed the Bletchley intercepts on his desk before him. The disruption caused by the recent air raids had temporarily forced internal German communications to switch from teletype to wireless equipment using the *Enigma* cipher, which the British code breakers at Bletchley were able to read without difficulty. The weekend's message traffic had been voluminous, and Ann lingered by McKinnon's desk, expecting his reaction. It was not long in coming.

"Oh, Miss Curtis, would you ask Major Hawes to come."

Ann disappeared, and moments later a knock on the office door announced the arrival of his assistant. When they were both seated, McKinnon pushed the intercepts across the desk to Hawes.

"I say, Jack, look at the latest development. Our people appear to be quite active."

Hawes read slowly through the intercepts and placed them back on the desk.

"Too bad that circumstances have made it necessary for them to use force. Pitting their handguns against the arms of a highway patrol is a very uneven fight. But apparently they have prevailed, so far, although I should think they have turned that piece of the Baltic coast into a hornets' nest by now. Wiping out a patrol of field gendarmerie—I cannot recall our people having performed anything equivalent in the past. Apparently the team has succeeded in picking up the Holzinger chap. It seems unclear to me whether they also have taken charge of his wife, and maybe even the cousin. To exit Germany with a group that size would present formidable problems."

McKinnon nodded.

"We are now talking about a group of five, or six, or possibly seven. The logistics of shepherding that many through an enemy territory that has already been stirred into a frenzy—I can hardly visualize the feasibility, when the opposition certainly will spare no effort to catch or kill."

Hawes was looking through the intercepts a second time; he slowly put them back on the desk before speaking.

"It may be that our entry into the picture is also entailing an involvement by the civilian authorities in their persistent attempts to pursue and ferret out German citizens of Jewish ancestry."

McKinnon looked thoughtful.

"If so, our proposal may have seemed timely to the Holzingers, to say the least. In any event, it looks like Lund has been successful to the extent of enlisting their cooperation. An attempt to escape through Denmark still seems to me the most likely possibility. Can you think of something, anything at all, we can do to weight their chances a bit?"

Hawes considered the question.

"As a matter of fact, sir, I have been thinking about ways in which we might influence events, but I haven't come up with anything concrete except for a preliminary step."

"Oh?" McKinnon knew his aide well enough to realize that any suggestion he would posit would be well worth considering.

McKinnon had filled his pipe and was concentrating on lighting it properly. The action prompted Hawes to open a pack of Players Navy Cut, extract a cigarette, and light it before speaking.

"Our experience has been that we gain real insights into German plans and actions whenever their teletype message traffic is temporarily interrupted, as usually happens after Bomber Command or the Americans conduct a major raid that paralyzes their telephone lines.

Until the lines are restored, they are forced to use coded radio communication, which Bletchley is able to monitor."

McKinnon confirmed his attention with a grunt, as Hawes took a puff on his cigarette before continuing.

"It seems to me, sir, that there are times when reading German radio traffic is of particular importance to us. Right now, for example, it would be of practical value to know the up-to-date situation of the *Emigrant* team. If we could force the other side to use radio instead of teletype, even briefly and temporarily, it might reveal something about the team and make a critical difference in our operations."

Between two puffs on his pipe McKinnon posed a question.

"Are you suggesting that we try to influence Bomber Command or the Americans to lay on their raids to suit our needs for information?"

Hawes shook his head.

"No, sir, I know that wouldn't work, but there may be another way to the same end. Both the Gestapo and the SD depend on teletype to communicate with their offices in the occupied countries in Europe. We also know that their military telephone landlines for the most part are strung in a temporary manner, often just tacked onto existing telephone poles, usually quite vulnerable. And in all of these countries we have contacts with resistance elements that have, or can quickly develop, the capacity to sabotage the landline connections. In the case at hand we might try to see if resistance people in Denmark can on short notice sever some of the lines for us."

McKinnon blew a large, fragrant blue cloud of Cremo smoke, as he weighed the merits of the idea before committing to a reply. At length he turned his gaze from the ceiling and fixed it on Hawes across the desk.

"By Jove, Jack, I think the idea is brilliant, and it seems almost providential that our list of drops has one scheduled for tonight in Jutland. Maybe Hansen would like to strap on a parachute to go along and arrange a teletype blackout."

McKinnon was referring to SOE's supplying of explosives to sabotage groups by parachute drops, a procedure that had been perfected from tentative and experimental to something bordering on routine. Hawes considered the suggestion pensively and at length until McKinnon finally broke the silence.

"I believe Hansen would enjoy the assignment. Do you have some concern or reservations about dispatching him?"

Hawes shook his head.

"Not at all, sir, but it just struck me that we might have him arrange a Lysander pickup of the German engineer, in case our *Emigrant* team has actually arrived in Denmark, when he gets there. I was just trying to imagine how Hansen would go about finding them."

McKinnon leaned back in his chair as he addressed this new wrinkle in the propopsal.

"I would leave that to him. Remember, he and Lund spent some time in Copenhagen on their last assignment and received help from several individuals, some of whom Lund will probably be contacting and relying on again. See if you can locate Hansen and get him in here right away, then we can get his opinion of your idea.

It was early afternoon when Hawes and Viggo Hansen sat down across from McKinnon, and the brigadier looked approvingly at the young agent. Viggo

Hansen had recently, on his very first SOE assignment, been part of an SOE team that had successfully extracted an atomic scientist from Gestapo's clutches.

"Well, Hansen, have you been enjoying some London sightseeing since your return from the continent?"

Hansen smiled.

"To tell the truth, sir, I didn't know how much damage the German bombers have done to the city, but there is still a lot to see."

"Hmm...yes, and air raids are becoming scarcer. It seems that Hitler needs his air force elsewhere. Now, the reason we have called you in here so suddenly is that a situation is forcing us to intervene in Germany's communications."

McKinnon went on to outline the need to interrupt teletype transmissions between Germany and Denmark. How would Hansen suggest accomplishing that in Denmark?

Hansen thought only for a moment.

"When I was bicycling in Jutland on my last trip, I noticed that what looks like a main communication cable is attached to the telephone poles along the north-south highway on the west coast. It looks like a temporary military installation that has become permanent. The cable is rubber covered and about the size of my wrist. It would be easy to sabotage by simply cutting and removing a section of the cable, and it would be easy enough to keep it interrupted by repeated cutting and removal elsewhere at night. It would be impossible for the Germans to guard the cable on the entire length of the road."

McKinnon came to the point.

"We are dropping a quantity of weapons and explosives in Jutland near the town of Ringkobing tonight. How would you like to go along and remove a section of that cable? Maybe you can ask the people receiving the shipment to give you a hand and get it done on their way home?"

Again, Hansen did not hesitate.

"I would like that, sir."

McKinnon turned to Hawes.

"In that case, Major, why don't you notify Tempsford that we have a passenger to go with tonight's shipment. And please bring Hansen up to date on the status of Mr. Lund's whereabouts to the extent we know it, so that he might be able to help his colleague, as he did recently in Holland. Give Hansen a tentative pickup date...or better, give him two dates and two radio codes such as we used before. Then we can arrange for a second Lysander pickup, to retrieve the whole *Emigrant* team."

14

Copenhagen

With a harbor pilot at the wheel, the coastal freighter *Rita* slowly nosed to her assigned berth in the commercial section of Copenhagen's extensive harbor complex. It was Monday morning, and the harbor was waking to a workday's routines, as the peals of the city hall bells announced the hour of nine. When the gangplank clanged into place, a bored customs officer appeared and posed a few routine questions to Captain Jorgensen, although no vessel incoming from Germany would have anything that could remotely be considered contraband. The possibility of stowaways had not been considered.

When the inevitable paper work had been completed, the crew quickly scattered to spend a few hours with their respective families. Only Jorgensen stayed aboard with his mate Karl Olsen, the latter because his family lived too far away to allow time for visiting before loading another cargo was to begin the following day. While they were at sea, Jorgensen had introduced to him their two unscheduled passengers, and as the four of them now sat down to a relaxing cup of morning coffee in his cabin, conversation began to flow freely in a mixture of English and German. Lowell told them that Lund had given him the address of a woman who could arrange their further transport to Sweden. Olsen cheerfully allowed that the Underground network making this traffic possible had grown so extensive that escape to the Swedish haven was now thought of as an ever-ready safety valve to Danes running afoul of the German occupiers.

By midmorning, when the activity in the harbor had reached a level at which their movements would attract minimal attention, Jorgensen and Lowell left the ship and walked at a measured pace through an adjoining seaside park toward the city hall square. Esther followed them a short distance behind, carrying a large shopping bag Jorgensen had lent her to make her blend in with housewives in the nearby streets. Well away from the harbor they joined together and Jorgensen hailed a cab to take them on the short ride to his home. They rode in silence, and Lowell began to realize how immensely more complicated his task would have been without Jorgensen's tutelage.

After a short ride they arrived at an apartment building in the northern part of the city. Jorgensen paid the driver, led them to his third-floor apartment, and introduced Esther and Lowell to his wife, Inger, explaining to her the situation in a few words with just enough details to put her in the picture.

Inger Jorgensen was a handsome woman of forty-eight, her blond hair showing barely a tinge of silver. She beamed at the guests and immediately took Esther to the privacy of the bedroom and offered her a bath and change of clothes. When Esther emerged half an hour later in a dress of Inger Jorgensen's, Lowell went through a similar process of clean-up and rejuvenation. By then Inger was preparing lunch, and her husband and Lowell began a discussion about the best way for the travelers to proceed.

Jorgensen was aware that resistance against the German occupation was gaining strength in Denmark, but like most people he had until now complied with the old king's admonition to behave with dignity, and with the government's frantic urgings to avoid violence. However, placating Hitler had led only to ever escalating demands that gradually were pushing public opinion to the boiling point. Jorgensen's discussion with Lund aboard *Rita* had come at a time when he was, like growing numbers of his countrymen, psychologically ready to take a stand against the Germans, and the crucial step to do so had been the transport of Lowell and Esther. He was well aware of sliding into a growing commitment, and he decided to establish a basis of understanding between them. Getting up from his chair, Jorgensen went to the kitchen, got two bottles of Carlsberg from the refrigerator, and handed one to Lowell as they settled in a corner of the living room. Hefting his bottle with a quiet "*Skål*" the captain sat for a moment in deep thought before he looked at Lowell and began to talk.

"I don't know how well informed you are about the current status in this country, but very recently certain events have made the overall situation more and more unstable. It started when the German administrator in Denmark issued an ultimatum: The Danish government must prohibit assembly and strikes; enforce curfews and German-monitored censorship; establish special courts; and, worst of all, adopt the death penalty for sabotage. Our government, captive as it is, refused to do this.

"The next German move was that their troops one night attacked and disarmed the small Danish military contingents they had allowed to exist. In the skirmishes some Danish soldiers were killed. We cannot be sure of the number, but probably about two dozen. A few of our navy ships escaped to Sweden, while the rest were scuttled by their crews. The following day the German military commander, General von Hanneken, formally assumed power. Referring to the Haag Convention of 1907, he declared a state of emergency, and declared our king and government to be superceded and replaced as functioning entities. On second thought, General von Hanneken decreed that the Danish government must first direct all civil servants to continue their work, and that it must then resign. Our cabinet pointed out that the Haag Convention did not apply because no state of war had been declared or existed, and that it would not order the civil service to continue, being anyway powerless to do so as it had been forcibly replaced. Our cabinet finally told the Germans that no constitutional provision allowed it to resign under such circumstances. Then the cabinet requested from the king permission to resign. So far, King Christian has chosen not to reply, so that legal government is in limbo just now, and General von Hanneken is ruling by decree."

Jorgensen took a good swig of his beer before continuing. Lowell did the same while paying rapt attention to this unprecedented and intriguing story.

"Now, Lowell, everybody is jittery and on edge, so it seems to me a very risky proposition for you to try to contact the woman whose name Lund has given you. The prospect of your doing so and speaking English opens untold possibilities for a slip-up and attracting attention. When I talked with him, Lund struck me as a very capable man, and I believe the best plan is for you and Esther to wait for his arrival, at least three or four days, before making any further moves. You are welcome to stay here with us, and it is certainly the safest place right now."

In Lowell's mind the imperative of safety was contending with his natural inclination to pursue their speedy return to London by trying to go through Sweden, but he was well aware of the natural obstacles to functioning in a linguistically alien environment. It was an unexpected stroke of luck to have encountered Jorgensen and enlisted his help. Besides, leaving without knowing the fate of the rest of the SOE team and the Holzingers—the real objects of Operation *Emigrant*—was not acceptable.

Jorgensen sensed the other's feelings and, recognizing his preference for taking action, added an afterthought.

"You know, I could pay a visit to Anna, the woman who is your contact person here in town and find out about the current situation in regard to transport to Sweden. A matter of scouting the prospects, shall we say. Besides, if I understand your plans correctly, that Anna person is a critical point of contact to link up with the rest of your team, when and if they arrive in Denmark."

The suggestion appealed to Lowell. It amounted to taking *some* action, rather than passively waiting, and as Jorgensen had correctly seen, it was one way of making contact with the rest of the team.

"All right, let's do that but, just in case her situation has changed, I will follow you for backup in case of trouble."

Jorgensen smiled.

"Oh, I can't imagine that will be necessary, but, if you think so...."

Cooperation

By midmorning on Monday the RSHA security center was functioning in its usual subdued manner, but the chiefs of Gestapo, the secret state police, and SD, the all-seeing security service, were not happy. The two department heads, Brigadefuhrer Erhardt and Best had been working through the night, in fact since their bruising conference with Himmler on Sunday afternoon. Being chastised by a paranoid and unpredictable chief could unsettle anyone, and the incontrovertible evidence of being caught behind the power curve could not be explained away or excused. They both realized that Jantz was the source of Himmler's insight and conclusion, and removing him would be their longer-range aim, as he presented a permanent threat to their standing with Himmler, but at the moment they could only repair the damage by trying to catch up.

After Himmler dismissed them on Sunday afternoon they had agreed on a joint overall plan of action. Erhardt would handle the screening of all road traffic, relying on field gendarmerie to establish and man the checkpoints, and also direct the railroad police to screen rail traffic in concentric circles around the city of Stralsund. Best would use his SD resources to monitor harbor facilities, longshore traffic, and canal traffic, the last carrying a substantial part of the inland transport of bulk goods.

The two chastised security managers agreed to coordinate their efforts, starting with a high priority teletype message ordering a search for enemy agents, probably four, as well as three Germans, Hans Holzinger, his wife Ilse, and Ilse's cousin Esther Lidman, believed to be accompanied by the enemy agents, fleeing from the Stralsund area and assumed armed and dangerous. The message gave descriptions of the three Germans and emphasized to apprehend at any cost.

After firing off the teletype, Erhardt made a series of telephone calls to Gestapo offices as far away as Kiel and Stettin to prod them to a maximum effort. Best did the same to rally his personnel, haranguing them to leave no stone unturned. Comparing notes, they agreed that they had used all means available to them, although neither of them felt confident about a successful outcome. When their need for sleep overwhelmed all else, they agreed to proceed with joint planning and action whenever either of them got any further information. Between Germany's most powerful security agencies a tentative state of cooperation had been established.

Confusion

It was five o'clock on Monday afternoon when Anton Scherer brought his barge to a gentle touch with the seaward end of the Warnemuende quay. There was almost no commercial traffic to this port, as the ferry service from Denmark had been reduced from four daily train transports—busy ones—in peace time to one single midday run, often just two cars, to be joined to the Rostock-Berlin connection. He put the loops of his mooring lines around the bollards embedded in the quay's concrete and very slowly pulled the vessel with its heavy brick load snug against the fenders. Then he returned to the wheelhouse and lit the Primus to cook his dinner, a piece of cabbage and two potatoes, together with a "soup maker," actually just a large bouillon cube made from God knows what meat offal, plus salt.

When the pot was boiling, Scherer turned the heat off, put a lid on the pot, and covered it with a scrap of blanket to keep it simmering. He climbed ashore and walked to a small store in town to buy a newspaper and a couple of bottles of beer. There were no other customers, and the woman behind the counter turned out to be talkative. She made comments on his Pommeranian accent, quizzed him about his background, and was delighted to discover that he was a native of Stettin, as she was too. Starved for company and conversation, Scherer responded in kind, and in the course of the ensuing exchange, she told him that plainclothes police from out of town this same afternoon had made several inquiries, asking her about today's customers and posing many other questions.

Back on the barge, Scherer ate his cabbage and potato soup, supplementing his modest dinner with dry bread and a bottle of the local beer. He had just finished when he heard the sound of shoes hitting the steel deck, as someone jumped aboard from the quay. He opened the wheelhouse door and looked into the face of the intruder, who flashed an ID with a curt "German Security Police." Horst Kruger, the SD agent, then held out his hand and posed the inevitable demand, "Papers," to examine Scherer's identity papers.

Next came a series of questions about his departure point, manifest, destination, and further orders. At the end, the agent admonished Scherer not to mention his visit onboard.

"Of course," Scherer said, "your colleague already told me that in Stralsund."

Kruger had turned to step ashore, but his foot stopped in midair. He retracted it slowly and turned toward Scherer.

"What are you talking about?"

"Uh...the other SD representative who came aboard in Stralsund on Saturday."

Kruger stared hard at the barge skipper.

"What was his name?"

"Uh...I don't remember exactly, but he showed me his ID. It was just like yours."

"What did he ask you?"

"Same questions as you did."

"Did he tell you anything else?"

"Only not to discuss his visit with any one else."

"Was he alone?"

"No, there was another man waiting on the pier."

"Tell me exactly when this took place."

"It was Saturday afternoon, I think around three or four o'clock."

Kruger stood silent, contemplating the unexpected information before turning to address Scherer.

"Now, this time, keep your mouth shut. Do not mention my visit to anyone, including the other...uh...my colleague, if he should come back."

Without further comment he stepped ashore and strode quickly toward town, where he was booked in at Hotel Baltic. From the wheelhouse Scherer followed his rapid departure. What was going on with the SD? Was there confusion so that one hand didn't know what the other hand was doing? Oh well, nobody could ever figure out what security people were up to. One thing was certain, though. If that other agent should come back, Scherer would know to keep his mouth shut.

The *S45*

Lieutenant Commander Bernd Klug leaned over the coaming of the flying bridge to get the best look at the rooster tail he kicked up as he went to full power. Under the 5,000 horsepower thrust of the two twenty-cylinder MAN engines, MTB *S45* surged to maximum speed—just under 41 knots—in only fourteen seconds. This was top performance, what the manual called for but few vessels achieved. Klug leaned back in the captain's chair and throttled back on the power to the economic cruising speed of a leisurely 15 knots, as prescribed by current admiralty regulations. Fuel was in shorter supply these days after the Wehrmacht lost control of the Baku oil fields in the Crimea. In fact, everything seemed to be in shorter supply, the longer the war went on. The Russians were proving able to rally again and again, drawing on seemingly endless resources of manpower and supplies in their enormous Siberian hinterland beyond the Ural mountain chain.

The *S45* was part of Motor Torpedo Boat Flotilla 5 out of Swinemunde, now returning from a routine patrol in the upper Baltic. The Finnish approaches and the Leningrad coastal batteries received periodic checking and probing. For some reason, the Finns had never fully accommodated to being a German ally. They cooperated grudgingly and always tardily, requiring constant watching and prodding. And Leningrad had proven a hard nut to crack, actually too hard, even though Hitler had spared no effort to erase this symbol of Soviet might. Well, in time the city's stubborn citizens would probably be starved into submission.

At the reduced speed the sleek miniature warship sliced lazily through a moderate sea, its twin diesels humming contentedly. It was amazing how these boats had become the German navy's mainstay force. At the beginning of the war, Hitler had nurtured hopes that his novel battleship design could seriously challenge Britain's naval superiority, and some early victories had briefly made it seem possible. But the Royal Navy had methodically hunted down the challengers and put them, one after the other, out of commission. By default, naval action had then devolved on the remaining MTBs.

Well, it was certainly fine with Klug to assume this responsibility and become the center of attention. He closed his eyes and savored the moment. It was fall in these latitudes, but as the late afternoon sun hung glowing red just above the western horizon, it still bore a hint of warmth. The breeze stirred the surface, but Baltic waves were usually too short and choppy to cause any motion in a vessel the size of *S45*. He closed his eyes with an overwhelming feeling that the world was as near perfect as one could hope for. The only possible improvement at this moment would be some action, something to display the capacity of this magnificent craft under his command and the abilities of his well-trained crew.

Tonight he would be patroling the Swedish coast, cautiously probing the defenses and alertness of this neighbor on the other side of the Baltic Sea. It never hurt to keep the good Swedes on their toes. To be sure, they were keeping up the deliveries of iron ore to Germany's voracious armament factories in the Ruhr, but on the whole, Scandinavians could not be depended upon. Too steeped in undisciplined democracy, needing a firm guiding hand.

He listened with utter pleasure to the hum of the engines, the wind, and the waves, totally content and at ease with the world, and particularly pleased that his *S45* was in top shape. One never knew what the future might bring. After his Swedish patrol he would make an inclusive circuit through the Fehmarn Belt before returning to base.

15

Night Trek

It was early evening on Monday when Lund returned to the hotel from a walk around Rostock to reconnoiter and to estimate what security measures their fight with the gendarmerie patrol had caused. Upon his return he quietly reported to the SOE team about his findings. The Rostock railroad station was bristling with police, so that going by train to Warnemuende was out of the question. Checkpoints had sprouted on the main arteries where they crossed the city limits, but he had carefully ascertained that the checkpoint blocking traffic on the Warnemuende road could be bypassed by using some side roads that led through a quiet residential area.

"So, you suggest that we walk?"

It was Morian who posed the logical question. Lund nodded.

"Yes, but we cannot proceed as a group. We'll have to come up with a configuration that takes advantage of our useable IDs, actually just Lowell's and mine. I have been thinking about how we can best do that. The trick will be to guard against being separated and becoming unable to find each other in the dark. Lowell and I will walk ahead, the rest will follow as far back as possible without losing contact. If Lowell and I are spotted by a checkpoint, we'll try to talk our way through. If we get separated, we will try to reunite at the barge, which I hope will be moored in the Warnemuende harbor. It is loaded with bricks and should be easy to find."

A general discussion with questions and answers followed to firm up the sketchy plan. By nine o'clock the darkness was sufficient and the group quietly filed out through the hotel's back entrance and began their trek by foot to Warnemuende. The checkpoint Lund had observed in the Rostock outskirts was easily bypassed, and they continued on a road devoid of traffic of any kind. The countryside lay dark and silent, a passive response to the RAF bombers that posed an unpredictable but ever-present menace in the German skies. It was a little after midnight when they passed through the small town of Warnemuende and took shelter in an empty shed on the quay, while Lund and Morian went ahead to look for the barge.

Rain had started to fall when they found the barge just inside the harbor entrance. They had been discussing the best time to start out, Lund thinking of an inconspicuous daylight departure by which their defection would not be discovered right away. Morian disagreed, and in their native Danish he portrayed their prospects in different terms.

"First of all, the harbor master is likely to notice already before we get underway in the morning that the skipper has been replaced with one of us. Secondly, the Krauts will have a welcoming committee waiting for us before we can make a landfall in Denmark. The distance is about twenty-five miles, and we cannot expect a loaded barge like this one to make more than five or six knots, if that much. We'll actually be underway long enough for the other side to sound the alarm and bring in one of those fast motor torpedo boats they use, from Kiel or wherever they keep them. I think we need to get a head start on the bastards, and that means getting the hell out of here, quietly but as soon as possible."

Lund had been trying to visualize their situation after departing Warnemuende. He recognized that some of his assumptions had been wishful thinking and that the picture Morian was drawing in a few sentences was more realistic and offered a better chance of success.

"Alright, Morian, I have to agree with you. And it looks like we can get out of here without being noticed. If you'll bring up the others, I'll go aboard and prepare."

Morian disappeared in the darkness, while Lund crossed the pier and silently stepped aboard the barge. The door to the wheelhouse had no lock, and when Lund opened it, he was met with the sonorous snore of Scherer, who slept on the only bunk. Lund remembered the wheelhouse configuration from his first visit, but he played the flashlight beam around the space, noting again the details of the layout. The barge had been built for inland canal traffic, which meant provision of enough room for the bargee and his wife, possibly even a small child or two. In practice, the typical canal barge was a moving home enabling a small family to adapt to an itinerant existence, a way of life eminently suited to an occupation that was useful to society at large.

Lund put his hand on the sleeping figure and shook Scherer awake, addressing him brusquely.

"Scherer, wake up, we're leaving." He waited a few moments for the other to leave dreamland entirely, then shone the flashlight at his own face. "Remember me? I am Martin Hagen from SD."

"Uh...*jawohl*, I remember." Scherer was straining to clear his mind while pulling on his pants.

"Start the engine."

"The engine..." Scherer sounded as if not comprehending.

"Yes. Now!"

"But we cannot leave before daylight...the regulation says."

"Start the engine now, on my authority."

Scherer slowly checked the compressed air supply, turned on the fuel, and opened the starter valve. The four-cylinder diesel coughed only once before catching with a low rumble. Scherer kept his engine in respectable condition.

The door swung open and Morian appeared followed by the rest of their group. Speaking in Danish, Morian turned to Lund with a grin.

"Hey that engine sounds fine, it'll take us to Denmark, if we can find our way. Does he have a chart?"

Lund repeated the question in German to Scherer, who had been staring speechless at the sudden invasion of his cabin with the apparent intent of taking over his vessel. He was a veteran of World War One, a loyal citizen who had accepted the takeover of the state by Hitler and his party without enthusiasm, but also without complaint. He fully understood the Nazis' system of rule by ruthless intimidation, and he did not want to become a target for their wrath.

Ignoring Lund's question about a chart, he summoned his courage and, speaking very formally, stated his own position.

"Herr Hagen, it looks to me that you are involved in some illegitimate enterprise in which I do not wish to take part."

Lund looked at Morian and switched back into Danish.

"I think we will have to count him out. He surely has a chart, and it should not be hard to find."

"I have the chart right here, it is Nautical Chart D-60 in the Baltic Series." Since the chart was first mentioned, Janiak had used his flashlight to search the shelves above the binnacle, and he now put the desired item on the table.

Speaking in English, Lund said, "Morian take charge of getting us out of here. Janiak, you're in charge of Scherer, and you had better tie him up. We're going to have to get underway without his help."

"It shouldn't be too difficult," said Morian, perusing the chart. "We are almost at the harbor entrance and pointed in the right direction. Give me a few minutes to check on the machinery and we'll be ready to cast off."

Retreat

SD agent Erich Kruger read the wireless message again and took a sip of coffee. He had driven back to his home office in Lubeck, where they had radio contact with RSHA in Berlin, to follow up on Scherer's revelation that he had been quizzed by the SD in Stralsund. The trip by road to Lubeck had been time consuming, as he had to pass four checkpoints, all manned by quite jittery field gendarmerie. They had damn near opened fire at one of them, when he drove his Opel a little too close before stopping, but the information he possessed was critical and had to be sent to RSHA quickly to be checked out. Did Berlin have agents roving this Baltic region without informing Lubeck? Possible but unlikely, and if it was not someone from Berlin, the person who visited Scherer would have to have been a British agent posing as SD. Unheard of brazenness, yet this opened a flood of possibilities, most of which he could not cope with by himself. The reply he was reading ordered him to put the barge under continuous surveillance and take "all necessary measures" to apprehend anyone attempting further contact with Scherer. Four additional agents under the command of Dieter Randschau were being sent to back him up. Randschau would be senior agent and would take charge of the operation. Meeting place: Hotel Baltic.

Well, the message he had sent to Berlin had obviously been a surprise. That meant that Scherer's contact in Stralsund *was* an enemy agent. Had to be. Which meant that he, Erich Kruger, had produced a critical clue to the whereabouts of this team of intruders that was stirring up the region, killers taking on field gendarmerie point blank, and behaving in a most unorthodox manner. What were they after? He would bet that Berlin didn't know. Helping a couple of Jews escape to Britain? Surely not worth such an effort. Whatever the explanation might be, they should soon know. He usually didn't like having outside agents in his area, but in this case his own firepower was far from sufficient. Even the reinforcements from Berlin might not be enough to deal with the Brits. He was alone in the Lubeck office except for the radio operator who was on night duty, but he called the station chief, Horst Marquart, at home, rousing him from sleep. Marquart was not impressed.

"What, Berlin is sending four? That should be plenty, Erich. After all, you are acting on a hunch, and that doesn't justify tying up more people. We should have the phone lines back in service by tomorrow, so stay in touch."

Marquart hung up and went back to sleep. Kruger reluctantly gave up any further attempt to beef up his forces and resigned himself to making do with the means at hand. He refueled the Opel from two jerrycans in the garage and put an extra PPK clip in his pocket before leaving. He had a feeling that his hunch was about to come true.

Kruger's return trip to Warnemuende took even longer than the other way. One more checkpoint had been added, and the insistent urgings from Berlin had caused the procedures of traffic checks to become still more thorough and time consuming. It was almost two in the morning before he was back at Hotel Baltic, where a sleepy clerk in response to his question informed him that there had been no arrivals from Berlin or anywhere else. By this time, Kruger was exhausted and went to bed, setting his alarm clock to wake him at seven. At four, Randschau shook him awake with some difficulty.

"Hey, aren't you supposed to keep an eye on a barge or something?"

Kruger swore at the other, then switched to a verbal counter attack as an experienced bureaucrat.

"For Christ's sake, I've been driving all night, just lay down an hour ago, waiting for you guys to show up." He fumbled for his shoes and began to put them on. "And why the hell does it take you guys a whole night to get your asses up here from Berlin?"

The bickering went on while they all piled into Randschau's car and started toward the harbor. Three minutes later they were driving toward the end of the pier.

"Slow down! No...stop!! They're getting away!"

The headlights swept over Lund who had just cast off the mooring lines and was straining to push the bow clear of the pier. Randschau slammed on the brakes, Kruger jumped out, and the quiet of night was rent by frantic activity, as he screamed at Lund.

"Get your hands up and stay where you are!"

Coiling up the moorings on the barge, Lowell had seen the car arrive and already had his gun out. Unable to aim in the darkness, he fired two shots in Kruger's direction and two toward the car, while yelling at Lund to get aboard. Lund ducked and jumped across the widening gap between the pier and the barge, with Kruger firing wildly at the dark silhouette of the barge. One of his bullets struck Lund in the shoulder, another crashed into one of the plate glass windows of the wheelhouse. Morian yelled "Get down!! Get down!!" and gunned the engine, competing with the sound of shattering glass. Lund staggered into the wheelhouse, where Janiak had finished tying up Scherer and was pushing the confused Germans to the floor.

The SD agents were tumbling out of the car and took up random firing at the barge, breaking two more wheelhouse windows. The heavily loaded barge gained forward speed slowly, gradually widening the gap between vessel and pier. At the wheel Morian sought partial cover by ducking behind the solid oak wall below the windows, while pulling out the P38 he had taken from the gendarmerie patrol and sliding it across the floor to Janiak.

"See if you can scare them off with this piece."

Janiak grabbed the heavier gun and started rapid firing at the dark silhouettes of agents walking on the pier, making them scatter and seek cover. By now the distance was getting too large for the pistols to have any effect, and the firing petered out. Prone on the floor Morian was reading the chart with the help of a flashlight, keeping the barge in midchannel. As they passed through the harbor entrance he got to his feet with a grin, commenting to no one in particular, "Well, this time we chose to retreat."

Janiak, kneeling in a corner of the cabin while loading a fresh clip in the P38, asked of no one in particular, "Isn't it what in English is called "a fighting retreat?"

Alarm

On the Warnemuende pier Randschau gathered his forces and took stock. One of his agents was lying close to the car, groaning, with a bullet in his abdomen. The car itself had a hole in one window. He turned to Kruger.

"Let's get to the harbor master and call for an ambulance to take Lang here to a hospital. Gottfried, you stay here with Lang. Kruger where is the harbor master's office?"

"It's back there by the loading crane."

Three of them got back in the car, and moments later Randschau was shouting at the nonplussed harbor master who had been roused out of bed.

"Call for an ambulance, and tell them to hurry!"

The harbor master was not used to being addressed in this manner at this hour.

"Wh...what...who needs an ambulance, and who the hell are you?"

Randschau stuck his SD credentials under the harbor master's nose with a menacing, "This is who I am, and you'd better pay attention when I give an order. Now, get the ambulance here, and fast!"

After three calls and almost ten minutes the ambulance people were on the way, and Randschau changed the subject.

"Now, the barge you had moored at the pier has left. When did you release it?"

"Wh...what barge?"

"I'm talking about the barge loaded with brick that moored last night. When did you release it, and for what destination?"

Revealing their SD identity normally had a calming effect, but the harbor master was not used to taking orders and stood his ground.

"I haven't released anyone or anything, and the barge skipper didn't need a release, anyway. He's free to go any time after daylight. He may have jumped the gun a little, no big deal. He's headed for Kiel."

"I'll decide what's a big deal. Where is the nearest navy installation?"

Invoking the navy in this off-hand manner was a reminder of the power and reach of SD. The harbor master did not miss the point, as he rubbed the stubble on his chin.

"Kiel...no...maybe Swinemunde...they are at about the same distance."

Randschau pondered the answer before following up with another question.

"How long would it take the navy to get here?"

The harbor master liked that question. It was in his area of expertise, sort of, and he instantly assumed an appropriate air of authority.

"Oh...with one of the MTBs...I'd say about two hours."

Randschau again pondered the answer before issuing a final order.

"Stay here in your office, so that I know where to get you. I'll be at Hotel Baltic."

He got up, motioned to his two colleagues, and the depleted SD team returned to the car and drove back to the hotel. The hotel clerk informed them that telephone service had been restored, and after a couple of tries, Randschau succeeded in getting the RSHA operator to relay a message to Brigadefuhrer Best at his home. Minutes later, Best was on the phone.

"Randschau, what are you reporting?"

"Herr Brigadefuhrer, we just made contact with the intruders, as they were fleeing from Warnemuende harbor in a barge. We had a firefight, one of my men is in hospital."

"Are you saying that you were unable to stop them?"

"Herr Brigadefuhrer, they were already underway in a barge when we fired at them, but our PPKs were insufficient, and they had heavier weapons."

Best exploded with a couple of obscenities, but Randschau deftly inserted a positive note.

"Herr Brigadefuhrer, I believe we have a very good possibility of stopping them, if we pass the alarm to the navy. If it will dispatch one or two MTBs from Kiel or Swinemunde right away, it should be a simple matter to catch up with the intruders. The barge is very slow."

Best considered the suggestion. It did look promising.

"I will see what I can do. Wait at the hotel."

Follow-Up

After his telephone conversation with Randschau, Best sat on the edge of his bed and considered the situation. At length he decided to follow up by involving the Gestapo. He picked up the phone and called Erhardt.

"Heinrich, good news. My people have made contact with the enemy agents and we now have a real chance to catch them. This is going to be a major operation, so I thought you and your people should have the opportunity to take part. Meet me in my office. I will be there in a few minutes."

The two Brigadefuhrer were keenly aware of the advisability of cooperation rather than competition on this particular project as they sat at opposite sides of Best's desk studying a chart of the Baltic Sea. Best had spent much of the previous day imagining and analyzing all manner of scenarios, as they might appear to the fleeing intruders.

"As I see it, Heinrich, the agents would prefer to aim for Swedish territory, because that presents safety as well as an immediate return to their homeland, but the distance is too great. They would be exposed to our search during all of the daylight hours today; that would easily be enough time for us to locate them and stop them."

Erhardt hesitated, scanning the chart and measuring distances.

"I agree, Werner. So long as they are at sea, they are—in a manner of speaking—trapped on that barge and completely at our mercy the moment we locate them. The question is, can we get to them before they land in Denmark?"

"I think so, but even in Denmark we could still pick them up quite easily. There they would still have the problems of remaining in hiding and finding transportation to Sweden."

"Yes, but as our recent experience showed, that can be done."

Erhardt was referring to a pursuit of another team of SOE agents which had eluded the combined efforts of the two Brigadefuhrer.

"True, Heinrich, but in this case they have the problem of being encumbered with a larger group and probably also with unforeseen problems due to the crash of their aircraft on the beach during the insertion."

The discussion was eventually terminated in an agreement to request assistance from the navy. Best picked up the telephone and called Himmler at home.

16

Encounter

Beginning after sunset, fog had been enveloping the southern part of the Baltic area, making nearby objects appear like floating images without earthly attachment. The barge carrying its heavy load of bricks plus the party of impromptu hijackers was chugging through a placid sea in the middle of the waterway that was labeled Fehmarn Belt on the chart spread out on the navigation table.

Janiak had quickly tied up Scherer and put him in the engine room below, where he was sitting on the floor, tethered to the banister. Hans Holzinger had found a broom and was sweeping up the glass shards from the broken windows, scooping shards and debris into a bucket and dumping it overboard. In the firefight with the SD agents at their hurried departure, Lund had been the group's only casualty when he was hit in the course of the random shooting. As soon as they left the harbor behind, Morian had Janiak take the wheel and follow the compass course he had laid out, while he cut open the sleeve of Lund's jacket and examined his upper arm and shoulder which was bleeding freely.

"Hmm...there is no exit wound, which means the bullet is still in there. I don't feel competent to start fishing for it, so we're going to have to get you to a doctor right away. In the meantime, we'll try to slow the bleeding."

Ilse had been assisting Morian in his examination of Lund's wound and was trying to follow their conversation, which was in Danish. Early in the war she had been trained in first aid procedures, and she had quickly searched the barge's cupboards for medical supplies, finding none. She looked from Lund to Morian before speaking to both of them in German.

"It seems the barge doesn't have any first aid supplies, but in my suitcase I have a nightgown that I can cut into strips, and some other material usable for a compression bandage to staunch the bleeding."

Morian's German was far from fluent, but it sufficed in situations such as the present one. He nodded and answered her in English.

"Good idea. That will have to do until we can get him to a doctor."

Ilse's English was on a par with Morian's German, barely sufficient to convey meaning. The contents of her suitcase yielded enough to produce a compression bandage and sufficient strips to strap Lund's arm firmly to his chest. The arrangement reduced the bleeding but did not stop it entirely. Lund and Morian both observed her approvingly, and Lund said, "If I stop another bullet, I will come to you and ask for another nightgown."

Ilse laughed.

"I'm afraid that was my one and only nightgown. Besides, I don't want you to stop any more bullets. You must..." she was interrupted by a shout from Janiak.

"Hey, what have we here?"

They all looked in the direction he was pointing, where the bulk of a vessel was becoming apparent in the darkness. It was a fishing boat, properly hove to with a wan light at the masthead. Morian jumped to take over the steering, cut the diesel engine and turned toward the apparition. As the barge slowed its forward motion, the distance between the two vessels diminished, and Morian brought them to a gentle touch. Janiak looped a line to a railing cleat, joining the two vessels dead in the water, and he suddenly let out a shout of surprise.

"Hey! This is *Rylen*, the Danish fishing boat that saved me when I was near giving up rowing to Sweden..."

The rumble of a hatch being slid open drowned Janiak's further comments, and an angry expletive in Danish brought bursts of laughter from Morian and Lund, as the vessel's skipper emerged on deck to survey the situation. Morian climbed aboard *Rylen* and shook hands with the surprised Egon Frandsen.

"You may not like being pulled out of your sleep, landsman, but let me tell you, this encounter makes us mighty happy."

Being addressed in Danish momentarily baffled Frandsen further, as he looked at the group gathering behind Morian.

"Are you people all Danish?"

"No," Morian said expansively, "just enough of us to keep things moving along on an even keel and staying one jump ahead of the Gestapo."

Frandsen turned, leaned over the open hatch, and bellowed into the dark void, "Jens, make us some coffee." Then he turned back to Morian with a quieter comment. "Get the Danes over here. We'd better have a little conference."

SD

At SD's Copenhagen office in the Dagmar building, Luther Schmitz was contemplating how best to take advantage of the scanty data they had obtained from Anna Hansen, their latest catch. She had proven to be a tough case even though they had worked her over most of the night. Funny how strangely prisoners could behave, reacting in totally different ways when the game was up. Some just spilled all they knew after a good kick or two, while others would hang tough, no matter what, some of them actually dying under heavy squeezing without revealing anything of value. Well, the agents would make do with what little they got and hope to catch somebody more talkative. Intelligence work was piecemeal stuff, one little nugget at a time, with the occasional avalanche of information when some key person broke down under the strain.

Schmitz turned toward agent Dieter Wagner, who was reading the carefully censored news in the morning newspaper.

"Dieter, we'd better set up a full-time watch in the Bodega bar and keep it up for a couple of days. Go through our list of local informers and pick someone to manage the counter. Then you and Albrecht can take the first watch, and we'll see if we can catch any fish in such a little net."

Wagner put down the newspaper.

"*Jawohl, Chef*, we'll try and bring you some more fish, maybe even some big ones. By the way, I saw in yesterday's report that local police in some cities have been siding with the demonstrators. How long do you think we're going to tolerate that kind of nonsense? Won't General von Hanneken clamp down before the Copenhagen police gets any such ideas?"

Schmitz took a sip from the coffee cup on his desk.

"We'll see. I think our next step to keep things under control will be to start executing some of the saboteurs we've caught. My feeling is that the Danes are fundamentally cowardly, and if we start shooting a few, the rest will fall in line. It's in everybody's interest that we coexist peacefully, and that means doing things our way. I saw how we quieted everybody down in the Ukraine by scooping up their Jews and shooting them in wholesale lots. Everybody got the message, and fast. Here we still have to show ourselves as being in charge."

Schmitz had been part of Einsatzgruppe B in Belorussia, where he had taken part in the wholesale massacring of civilians until his left knee was shattered by a partisan's bullet, rendering him unfit for service. He lit a cigarette, his hand slightly unsteady.

"Now, you and Albrecht get on your way and bring me some more troublemakers. I'm in the mood to make them talk."

Two hours later the SD agents had installed a local informer as Bodega's temporary bartender. Their instructions to him were simple: "Keep business flowing smoothly, and if anybody asks to see Anna Hansen, pass the word to us in the room right behind the counter."

With their preparations in place, the two agents settled themselves in the back room with the door cracked and had a drink.

Wounded

Morian stuck his head back into the barge's wheelhouse and addressed Lund who was sitting on the couch.

"Hey, Lund, this is the best coffee invitation we've had for a while."

Lund smiled as he slowly got up and walked outside to step onto the other vessel, which was somewhat lower. The effort made him stagger, but Morian caught him, noticing that blood had soaked through Ilse's bandage and was trickling down the side of his pants.

"Easy there, you are not ready to jump around just now."

"I guess you're right," Lund agreed weakly.

Frandsen quickly took hold of Lund's free arm and helped him to the companionway, where he leaned over the hatch opening and yelled, "Jens, lend a hand here."

As Lund was being helped below and seated, Frandsen turned to Morian. "What happened to him?"

Morian had been steadying Lund on the other side and quickly filled Frandsen in.

"We had a disagreement with the Gestapo in Warnemuende. They didn't want us to leave German hospitality and tried to stop us, so, one thing led to another, and there was a bit of shooting. Lund here caught a stray bullet. We haven't been able to stop the bleeding, so we need to get him to a doctor first of all."

From the barge, Janiak's voice unexpectedly broke into their conversation.

"Mr. Frandsen, we need your help again!"

Frandsen turned toward the barge.

"Who is...well, I'll be damned...the Janiak chap, and in better shape than the last time we fished him out of the sea. Any other surprises?"

Frandsen was not a slow thinker. He turned to Morian.

"How many are you on the barge?"

"We are five, three British agents and a German couple we need to take to London."

"Well, get everybody over here and let's get underway before Lund here bleeds to death."

Moments later Janiak cast off the line holding the two vessels together. *Rylen* got underway with Frandsen and

Morian in the wheelhouse and everyone else crowded into the cabin below.

"Listen," Frandsen spoke quietly to Morian, "the best would be to lay a straight course for a Swedish harbor, but that's out of the question. Lund would bleed to death before we could get there, and that's equally true if we aim for Copenhagen. We might make it to Rodby, my home base, but I prefer to run for Nykobing, where I think I can locate a doctor we can trust to help us. We can make it to there in about four hours at top speed, if we don't ram another fishing boat on the way in the darkness. Maybe your eyes are better than mine, but either way, you can help me as a lookout."

Morian laughed quietly.

"Isn't it pure irony that with the Gestapo and SD and maybe even some warships arrayed on our tail, the greatest danger may be from some innocent fisherman who happens to be in our path?"

As *Rylen* surged toward the small town of Nykobing on the island of Falster, both men stared intently into the murk ahead. As yet there was no hint of dawn. In the cabin below Ilse was pressing an additional bandage on top of the first, reducing the bleeding to a slow ooze.

Left behind, the barge drifted heavy and silent in the pre-dawn darkness.

Crash

In his chair on the bridge Navy Lieutenant Bernd Klug read the message from the admiralty with the help of a flashlight. The previous evening a developing fog had made even close objects appear insubstantial and unreal, and in the very early morning hours the last of the darkness had combined with the fog to virtually obliterate visibility, slowing his last patrol circuit through the western Baltic from a leisurely amble to a virtual crawl. Now the telegram he was reading placed him and his ship abruptly under high priority orders to find and intercept a barge taken over by enemy agents. They had escaped from Warnemuende two hours ago and were presumed to be heading for a Danish or Swedish harbor. *Stop at any cost.* Was this the opportunity he had been wishing for to show off his ship and his crew? Hard to tell, because war rarely offered you choices.

Klug waved the telegram at his waiting radio operator and snapped an order to acknowledge receipt. Then he turned to the companionway and quickly descended the ladder, stepped to the navigation table, and by the attached light read the message once more. *A canal-type barge...taken over by enemy agents... escaped from Warnemuende harbor two hours ago...speed probably six or seven knots...presumed to be heading for Denmark or Sweden....*

Klug aimed the light at the Baltic chart clipped to the table and glanced at the familiar features. Sweden was much too far for the barge to reach under the cover of darkness. Without question, the Danish harbor of Gedser would be the logical choice of the intruders, and in that case his best chance would be to lie in wait just outside the entrance to the Gedser harbor. He checked the distance and made a quick calculation. There might be just enough time for the *S45* to reach that critical point and take up position to cut off the barge. It took him only moments to make his decision to move fast.

To be sure, there were a few fishing boats in the area, usually poorly lit at night and in any event nearly invisible in the present murk, but that was a chance he would have to take. At worst he could slice through one of them with only minor damage to his ship, and the loss of a fishing boat and a few fishermen was of negligible consequence when compared with the importance of his mission. And it would only be a twenty-eight minute run to reach Gedser. The barge itself must be about midway between his present position and Gedser; that called for a curve to the east to avoid running into it.

Klug bellowed out the new course to the helmsman, went to full power, and ordered battle stations. The entire crew, including off-duty sleepers, began tumbling to their assigned posts, while the rising roar of the diesels and the vibration felt throughout the ship combined explosively to infuse the *S45* with the urgency and excitement always attending action. Everyone felt the centripetal pull as the engines were spooling up while the ship was making a starboard turn onto the new course, followed by a slight upward inclination as it climbed the bow wave and reached maximum speed.

At that precise moment, the world of MTB *S45* dissolved in a cataclysmic crash. The vessel was stopped dead in the water by running into what seemed like a solid rock wall. Klug was thrown violently against the forward bulkhead, impaled on the steel rungs of the companionway ladder. He fought to stay conscious, groping to get free, find the companionway, get on deck, take charge of the situation.... Stabbing pain from crushed ribs in his chest overwhelmed all else. His efforts ceased as he lost consciousness and dropped to the steel floor.

Dispatches

WAAF Lieutenant Ann Curtis first put the tea on McKinnon's desk, allowing the steaming hot liquid to spread its exquisite fragrance through his office. She then placed a sheaf of dispatches from Bletchley beside the cup with an explanatory comment.

"The messenger came early this morning, sir."

McKinnon's hand had already lifted the cup, but it hesitated in midair, as his glance fell on the first of the dispatches.

"Oh, Miss Curtis, please ask Major Hawes to come."

"Yes, sir."

Ann left quietly, and shortly a knock on the door announced the arrival of Major Hawes. McKinnon had just finished the dispatches, all of them decoded and translated from intercepted German radio traffic.

"I say, Jack, these dispatches reveal quite a story."

McKinnon was filling his pipe while his assistant was reading through the sheaf and making notes along the way. Having finished, Major Hawes allowed himself a rare smile.

"Indeed, sir, and our team seems to be taking the course of action we expected. The involvement of the German navy may pose a serious problem for them, but perhaps our people and their German wards can stay a jump ahead."

"I'd say that a short jump apparently has been possible so far," McKinnon agreed, "and their chances of getting to Denmark ahead of the blood hounds seem to me substantially improved. Did you send Hansen off yesterday, and did you prepare him for possibly making contact with the *Emigrant* team?"

"Yes, sir, he was fully briefed, and we should shortly know from Bletchley intercepts whether he was successful in cutting the teletype cable. I am arranging a Lysander pickup for him plus possibly two members of the *Emigrant* team, with subsequent pickups pending in case they are needed. He has with him a code to let us know when he is ready to return, and when to schedule further pickups."

McKinnon nodded and took a sip of tea.

"Very good, Jack. We haven't tried anything like this before. Let's hope it works, but in any event, it will certainly be instructive."

Presentation

It was close to ten in the morning, and Brigadefuhrer Werner Best had difficulty keeping his eyes open after staying awake much of the previous night, when various actions by his people had repeatedly claimed his attention. It now appeared possible—almost likely—that his agency would redeem itself, thanks to the navy's patrol boats, modest remnants of the once proud German navy. He had his secretary, Giselinde Thoene, bring him a cup of coffee, not ersatz but the real thing, of which the top people still had a small hoard. It did keep him awake, and now Miss Thoene brought him a teletype dispatch from Lubeck. He grabbed it eagerly and scanned the message.

"Shit!!"

His outburst, loud enough to be heard in the surrounding offices, startled even Giselinde Thoene, who was not easily upset by his occasional explosions. Seizing both coffee and teletype, he stormed down the hall to the office of Brigadefuhrer Heinrich Erhardt and threw the offending document on his desk.

"Now, see what the goddamn navy has done."

Erhardt read the teletype twice before making any comment. *German fishing boat "Dorsch" reports MTB collided with unknown object...MTB sunk...four survivors, none of them officers...*

"Werner, calm yourself, you are not thinking clearly. This may not be bad news, but we have to be careful how it is phrased and presented."

"But it means the SOE agents have once more slipped through our fingers."

"No, no, not necessarily. We can say that we used all means to stop their escape, and that we appear to have succeeded. After all, who knows what's lying on the bottom of the Baltic?"

Best slumped into a chair and downed a mouthful of coffee while reconsidering the message from this aspect. Yes, indeed, a presentation to Himmler in the format Erhardt was suggesting might actually sound plausible enough, at least temporarily, and if no further evidence could be found, it might even become the permanently accepted version. In fact, it might *be* the truth, but so long as it was accepted by Himmler, who cared? Best was without any sense of humor whatsoever. The tight smile that crept onto his face was one of relief.

"You know, Heinrich, I think you are right. I guess our previous experience in Copenhagen made me jump to the worst conclusion. And as I now look at the matter, it is actually unlikely that any contrary evidence will turn up—*can* turn up."

"Quite so, Werner. Let us pay a visit to the Reichsfuhrer and tell him the good news."

17

Surgery

Dressed to blend with the fishermen unloading a few boats in Nykobing's harbor, Claus Nielsen stepped gingerly from the pier onto *Rylen's* deck. He was carrying a burlap sack concealing a black leather case with a few instruments and medications, a far cry from what he was used to having on hand as chief surgeon at the town's hospital. While the equipment was minimal, the operating room was even less impressive. Jens had procured three six-foot planks to extend the table on which Lund was now placed. After Jens and Morian had been sent on deck to serve as lookouts while pretending to work, *Rylen's* small saloon was still crowded with three persons beside doctor and patient. Undaunted, Nielsen snapped a few orders, telling Frandsen to boil some water and designating Ilse to be his nurse. Then he went to work.

An hour later, Nielsen tied the last suture, closing the wound in Lund's shoulder. While Ilse was cleaning up after Nielsen had finished bandaging, he turned to Frandsen.

"I gave him just enough sedative to dull the pain while I was fishing for the bullet. The effect is wearing off, and he will be clear again in another hour. Ideally, he should have a transfusion, but his constitution is strong, and I think he will do well enough without. However, it is imperative to keep him immobile in bed for the next few days. It's damn lucky this was not a heavier caliber," he pointed to the slug he had extracted with his probe, "or he would have quietly expired from blood loss hours ago. Now let's see if we can transfer him onto the cot over there."

They all struggled to move Lund as gently as possible in the cramped space, at length getting him settled. Nielsen put his instrument bag back into the burlap sack and departed, waving off all expressions of gratitude.

Assisted by Morian, Frandsen and Jens started unloading their catch of sprat, while the Holzingers stayed out of sight but made themselves useful by cleaning up the cabin and watching Lund, as he overcame the sedation and regained consciousness. By late afternoon, when *Rylen's* hold had been emptied, Frandsen and Morian sat down next to Lund's berth. The fishing skipper smiled at the patient who had suddenly and unexpectedly become his responsibility.

"So, are you able to make some plans for our further moves? It seems that we had better put our heads together."

Lund was also able to smile. His mind had already been working on their immediate need for constructive action, and he had formulated an outline.

"Our most urgent need is to get the Holzingers to London. If you will take us to Copenhagen, most of our problems will be solved. From there, I should be able to arrange for our team to proceed to Sweden and then on to London."

Frandsen looked doubtful.

"The doctor's orders were for you to keep immobilized in bed for a few days. Any exertion could have serious effects. How are you going to meet that requirement?"

"I have a friend who is a doctor at the Bispebjerg hospital. He has been helpful before and I am planning to ask him to help us again."

Frandsen laughed.

"Doctors have proven to be a really handy resource in illegal activities. All right, I will take all of you to Copenhagen."

He got up and turned to Jens, who had been following their planning session with unfeigned interest.

"Check on our fuel. I'll be right back."

He climbed the companionway ladder and headed for the office of the harbor master to report leaving to resume fishing. Ten minutes later they cast off and got underway. When Nykobing was out of sight, Frandsen laid a course for Copenhagen.

Reporting

Reichsfuhrer Heinrich Himmler looked up from the document he was reading and acknowledged without enthusiasm the two Brigadefuhrer who had requested a conference. Addressing himself to Heinrich Erhardt, head of the Gestapo, who was slightly senior to Werner Best from the SD, he made a simple question sound like an accusation.

"And what further bad news do you have to report?"

"Herr Reichsfuhrer, our news is distinctly good this morning. The navy reports that its MTB *S45* has intercepted the barge on which the British agents and the German defectors were trying to escape." Erhardt paused slightly before adding, "In the event, the MTB actually collided with the barge, and both vessels sank, but I believe we can consider that an acceptable price for eliminating permanently both the intruders and the defectors."

Himmler's instincts as an experienced schemer combined with his paranoia to demand certainty.

"Are you saying that there were no survivors?"

"Only four ordinary seamen from the MTB, Herr Reichsfuhrer."

"And what about dead bodies?"

"None has been found so far, Herr Reichsfuhrer."

"Hmm...in other words, you have no concrete, positive proof, only a supposition."

Sensing the need for reassurance, Best hurried to support the assumption of successful closure to the case.

"Herr Reichsfuhrer, from the point when my men exchanged fire with the intruders in Warnemuende, only two hours passed until both intruders and defectors were permanently eliminated by being sent to the bottom of the sea."

Himmler was unconvinced.

"I suggest that you both pursue this case diligently until we can be sure. There will be debris, including dead bodies that will float around. Find some. And I want daily reports of your progress."

He dismissed his underlings, leaving the case open.

Bodega Shootout

Captain Jorgensen strolled leisurely down the Vesterbrogade, a street in the central part of Copenhagen flanked by four-story buildings with apartments on the upper three floors, the ground floors occupied by commercial establishments. It was late afternoon, the hour when bar clientele drift into their favorite haunts after work. Jorgensen stopped where a large sign announced the occupant as a bar named Bodega and entered, two steps down from the street level. On the sidewalk about a hundred feet behind him Lowell slowly approached, observing window displays with feigned interest. He had maintained his insistence on following Jorgensen in case a backup might be needed.

The room was half full, with a soothing hum of conversation mixing with the tinkle of glasses as a barkeep and two waitresses attended the throng of customers. Jorgensen took a seat at the end of the counter and ordered a beer. When the barkeep was drawing the beer, Lowell entered the room, looked around, and chose a seat near the opposite end of the counter. Receiving his glass, Jorgensen quietly posed a question.

"Is Anna around?"

Scooping up payment and tip, the barkeep faltered slightly with his reply, "I'll take a look in the office," and disappeared through a door to the back room.

Jorgensen had lifted his glass for a first sip, when two men rushed in from the back room with guns drawn, one facing Jorgensen directly with a menacing, "*Hände hoch!*" as he rested his Walther PPK on the counter between them, the other tearing around the end of the counter and poking his PPK into Jorgensen's ribs.

The two SD agents moved so fast that only the nearest of the afternoon drinkers were aware of anything unusual taking place in their midst, but Lowell leisurely strolled toward the scene of action looking around as if searching for a table while closing his right hand around the PPK in its holster and clicking the safety off. Within four feet he fired at the agent pressing his gun into Jorgensen's back, then lightning fast switched his aim and shot the one across the counter in the forehead. With the two Germans tumbling to the floor almost simultaneously, Lowell in a sweeping motion with his left hand grabbed Jorgensen by the arm, spilling his beer on the counter and yanking him toward the street door. They exited in a run while the bar customers were just beginning to sort out what had happened in the few seconds when gun fire interrupted their afternoon relaxation.

On the sidewalk Lowell changed to a fast walk, let go of Jorgensen's arm, and in a quiet conversational tone addressed his companion.

"Where do you think we can find a taxi?"

Gathering his wits, Jorgensen cleared his throat.

"On this street, just a little farther on."

"When we get a cab, tell the driver to take us to some place not too close to your home. We can walk a block or two."

Lowell looked at his companion and smiled. Jorgensen realized that the suggestion was a safety measure to prevent giving the SD or Gestapo any leads. He was also aware that Lowell was trying to restore his mental equilibrium after he had unexpectedly taken a very active part in the life-and-death struggle of the war itself, a crucial step from being merely an observer to becoming an active participant. The death and mayhem he had just witnessed in a peaceful Copenhagen bar was the struggle some people—both young and of his own age—were waging to subdue the scourge of Nazism. What was he getting into? Was he up to this kind of fight that could abruptly turn bloody and deadly? To his own surprise, he did not feel fear, only excitement at the prospect of doing his small, local part in this struggle that was truly a worldwide contest.

He smiled back, as his eyes met Lowell's.

"Yes, I'll tell him. You know, I really resent that I never got to drink my beer. A good thing that we have a few bottles of Carlsberg at home."

In the quiet of the living room Inger and Esther joined them for a predinner drink, which enabled Aage Jorgensen to report to his wife what had transpired in the bar. He spoke casually in Danish, trying not to dramatize the happening, but Inger was an intelligent and perceptive woman.

"Are you saying that Mr. Lowell shot and *killed* two Germans?"

"Well, yes, it happened in a flash, and it certainly saved my life. Now, I think that's well worth drinking to."

He lifted his glass in the traditional Danish toast.

"*Skål!*"

Inger lagged slightly behind the others as she mechanically gave the traditional response and raised her glass toward the others, then touched it to her lips and took a sip. Lowell divined what Jorgensen was saying and perfectly understood his intention to make light of the event for his wife's peace of mind. He smiled at Esther as he in a few words in German related the event to her. Esther looked thoughtful as she responded in German, which was understood by the other three.

"It is terrible what war makes us do. How I wish the killing to be over soon. Is there any positive news from the Russian Front?"

Esther's reaction was heartfelt, and it placed in perspective the events in the bar as being trifling in the context of the war events elsewhere. Jorgensen seized the opportunity to downplay their experience in replying to Esther.

"It seems that a pivotal battle is shaping up near Kursk on the Eastern Front. The Russians are definitely pushing the Germans back to their own country. Let us hope that will hasten the end of the war."

Lowell brought the discussion back to the here and now.

"We have a serious immediate problem. When Lund and the others arrive, which could happen any moment, he will probably attempt to contact Anna the way we did, and the outcome could be fatal, as we have just stirred up a hornets' nest, causing the Gestapo to be on high alert. In order to prevent a repetition of today's action, they will surely take steps to reinforce the watch they have in the bar. We have to devise a warning system to keep Lund from walking into the trap." He paused briefly to allow the others to focus on the new problem before going on. "Esther and I both know what Lund looks like, but it would be best if I don't show my face in or near the bar, and as Esther does not speak Danish, she would quickly become conspicuous by standing silent watch on the street."

Lowell took another sip of his drink and looked around at his companions. When nobody spoke, he went on.

"Besides Anna, Lund gave me one other contact in Copenhagen, this one at a hospital called Bispebjerg. I think I must try to make that contact right away, as he perhaps can help us solve the problem."

Jorgensen looked at his watch.

"I'll call a cab. We'd better get to the Bispebjerg hospital quickly."

Bad News

SS Brigadefuhrer Heinrich Erhardt walked into the office of his SD counterpart, Werner Best, and dropped a teletype on the desk.

"Heinrich, read this, it's from my office in Kiel. It seems the Reichsfuhrer was right about expecting debris and bodies, but this is not good news, as I see it. What do you think?"

Best carefully studied the teletype before answering. The message stated that two MTBs were still combing the area, but so far they had recovered only minor debris and two bodies, both the remains of German sailors.

"Hmm...so they haven't found any bodies of the intruders we're looking for. That leaves still unsolved the question about their possible survival. You are right, Werner, this is not good news."

Best answered a knock on his door which let his secretary, Giselinde Thoene, enter with a teletype.

"Herr Brigadefuhrer, this just came in from our office in Copenhagen."

Best snatched the paper from her hand and scanned it. Then he let out a string of profanities and thrust the offending document across his desk to Erhardt.

"Now look, Heinrich, could this be the start of a replay of our recent goings-on up north?"

His colleague read the message twice.

Two agents killed in a public bar...apparently by trained professionals, probably SOE...

Erhardt pursed his lips and met Best's glance.

"I certainly hope not. This might actually be the intruders we're looking for right now. Could they possibly be in Copenhagen rather than on the bottom of the Baltic?"

Best shrugged.

"At this moment, there is no way to know, but such bold and ruthless killing does look similar to the behavior we have just seen here on the Baltic coast in our present pursuit. I will get as much detailed information from Copenhagen as possible, then we can compare the events. And I would suggest that we keep this from the Reichsfuhrer at the moment."

Erhardt nodded emphatically.

"Yes, that's certainly desirable, but at the same time we must take all possible steps to apprehend the killers in Copenhagen, who in fact may be our SOE intruders. I will instruct my people to use every means in pursuit, and you had better do the same without delay."

Best concurred. The two colleagues recognized that once again cooperation must override competition between their agencies to deal with the present dilemma.

Lindbergh

Internist Helge Lindbergh was getting ready to leave the hospital and return to his two-room bachelor apartment, when a call from the registering nurse informed him that two visitors were requesting to see him. They would not divulge the nature of their call, only that it was urgent.

"Oh, all right, send them in."

Lindbergh looked notably uninterested as Jorgensen and Lowell walked into his office. After introductions, Jorgensen came straight to the point, speaking English.

"We are contacting you on behalf of Svend Lund."

Lindbergh got up and closed the office door.

"Tell me more."

Lowell explained briefly the shootout in the bar earlier in the afternoon; their expectation that Lund would shortly arrive in Copenhagen; that he would have with him a defecting German engineer with critical knowledge of Germany's rocket program; that they expected he would attempt to contact Anna in the bar which was now a Gestapo trap; and that they had no means to keep watch in the bar, as they had both been compromised in the shootout. Did Lindbergh have any ideas or suggestions?

The young doctor immediately understood their dilemma, as he leaned back in his chair and pondered the question. He had very recently helped Lund carry out a desperate project of rescuing an SOE colleague, and he was willing to do anything within his capability to help. This sounded like the kind of project Lund would take on.

"You say that Lund could come any time?"

Lowell nodded confirmation.

"Of course, many things can delay him and his group, but I would expect them to show up about now."

Lindbergh looked at his watch and shook his head.

"I don't have any good ideas to offer. You see, I don't know of anyone in town who could identify Lund except myself. But if you really expect that his arrival is imminent, I imagine he would try to make contact in the afternoon or evening, when bars normally do most of their business. So, I'll go to the bar right now and keep watch tonight. Maybe we can think of some other arrangement, but this is the best I can come up with on the spur of the moment."

Good News

The Bletchley messenger was late Wednesday morning. McKinnon had finished his tea when WAAF Lieutenant Ann Curtis placed the dispatches on his desk and busied herself collecting the cup and silverware on the small tray while anticipating McKinnon's request. It came almost immediately.

"Uh...Miss Curtis, would you ask Major Hawes to come."

"Yes, sir."

Ann Curtis disappeared with the tray and shortly a knock on the door announced his assistant.

"I say, Jack, I thought your idea was a good one, but I did not anticipate results *this* fast."

McKinnon never failed to acknowledge when Hawes, or anyone else in the Special Operations Executive, deserved credit for their performance.

Hawes sat down and read the intercept McKinnon handed to him. It was from the SD office at Dagmarhus, the security headquarters in Copenhagen, and destined for Brigadefuhrer Werner Best at the RSHA headquarters in Berlin.

Two SD personnel on stakeout murdered in a bar...apparently by trained professionals...probably SOE but no positive identification yet...stakeout watch on recently broken escape route to Sweden.

Hawes put the intercept down and looked at McKinnon.

"It looks like the work of either Lund or Lowell. In any case, our *Emigrant* team must have arrived in Copenhagen and is trying to arrange escape to Sweden. They nearly got waylaid but apparently were faster on the trigger than the SD."

"That was also my reaction," McKinnon said, "but we can dispense with guessing." Handing Hawes a second intercept, he continued with a smile, "Thanks to your idea of forcing the other side to tell us what's going on, here is what amounts to proof positive."

Hawes read the second intercept twice. It was from Best to his SD office in Copenhagen, a reply to the first intercept.

Intruders traveling with defecting German engineer heading for Denmark...suspected SOE agents...may be the reported killers in the Bodega bar....

The message went on to provide descriptions of the three Germans and ended on some ominous notes.

MTBs will double patrols in The Sound...stopping the intruders has highest priority...shoot on sight....

Hawes handed the second intercept back to McKinnon.

"That does appear to establish that our team is in Copenhagen and active. We must hope that Hansen gets to them before they attempt to reach Sweden and run into trouble on The Sound."

"That would seem to be the case," Hawes concurred. "Now the question becomes, can Hansen make contact and arrange for us to pick up the German engineer rather than exposing him to further risk."

"Quite so," McKinnon agreed, "and isn't it convenient to be in a position to know what the other side is doing and thinking?"

18

Bispebjerg

The scattered clouds were flushed with sunrise when Frandsen maneuvered *Rylen* gently to a berth in the commercial fishing section of *Sydhavnen*, the south end of Copenhagen's large harbor complex. After mooring, he stepped ashore, walked to the harbor master's office and reported having an injured crew member but needing no assistance, explaining that he would contact his cousin, who was a physician at the Bispebjerg hospital. Leaving *Rylen* in the care of Jens, Frandsen took a taxi to the hospital.

Located in the western outskirts of the capital, Bispebjerg was situated on a slight rise, not much elevation, but in Denmark's level topography enough to justify the proud titular inclusion of "bjerg" which means "mountain" in Danish. Mountain or not, the rise gave the hospital a panoramic overview of the city and an infusion of health-inducing beauty to patients temporarily confined to its restorative care. At Bispebjerg a group of the hospital's personnel had banded together in a tight-lipped fraternity that was providing emergency surgery and momentary bed rest for people wounded and pursued by the Gestapo.

Frandsen found Helge Lindbergh in his office, where the two men shook hands, and Frandsen came to the point.

"I have a greeting to you from Svend Lund."

Lindbergh got up from his chair and closed his office door.

"Tell me about it."

The fishing skipper explained the situation briefly, starting with *Rylen's* early morning encounter with the barge, his fullspeed run to Nykobing with Lund and the four others, and finally the primitive arrangements for the emergency operation to remove the bullet. Lindbergh listened and observed him intently, as his visitor finished the story.

"And the doctor in Nykobing told us that the injury caused by the bullet makes it imperative that he spend a couple of days in bed under medical observation. It was Lund's idea that I contact you to see if you might help us out."

Lindbergh grunted his consent as he considered the new problem being dumped in his lap. In each such case it came precariously down to an individual judgment: was there a bona fide need or was it a ruse concocted by the Germans? In the case at hand the decision was an easy one. He knew Lund, and Frandsen was clearly the fishing skipper he claimed to be, but a piece of the picture was missing.

"Are you aware that two people of Lund's group have arrived in Copenhagen and are waiting for him?"

Frandsen was taken aback.

"No, Lund didn't mention that."

"Hmm...well, that doesn't actually surprise me," Lindbergh was thinking out loud. "In the kind of work Lund is doing, it comes down to a question of 'need to know' before any information is spread around." He got up from his chair. "Wait here, and I'll see what I can do."

A few minutes later Lindbergh was back and explained his moves to Frandsen.

"I am sending an ambulance to pick up Lund. You had better

ride along and show them where you are moored. We can put him up here for a couple of days. Keep the others on your boat until we can figure out what to do next."

Frandsen nodded his consent to having his fishing thus put on hold. The sprat would have to wait.

Reaction

Luther Schmitz finished his terse report to Berlin about his loss of two agents in the Bodega bar. This was quite unheard of in Copenhagen, where the population usually presented an unruffled sea of agreeable people, too concerned with their comfort and, in Schmitz' opinion, too cowardly to constitute more than a nuisance to the German administration. He swore under his breath as he contemplated his next move and angrily kicked his waste basket across the floor to collide with the late Dieter Wagner's desk. And Dieter had been a good agent, a fluent Danish-speaker, quickly picking up the particulars of his job here and not needing prodding to study up on the local problems. What a waste, losing him to some crazy resistance fighter just as he was starting to be useful.

Schmitz thought of himself as hard-core SD. As far as he could see, the SD was the backbone of German society, in essence the fiber and sinews that held the national body together and kept it functioning properly. He had joined the SS at the time when Heinrich Himmler took charge of that organization and expanded it. After the war came to include the Soviet Union, Schmitz had with glee served with a so-called "Special Service Squad" following behind the Wehrmacht troops, rounding up and killing masses of Russians, mostly Jews, in the conquered areas.

The shooting of unarmed civilians never bothered him. In fact he had rather enjoyed the strange excitement of it, observing and afterward discussing with the others the best and least risky way to get the job done. And it was also interesting to watch just how people died when their time came. The behavior varied widely, from mindless rage and attempts to strike back at the black uniformed executioners, to petrified fear, but most victims went quietly resigned. He never wondered how he would react in that situation. No point in drawing comparisons. After all, they were merely subhumans without souls. Not comparable.

Schmitz lit a cigarette. He had questioned the bartender at length but without gaining any useful information. The man had stayed safely in the back room until the shooter and his accomplice were long gone. The few guests who had stayed until the police came had been no better. And their information, if they gave any, would be notoriously worthless. You couldn't trust any of the local people...Fuck!

He would have to post another two-man watch at that Bodega place, and right away, for it looked like it might attract still more people looking for transport to Sweden. He turned the problem over in his mind. Maybe he should go himself. That wasn't something he did very often, stakeouts were ideal training for newcomers but really beneath his talents; and yet, a catch would in the present case be a satisfying demonstration of his ability to handle tough cases. He swiveled his chair toward Oscar Jaffe.

"Oscar, I'm taking you along on a stakeout. Be ready in ten minutes."

Philosophy

At the RSHA, Erhardt walked into Best's office and sat down. The strain of recent events and the lack of sleep were beginning to show in his demeanor and to affect his temper by noticeably shortening his patience.

"Listen, Werner, let me tell you what I have done. I have sent orders to my people in Copenhagen to be vigilant in looking for a group of three German defectors, one man and two women, accompanied by SOE agents, and intending escape to Sweden. I have obtained and forwarded to Copenhagen accurate descriptions of the three Germans and warned my people that the SOE agents traveling with them are unusually dangerous. In fact, they may well be the ones responsible for the recent killings of our personnel in the Copenhagen bar, and this is what can be expected."

Best looked thoughtful, drumming on his desk with the fingers on his left hand, a nervous habit he had developed in the last few days.

"Hmm...that makes good sense, Heinrich, and I have informed my people up there along the same lines. I have told them to watch train arrivals from the Warnemuende-Gedser ferries and to expect that our defectors and the SOE intruders will attempt to escape to Sweden."

Best drummed some more on the desk top before continuing.

"You know, Heinrich, it doesn't make sense that we cannot shut off the persistent outflow from Denmark to

Sweden of criminals who escape our justice by sneaking away. We need more patrols and more severe penalties."

Erhardt snorted derisively.

"The Danes are cowardly and cannot be trusted. They had sense enough not to try to fight when we occupied their country, but they have been unreliable from the start and have resisted our orderly administration in minor but annoying ways, such as letting lawbreakers take refuge in Sweden. And you saw how they helped the SOE to spirit that Dutch-Jewish scientist away to England, when he should have been dispatched to the gas chamber. It was typical. Danes feel neither respect for nor obligation to their own heritage of Aryan blood. They are weak, degenerate, and unprincipled. I agree with you that we should be firmer with them, but the Fuehrer is surprisingly tolerant."

Best had never taken a philosophical view of Germany's neighbor to the north, nor bothered to ponder the motivations of any other opponent of the Fuehrer's plans for reordering Europe and, in due time, for reordering the world at large.

Erhardt, on the other hand, was trying to overcome an academically minimal background, and he thought that a measure of philosophical pondering suitably leavened his commentary and was useful by helping to veil his lack of formal education. One way that made him feel on a par with better credentialed colleagues was to speak in familiar tones about leading thinkers and to second guess acknowledged authorities.

In the face of Erhardt's specific critique, Best was briefly floundering, unprepared to shift mental gears, but he quickly temporized.

"So, you think the Danes have degenerated from a respectable racial background to become weak and cowardly?"

Erhardt saw an opening to show off his knowledge of the deeper principles on which the fuhrer liked to expound, and he seized it eagerly.

"Nietzsche would certainly have said so."

Warning

Helge Lindbergh watched as the ambulance attendants expertly transferred Lund from the guerney to a bed in the recovery room of Bispebjerg's surgery wing. Despite the economic restraints of wartime, the ambulance service still functioned flawlessly. Lund was half asleep but greeted Lindbergh with as much enthusiasm as he could muster.

"Hello, Helge, can I check into your hotel for a brief visit?"

Lindbergh smiled.

"You seem to qualify for it right now. Apparently you're too slow to step out of the way when bullets are flying. Well, at least it solves our problem of keeping watch for you in that beer joint in Vesterbrogade."

Lund looked uncomprehending.

"What are you talking about?"

"I guess you haven't heard that some of your team already arrived in town and ran into a Gestapo stakeout in the Bodega bar, where they left two of the bad guys dead. No doubt the Gestapo is now hoping for other callers to show up, and we were afraid you would run into the same trap. So, I had to eat dinner there last night, beer and sausages, waiting to warn you in case you might come. Well, at least that's one problem solved."

Lund suddenly tensed and grasped Lindbergh's arm, trying to get up.

"Helge, for God's sake, one of my team intends to go there, a Dane by the name of Morian Jensen, he may even be there right now, you've got to send somebody to warn him!"

Lindbergh thought fast.

"I have Lowell's telephone number—I assume he knows Morian Jensen, doesn't he? Maybe he can get to the bar and stand guard until we can contact this Morian fellow."

Without waiting for an answer, Lindbergh rushed off to his office and dialed Jorgensen's number. It was Inger Jorgensen who answered the phone and in turn put Lowell on the line. Lindbergh did not waste time. In two quick sentences he put Lowell in the picture and hung up.

Jantz

Horst Jantz, Himmler's special assistant, combed through the teletype trays, both incoming and outgoing. Since his inter-vention had revealed the overall scheme of the SOE intruders, the various steps taken by SD and the Gestapo had been simple and entirely predictable. He noticed that some of the incoming information had been withheld from Himmler, but there was no need to tattle about it at the moment—or was there?

Jantz lit a cigarette and in his mind reviewed the record these intruders had racked up to date. They had contrived to locate, contact and spirit away an engineer with critical knowledge about the Peenemunde top secret rocket development program; they had done so despite the efforts of several agencies insuring the program's security; then they had persuaded the engineer and two members of his family, no fewer than three Germans, to defect; they had transported all of them out of Germany, all the way to Denmark, successfully avoiding or fighting off so far all attempts to stop them; and they were now hiding in Copenhagen, one small step from Sweden, where they would be irretrievably out of German reach.

Immersed in thought, Jantz smoked silently. The idea that a small team of foreign agents should get away with a scheme so straight forward simple, even overcoming a crash landing on German soil, was more than galling. It was unacceptable. And it was so clearly due to the bungling of the two Brigadefuhrer and their *Dummkopf*, fathead, underlings, more than even he, an astute and highly competent investigator, could make up for.

The cigarette finished, he flung it away with a curse, got up from his chair, and stalked down the hall to Himmler's office. Seeing that the secretary, Frau Gruber, was momentarily away from her desk, Jantz simply knocked on Himmler's office door. The Reichsfuhrer offered him a seat and observed him attentively. It was rare for Jantz to appear unannounced.

"Herr Reichsfuhrer, I would like to bring you up to date in regard to the SOE agents and the three defectors who are now well on their way to Britain."

Himmler sat up in his chair.

"Do we have further information about their fate after the MTB incident?"

"Yes, Herr Reichsfuhrer, there is circumstantial but quite compelling evidence that the SOE group has arrived in Denmark, having slipped through our fingers. They may at any moment reach Sweden. In fact, they may already have done so."

Himmler frowned.

"Are you saying that our security people have been unable to stop them along the way?"

"I'm afraid so, Herr Reichsfuhrer. This is what has transpired."

Jantz proceeded, step by step, to lay out the events as they could be reconstructed from the teletype messages, while his listener's face took on an aspect even more gloomy than usual.

Hansen

On the Belt Sea railroad ferry, taking the train to the island of Zealand where Copenhagen is located, Viggo Hansen walked into the restaurant reserved for passengers traveling first class. There were several empty tables, and he chose one at the forward windows that offered a commanding view of the blue Belt Sea water ahead, sparkling in the early fall sunlight. He sat down with a pleasant feeling of satisfaction. Hansen was back in his native country after a successful parachute drop, had completed his assigned mission in record time, and he now felt justified indulging himself with a good lunch.

The resistance group receiving the parachute drop had willingly helped him sever and remove almost two hundred feet of the heavy communications cable along Highway 11 on Jutland's west coast, temporarily cutting the teletype communications between the German occupation forces in Denmark and their sundry headquarters in the Reich, wherever those might be located. Then he had caught an early morning train to Copenhagen, snoozing until awakened by the rumble of his train car being shuttled aboard the ferry.

Hansen perused the menu, marveling at the fact that the Danes still enjoyed a higher standard of living than any other European country touched by the war. As Hitler's prime foreign producer of food products, Denmark was being treated with kid gloves by the Germans ever since the initial, almost bloodless attack and occupation. He ordered eggs and coffee with fresh morning rolls and pastry. The coffee was ersatz, the real stuff being only a distant memory. Well, *some* hardship is to be expected. But overall, this was far better than the food he had become used to in London.

While eating, Hansen contemplated his next move. He had accomplished his initial task smoothly in just a few hours, but he still had to carry out the second part of his assignment, finding Lund and his team, if they had arrived in Copenhagen, and arrange Lysander pickups for all of them. Hawes had described Lund's project in some detail and had placed emphasis on the high priority of getting the German engineer safely to London. So, where should he be looking for Lund? He contemplated the problem until the end of his meal, when he was pensively dissecting a sizeable piece of *smorkrans*, the dessert properly recognized as the *pièce de résistance* of the ferry service. That brought to his mind the help they had received from Helge Lindbergh, when they were in desperate need of immediate medical attention for one of their team who'd been wounded in a fight with the Gestapo. Helge was a man who could be relied upon. But, in the matter of transport to Sweden, Anna Hansen at the Bodega bar was probably the one to contact. It was a good bet that Lund's first move would be to seek her out. Yes, no doubt the Bodega was the logical place to start probing the whereabouts of Lund and his group. While finishing the Smorkrans unhurriedly, he decided to begin his search by having a drink with Anna.

From Hovedbanegaarden, Copenhagen's central station, Hansen walked to Vesterbrogade, the street where the Bodega bar was located. He relished breathing deeply of the crisp, cool autumn air, squinting in the blinding sunlight and perfectly at ease. An aircraft mechanic by trade, Hansen was endowed with a naturally upbeat, positive outlook, finding life to be delightful despite war and other man-made calamity. He had observed and experienced enough of the horror the Nazis were causing to accept that they had to be removed from the face of the earth, and he had come to terms with the necessity for killing in order to reach that goal. Somehow, events beyond his control had suddenly shaped him into that rare human phenomenon: a person at ease with the world and appreciative of its beauty, yet at the same time an entirely cool-headed and efficient killer when his service with the SOE demanded, which it did from time to time, most often unexpectedly.

Reaching his goal, he descended the two stone steps, entered the bar room, and stood a moment by the door to let his eyes adapt from the brightness of the street to the half-light inside. Then he made his way across the half-full room and took a seat at the counter. He felt a momentary delight tinged with nostalgia at the familiarity of the setting: the polished mahogany of the counter, the shiny chrome of the pumps, and the old Carlsberg posters adorning the walls. The barkeep finished drawing a glass of lager and slid it to a man seated three stools away on Hansen's left. As the customer hefted the glass, Hansen heard him quietly addressing a question to the barkeep.

"Is Anna around?"

The barkeep hesitated only a second, turning toward a nearby table where two men were nursing their beer and smoking. Then he snapped a curt "I'll look" and disappeared through a door to a back room. As if on cue, the two smokers got up from their chairs, pulled out PPK pistols from shoulder holsters, and converged from behind on the guest at the counter. Reaching him, they simultaneously pressed their guns into the man's ribs, and one of them hissed, *"Hände hoch!"*

Afterward reviewing in his mind the events, Hansen realized that it must have been the German command that made his right hand move in a virtually automatic reflex to close around the PPK under his jacket, his thumb clicking the safety lever off. Before the other customers in the room had perceived anything unusual, he took two steps from his stool toward the German duo to get a clear shot and fired twice in rapid succession. One of the Germans tumbled backwards to the floor, the other fell forward onto his intended victim, who pushed him away, stepped over him and snapped, "Let's get out of here."

Hansen followed him in a dash across the room, out onto the sidewalk, continuing their run to the next side street, where they slowed to a quick walk. The stranger addressed Hansen with a grin and shook his hand while walking.

"My name is Morian Jensen. That was impressive shooting. I must admit that the bastards took me by surprise. That won't happen again."

"And I'm Viggo Hansen. I didn't know that the scene in Denmark had become so heated that a guy can't have a quiet glass of beer without covering fire. But you must be from Lund's team, and if so, I'm glad I just had that one-in-a-million chance of running into you at a somewhat critical moment. Tell me that I'm right, and bring me up to date on your situation."

Morian laughed.

"You're right. We just arrived, and Lund checked into the Bispebjerg hospital. He caught a bullet when we were leaving the Warnemuende harbor. It will keep him down for a couple of days, but otherwise the group is intact, all seven of us, if Lowell is here with Esther, one of our wards. Actually, it feels good to be back in Denmark, even with the Krauts crowding us."

Hansen nodded agreement.

"Did you say there are *seven* of you? And that Lund is at Bispebjerg? I'd better go see him and do some planning to get all of us back to London. That'll be some transport job." He thought for a minute, as they continued walking. "Yes, we'd better get to Lund right now. I need to know when to arrange for a Lysander pickup...or two pickups, I suppose."

Morian laughed.

"Better plan on three pickups, or we'll be overloading one of 'em, and that's not a good practice." He pondered their problems for another moment before adding, "And Lund should know where Lowell is hiding out."

19

RSHA

At the security headquarters in Berlin Heinrich Erhardt and Werner Best both arrived on the double at the door to Himmler's office, having been summoned by Himmler's secretary. As he lifted his hand to knock on the door, Erhardt whispered, "What is this about?" But Best just shook his head, "Don't know." They entered and saluted with heels clicking before their chief's desk.

Himmler glowered at his underlings but did not invite them to sit down. He addressed Erhardt.

"Heinrich, what can you report to me about the SOE agents who are still on the loose?"

Erhardt cleared his throat.

"Herr Reichsfuhrer, I am keeping in constant touch with our naval office in Swinemunde, but so far the search for debris or bodies from either the barge or the MTB has not yielded anything further."

"So, your conclusion is still that the intruders have simply gone to the bottom and disappeared?"

"Uh...yes, Herr Reichsfuhrer." Erhardt sounded rather less than convincing, sensing that his answer was unsatisfactory.

Himmler turned to Best.

"Is that still your conclusion as well, Werner?"

Best thought fast. Obviously, Erhardt's hesitant admission was unimpressive. Better consider the shootout in the Copenhagen bar as a new lead.

"Herr Reichsfuhrer, I was about to report to you that two of my men in our Copenhagen office were murdered yesterday, and the circumstances lead me to believe that the perpetrators might be the intruders we have been looking for."

Himmler leaned back in his chair before speaking.

"I can hardly believe that neither of you has brought this to my attention before. Your slowness in pursuing has enabled this enemy team to escape, transporting the defectors from Germany to Denmark, where the group now is but a step from completely escaping us by entering neutral Sweden. Why does it take you so long to act on information that is plain and easy to interpret? You now have one last chance to apprehend or kill these SOE agents. They must be bottled up in Copenhagen by closing the water routes to Sweden. Take all necessary steps to get that done. Now!"

Returning from their meeting with Himmler, the two Brigadefuhrer went to Best's office to coordinate their urgent planning.

"This is all caused by Jantz second-guessing our respective operations," Best said bitterly. "If not for his snooping in the teletype records and his sleazy meddling, we could have gotten this affair quietly off our hands by now."

"Certainly," Erhardt agreed, "but at the moment, we have to ignore him. Our time to throttle him will come. Let's see if we might still catch up with the British agents."

After discussing the various possibilities they could think of, the two Reichsfuhrer agreed to request increased patrols in The Sound but were stymied trying to think of other steps to take. As they were finishing their planning, Best's secretary, Giselinde Thoene, brought a teletype marked "Urgent." Best glanced at the content and exploded into a string of obscenities.

"Now look, Heinrich, goddamn, just look!! I've lost two more of my Copenhagen staff, including Schmitz who was in charge. This just guarantees that we are dealing with that SOE group. We have damn well better catch them, or we'll look like rank amateurs!" He broke into another string of obscenities.

Intervention

In the communications room at the security headquarters Horst Jantz had finished searching through the teletype and wireless traffic. He walked back to his office and started reviewing his notes. In the course of the next hour he patiently pieced together a sketchy picture of the actions and movements of the SOE agents: crash landing on the beach near Stralsund; then taking charge of three defecting German citizens and starting on their escape to Britain; forcing their way past a gendarmerie checkpoint; shooting their way out of the harbor in Warnemuende; succeeding to get as far as Copenhagen; finally brushing off two SD ambushes in that city; and through all of this they had suffered no casualties, as far as was known.

Overlying these events, Jantz established a complete picture of the response up to now by SD and Gestapo, including the support by MTB *S45* from the German navy, in their efforts to catch up with the combined group of defectors and intruders. The response was merely to dispatch more personnel to Copenhagen and to strengthen the patrols in The Sound. Jantz felt certain that those moves were unlikely to catch any of the escapees.

The whole story strained credulity and was absolutely unprecedented.

Jantz pushed the notes away and lit a cigarette.

Looking at the facts dispassionately, Jantz realized that the SOE group had been favored by luck, no question about that. But that they had contrived to get as far as Copenhagen was due as well to their unusually aggressive *modus operandi*: resorting to force immediately, rather than as a last resort, which was a more natural approach when deep in enemy territory. What were the chances of the SOE group getting to Sweden and on to London? Beyond question, their chances were excellent. Neither increased patrols in The Sound nor additional dispatches of clumsy personnel to Copenhagen would be likely to stop them.

His years of Kripo experience made Jantz automatically imagine himself in the position of his adversary. What would then be his next move? The SOE agents would be aware that all efforts were being exerted to catch them, or, at least, they would guess so. And they would likely know from local contacts about the increased patrols rendering the escape route to Sweden less secure. He did recall that SOE recently had evacuated a kidnapped scientist in an aerial pickup. If he were in their position, would he prefer that means, rather than the risk of crossing The Sound? Yes, he decided. Definitely.

Jantz picked up the phone and called Himmler. It was great to have this privilege of immediate access in matters he deemed to warrant such direct contact, and the implied power and prestige were ever so gratifying.

"Jantz here, Herr Reichsfuhrer. May I come to your office and impose on your time for a moment."

235

He was careful not to abuse his privilege. Permission was granted, and when he entered, he was offered a chair. More than most mortals could hope for.

Seated across from Himmler, Jantz quickly summarized the SOE position and the steps SD and the Gestapo had taken, making the situation sound as unpromising as in fact it was.

"I believe, Herr Reichsfuhrer, that the SOE agents very likely will choose to call in a small plane from Britain and evacuate by that means. The Reichsfuhrer may recall that just such an event took place recently, and one of our fighters was shot down in the process. If the Reichsfuhrer were to notify the Luftwaffe that we expect another attempt of this kind to occur very shortly, we might perhaps have a fighter stand by for immediate action. If this should succeed, Herr Reichsfuhrer, you would thereby administer a valuable lesson." Jantz discreetly omitted identifying the possible beneficiaries of this lesson.

Himmler liked the idea.

Preparation
Autumn was definitely in the air, with the bright London sun conferring a most attractive visage on the old city. Through the open window WAAF Lieutenant Ann Curtis could hear the Bletchley messenger's Royal Enfield arrive in the street below the SOE offices, the sound of its explosions ceasing as the rider applied the valve lifter to turn the engine off. A moment later she was scanning the latest intercepts, motioning the messenger to help himself to tea from the small serving table. Sergeant Donovan gratefully poured himself a cup of the pungent brew, while Ann went down the hall to McKinnon's office. She found

her chief and Major Hawes poring over a map of the Baltic, but her appearance stopped their discussion, as McKinnon reached for the intercepts, trying not to appear eager. Following his example, Major Hawes slowly produced from his pocket a pack of Players Navy Cut and leisurely lit one of the cigarettes.

McKinnon looked up from the intercept he was reading and spoke with studied unconcern, as he passed the intercept to Hawes.

"It appears that Hansen has carried out the second part of his instructions. We can now take steps to retrieve them by Lysander pickup. Or several pickups, I should say, as the *Emigrant* team with...uh...supplementary helpers, plus the Germans, has swelled to...what will it be? Seven, I guess."

Hawes looked up from reading the intercept.

"Actually eight, sir, if we count Hansen as well."

"Right," McKinnon allowed, "and that will require several pickups. You had better prepare a complete schedule with the details for the following pickups to be sent with the first one, and that first one should bring us the Germans before anything further can happen to them." He was silent for a moment before adding, "Remember how close we came to disaster, when we retrieved that Dutch scientist?"

"Indeed, sir." Hawes well remembered the incident. "It was a stroke of luck that the locals succeeded in shooting down the German fighter. Rather unheard of."

Dinner

Captain Jorgensen felt a surge of exhilaration as he looked around the table where they were all seated. No one minded that they were somewhat squeezed, nor the feeling that the apartment seemed overflowing with pent-up energy waiting to find outlet in action. The conversation in three languages was flowing freely. There was a sense of release at having escaped the horrors of capture by Nazi police, spurred by the prospect of reaching security in London, and further animated by good Carlsberg beer. Frandsen had brought the Holzingers to the apartment two days ago, relieving the crowding aboard the *Rylen* where Morian was still spending the nights. The Holzingers looked relieved, almost cheerful, at having left Hitler's Reich behind.

Assisted by Ilse, Inger was serving a dinner of pork chops and a green salad, while the two women were discussing the wartime challenges faced by housewives struggling to feed their families diets sufficient in vitamins, and the numerous problems in providing a semblance of normalcy in daily lives that had been rudely upset by the contingencies of war and unexpected shortages. Inger was telling Ilse about the efforts of Danish municipalities in making up for a faltering supply of wool and cotton cloth by organizing local centers for exchange of children's clothes, as successive age groups of youngsters outgrew items still in usable condition.

Lund had regained his usual healthy appearance. Three days at Bispebjerg had worked wonders, Jorgensen thought, restoring what was obviously a strong and super-healthy constitution. He had engaged Frandsen in a discussion about the effectiveness of the German blockade of transit across The Sound, trying to assess realistically the risk of exposing his German wards to capture if they were to attempt a crossing. They were speaking German in order to include Janiak, who was keenly interested to learn more about the methods and ways of getting to Sweden. He described to them his own ordeal, and they were speculating about his eventual fate, had he not encountered the *Rylen* along the way.

Morian and Viggo Hansen were pursuing their favorite subject, engines, with Hans Holzinger. It had started with a discussion of the merit of BMW's radical motorcycle engine design of horizontally opposed cylinders. From there they had progressed to aircraft engines, comparing BMW's latest version to the latest Merlin, and Holzinger was now revealing to them the possibility of a fighter powered by a jet engine, which Messerschmitt was rumoured to be working on.

Lowell was seated next to Esther who appeared outright cheerful. Inger had observed and with female intuition interpreted the younger woman's reactions and behavior in the presence of Tom Lowell. Yes, Jorgensen mused, no doubt his wife was right about that. A bond had subtly been established between the two, maybe unspoken, but there, just the same.

Through a clandestine wireless operator in Copenhagen Viggo Hansen had arranged the first pickup. It would be at a place near Ringkobing on the Jutland west coast tomorrow night, and included only the three Germans. That was the full capacity of the plane, Jorgensen was told. How the rest of the group would return to London had not been decided yet. The pilot performing the pickup tomorrow might carry further instructions about that.

Jorgensen lifted his glass.

"*Skål!* Let us drink to a successful journey for the Holzingers and Esther. May they get to London safely."

Skrydstrup

Luftwaffe Lieutenant Emil Schulze leafed through *Politiken*, trying to understand at least some of the newspaper's headlines. He had served on the Eastern Front long enough to appreciate the change of scenery. The Danes were Westerners, really just a branch of the Germanic Aryan body, he thought, whereas Russians were Slavs, alien in every way. Prodigious fighters, though, he would give them that. By comparison with his experience in the East, this was a picnic, just rest and recreation. And the food was marvelous. He had gained back the weight he had lost during his Russian interlude.

He put the paper down. The Danish language was more difficult than he had expected before arriving at this post in the village of Skrydstrup a month ago. And yet, he *was* making progress in understanding a bit of it...if only they wouldn't talk so fast, and not swallow half the words. Schulze was an amateur history buff and had succeeded in garnering enough bits of local information to assemble a picture of his present location.

It appeared that the village had attained momentary fame a few years ago, when excavation of an early Bronze Age gravesite uncovered the remains of a 20-year-old female. The body had withstood some three and a half millennia of entombment surprisingly well, and it was immediately dubbed "The Skrydstrup Girl." Attention of a different sort came to this southern Jutland village when the occupying German troops in 1940 chose the area for a Luftwaffe airfield. In readiness behind a Himmelbett zone of the latest radars, Kampfgruppe 506, a nightfighter outfit, now kept a vigilant watch against enemy planes entering the airspace above the peninsula. Schulze's plane was the formidable Junkers Ju 88R, equipped with BMW 801 engines and the FuG 212 Lichtenstein C1 radar. During the devastation of Hamburg, he had added to his credit two kills on enemy bombers. They had been largely due to his radar, which had greatly facilitated the final phase of the acquisition and pursuit.

This was the third night he was on standby alert with his crew. Orders had come down to be ready for a small enemy intruder, a high priority target expected to attempt a pickup of enemy agents from an undetermined location. Schulze was convinced that it was a waste of time for him and his crew, but you didn't argue with orders of this kind. He poured himself a cup of coffee and helped himself to another pastry. The food here was excellent. Danes knew how to live, spending their money on creature comforts rather than military hardware. It probably made them soft, although he had heard that the ones who had volunteered to fight against the Russians had acquitted themselves well enough.

He got up and strolled over to the corner where his two crew members were playing a game of chess. Reinhardt, his rear gunner, was winning, but Teske, his copilot and forward gunner, refused to concede, obviously hoping for a miracle. He studied the position on the board and started a comment, "Look, Teske..."

The deafening sound of the alarm bell made them all jump and grasp their gear from the wall. As they raced out the door leaving the chess board overturned, Teske triumphantly yelled, "That game was a draw!"

Interception

The breeze was from the southwest and bore a hint of the North Sea, some five miles distant. In the darkness

Lund and Morian were leaning against the car, a Ford equipped with a "stove," an awkward contraption resembling a 40-gallon water heater. It produced gas for the engine from bits of beech wood, a method of propulsion that had replaced liquid gasoline, which was all reserved to provide power for Hitler's war machine. Inside the car the Holzingers and Esther were waiting uneasily for the next move in their travel venture. Without any alternative, they were placing their trust in the ability and courage of the SOE agents.

Bent Lauersen, the leader of the local resistance group, materialized from the darkness, his footsteps silent in the grass.

"I have checked the layout again. Everybody is still awake and things are quiet. The plane should be here about now, if our past experience is a guide. My group has received drops twice before, and they went smoothly. I think that speed is the most critical element."

He stopped, as they all strained, listening, until Morian broke the silence.

"The breeze has been backing some, it is more southerly now, which makes it less of a headwind on the return trip. That's good, for he'll have quite a load to haul." He paused and then chuckled. "You know, this is the first time I have been on the ground at one of these affairs, and I must say, I'd rather be sitting at the controls instead of passively hoping for someone else not to get himself lost or screw up."

Conversation petered out until, twenty minutes later, Lauersen exclaimed with excitement in his voice, "There he is." He turned on a flashlight and signaled into the dark. Two gasoline markers flared, one at each end of the improvised landing strip. The oncoming pilot swerved to the north, doing a "one-eighty" half circle and giving himself room to land into the wind. Listening to the subdued engine sound breaking the night's silence, the people waiting on the ground could follow the plane's progress on its final approach to the inland marker. Passing over the flare they glimpsed the plane, and Morian exclaimed, "Good job," acknowledging the fellow pilot's performance.

At that precise moment a thunderous roar abruptly drowned out the Lysander's engine, and seconds later a volley of machine gun fire added to the deafening din. At an altitude of barely a hundred feet the doomed Lysander was literally shredded before their eyes. Turned into a flaming pyre, its fuel tanks exploded, and the wreckage fell to the ground. With lightning speed Teske switched his fire from the interceptor's three MG 17 machine guns in the nose to his two MG 151/20 cannons firing obliquely toward the ground, plowing a swath through the grass as the plane passed over the end of the improvised landing strip. The little group of observers on the ground watched in frozen horror as the JU 88 night fighter swept past and darted away, to be swallowed up by the darkness as abruptly as it had appeared.

Turning to Lauersen, Lund was first to speak.

"Let's get out of here. Can you...." He was interrupted by a yell from one of the group, "Alfred is hit!" One man lay groaning on the ground with Lauersen kneeling beside him holding a flashlight. Lauersen got back up. "He's got a piece of shrapnel in his hip. Put him in the car with our three Germans, and I'll take him to the hospital. Lund, take his bicycle and wait for me at my home." He turned to the rest of his crew. "You guys pack up and scat. Don't leave anything that can be traced."

Lund spoke up again.

"Can you put up our three Germans with Lowell and Janiak while I dash to Copenhagen and make new arrangements?"

"Yes, but not for more than a couple of days. Holstebro is a small town, you know." Lauersen turned and yelled into the darkness, "Erik, take charge and pack up while I get the visitors out of here."

From somewhere, an invisible helper answered, "OK, we'll hurry." The voice, in a Jutland accent, sounded unhurried and calm, no trace of excitement. Lund smiled to himself. These guys were sturdy, once the chips were down.

Morian had kept silent as the drama played out before their eyes. Now he quietly said to Lund, "I had better stay with you, and we'll grab the first train to Copenhagen. Frankly, I don't feel like chancing another pickup. The Krauts seem to have gotten the hang of this."

20

Triumph

The teletype from Denmark was still out of service. Jantz swore to himself, as he began to check the incoming wireless traffic, but his attitude changed in an instant before he was half way through the stack.

From Luftwaffe base in Skrydstrup...night fighter shot down light plane intruder...enemy crashed and burned...no survivors....

Jantz felt a surge of elation. This was success! This was what scientific police work and astute planning could accomplish, showing counter intelligence by the military for what it usually was: clumsy, bumbling, and amateurish. He lingered for a moment with his hand outstretched, trying to decide how to make the most of this development. Then he picked up the telephone on his desk and called Himmler's office on his direct line.

"Jantz here, good morning, Herr Reichsfuhrer...I just wanted to report that your intervention with the Luftwaffe has paid off...yes, already last night...yes, one of our night fighters shot down an enemy light plane trying to make a pickup...yes, at a village called Skrydstrup...no, Herr Reichsfuhrer, without doubt it was after our defectors...*jawohl*, Herr Reichsfuhrer, I will bring you the wireless message...."

Jantz hurried down the hall, message in hand. Frau Gruber waved him right through, and he came to attention before the Reichsfuhrer's desk. Himmler looked up from his papers, took the message with a slight nod, and read it

245

leisurely. A rare, slight smile passed over his face as he put the message on the desk and motioned Jantz to sit down.

"So, Jantz, we have foiled their first attempt to get to London. What will they try next?"

Jantz had expected Himmler to pose the question in some form and had decided what his answer should be. He would not prevaricate or evade. After all, the SOE agents on the run with the defectors would have to choose one of only two means of transport to reach London: directly by aerial pickup, or through Sweden if they could devise a way to cross The Sound. It was obvious that the Luftwaffe's response had become swift enough to discourage another pickup try. If he, Jantz, were in the position of the SOE agents, what would he choose? Almost certainly the Swedish route. He would appear most professional by replying thoughtfully that only an escape through Sweden need to be considered. Jantz cleared his throat.

"Herr Reichsfuhrer the English planners are not foolish enough to try another pickup by plane. You have put a stop to that. Our only hope is to catch them when they try to cross The Sound, which they will certainly try next." He made a slight pause. "I do not know what steps we have taken to make our blockade impermeable, but that should not be too difficult to do."

There, if the bunglers failed to catch the SOE agents, he, Jantz, would still look good by having correctly predicted that SOE would make the attempt. And if they succeeded, he would have downgraded their accomplishment in advance.

Informer

Kurt Schmidt finished getting dressed and gathered his few belongings in a small suitcase, ready for discharge. His stay in the hospital had been lengthy, almost six weeks, for the gangrene in his frost-bitten hand had taken time to heal, more so than the loss of his right foot. Still, it was lucky that he had been sent home to Denmark, when the hospital in Frankfurt had to be evacuated after a raid by the RAF. Schmidt had been one of countless casualties from the Eastern Front, and a lucky one at that. Many had never made it out of Russia in the aftermath of the savage fighting around Smolensk. He had been one of a band of Danish volunteers to the Waffen-SS, looking for excitement and adventure under the swastika banner. Excitement he found, all right, although war had turned out to be less glorious, less romantic, than he had been given to believe at the recruiting center in Copenhagen last year. He was now a cripple, would remain so for life, but with undimmed enthusiasm for the Nazi cause.

They wheeled a gurney past his open door and into the next room. Snatches of conversation...shrapnell wounds could be nasty someone said.... Wait, there were no shrapnel injuries in this perfectly peaceful setting of central Jutland. He listened intently and heard the door close to the next room, then saw Bent hurry by, an old class mate from high school ten years ago. He knew Bent to be English friendly, most Danes were, of course, as they lacked principles and devotion to race and nation.

A nurse appeared with a wheel chair and helped him into it. In this country, the public health service functioned perfectly. He knew her, Edith Karup, another high school acquaintance.

"Edith, who's the guy moving in next door?"

She shrugged, "Don't know."

Hey, how could she not know? This was Holstebro, for God's sake, where everybody knew everybody else. Hm...maybe that was the problem. They all knew *his* story. His father was waiting in the lobby to take him away in a taxi.

When they got home, he picked up the telephone.

Ambush

SD agent Hans Mencke finished the telephone conversation, hung up, and turned to his two colleagues.

"Well, it's good to have a few reliable people who can report what's going on practically within our sight. This guy in Jutland just told me where we can find a local who tried to make contact with a light plane that one of our night fighters shot down last night. It sounds like we can pick him up easily. If we just swoop in swiftly, he'll still be confused, wondering what to do next. Always remember, those resistance guys are amateurs, while we're professionals. Johan and Rudi, be ready to go in ten minutes, and we'll show the higher-ups that we're alert, decisive, and quick. We'll pick him up and bring him here and work him over. When we have enough information, we'll send a task force and roll up the entire group." He picked up the phone again and dialed the garage. "Uwe, get an Opel ready for a quick trip to Jutland." Having ordered the car, he paused for a moment. "We should be able to make it back here by late tonight. Actually, that'll look pretty impressive. I can visualize the report: 'lightning swift action by seasoned SD agents in Copenhagen.' Good basis for promotion."

Mencke's colleagues Johan Peters and Rudi Hartmann replied with chuckles to their enthusiastic superior's proposed scenario and made ready to leave. The morning sun was still shining brightly, as the trio set off across Zealand with their driver, Uwe Meier.

Alternative

The party around the Jorgensens' table was a reduced and subdued remnant of the happy throng that had gathered there a few days earlier. Besides the hosts, Lund, Viggo Hansen and Janiak were present, and Lund had asked Frandsen to be there as well, as his counsel was needed. Without superfluous words, Lund described the disastrous outcome of their attempt to evacuate their German defectors by air. At the end of the brief story, he added the assessment Morian had volunteered: the Luftwaffe's attention and preparedness had reached a point to make this mode of transport too risky for high value subjects, at least for the time being. Would the alternative of running the risk of a nightly crossing of The Sound be preferable? He posed the question to Frandsen and Jorgensen as the ones most familiar with this aspect of sea borne traffic.

Frandsen shook his head. "I spoke today with a couple of fishing skippers, and they said the Germans have beefed up their surveillance so you can hardly move your boat without being in the gun sight of some patrol. I think the risk is at a peak just now. Never seen anything like it."

Jorgensen sipped his coffee, backing up Frandsen's assessment. Janiak made a hesitant suggestion about crossing by kayak, but that was discarded as unsuitable for the particular individuals. The little group lapsed into morose silence, until Jorgensen spoke up.

"I have an idea that conceivably might work." He went to his desk and returned with a map which he unfolded and placed on the table. "Here is the ferry line between Frederikshavn and Gothenburg," he pointed to a stipled line on the map. "An old colleague of mine lives there," he tapped Frederikshavn on the map, "Ejnar Mikkelsen, he used to skipper one of the ferries. The line is state-run but has been shut down since the occupation started—it was too much of a headache for the Germans to police —and the ferries have been tied up in Frederikshavn since then. Now, it just may be possible to grab one of them and take off for Sweden. The minefields that the Germans maintain are farther north, so there should be no problem in that regard. Whether we can start and operate one of the ferries, well, I'm not sure about that, but it might be worth looking into."

He paused to let the information sink in. Lund posed the first question.

"How large are these ferries? Are they the size of the Belt Sea ferries?"

Jorgensen laughed.

"No, that would be a bit too formidable. As you know, each of the Belt ferries can take a couple of railroad trains. The ones we have in Frederikshavn are of a more moderate size. We would be able to handle it, if we can find one that's in functioning condition."

Hansen was eyeing the map, trying to estimate the distance.

"Could we make it in one night, under cover of darkness?"

Jorgensen nodded. "No problem. We should be able to make the trip in five-six hours."

"Besides," Frandsen interjected, "you'd be in Swedish territorial waters when you're about half-way across, and the Germans respect that...at least, they *usually* do."

Thinking through the various possible scenarios, Lund brought up another point, thinking out loud.

"If we should be discovered and challenged by one of the patrol boats, we should be able to brush it off. I know where I can lay my hands on a Suomi machine pistol, and that would be sufficient to deal with one of the German patrols in The Sound, as we'd have the vantage position of the higher ferry deck. The patrols don't have anything heavier than a machine gun, and that wouldn't be enough stop us."

The mood in the room had suddenly changed, from somber to upbeat, to nearly cheerful. Everyone present could visualize the scheme and immediately liked it: here was an opportunity to pull off something novel and spectacular. The discussion continued with a few more questions until Lund brought it to a close, lifting his coffee cup in a salute to Inger.

"Thanks again, Inger, for your hospitality. It's time for some of us to get on a night train to Frederikshavn and go shopping for one of the state ferries."

Inger smiled, mentally shaking her head. She sensed and fully gauged the change of mood that had overcome the group. *Will boys always remain boys?*

She lifted her cup, returning the gesture.

"You are welcome. And good luck."

Raid

Lowell and Bent Lauersen were having a cup of coffee in the dining room, discussing the overall progress of the war. Ilse and Esther were in the kitchen, helping Sofie, Lauersen's wife, with dinner preparations, while comparing the Danish system of food rationing with the one in Germany. Hans Holzinger and Morian sat in a corner of the kitchen, also drinking coffee, involved in what seemed an endless discussion about aircraft engines. The Lauersens had only been married for a few months, and the drastic enlargement of their household was a new experience, but the influx of strangers had with surprising ease attained an aura of tentative relaxation after the night's events.

When the door bell rang, the hum of voices abruptly ceased. Lauersen and Lowell stepped into the entry hall, guns ready. In the kitchen, Morian pulled out his gun, listening to events at the front door while watching the kitchen door. When Lauersen turned the door handle, Mencke in a well-practiced move put his shoulder to the door and shoved it open, entering with his gun drawn and his two companions pushing from behind. Lauersen hesitated slightly, but Lowell's first shot killed Mencke before his companions had even crossed the threshold, and he fired two shots at each of the other two SD agents in a sequence so swift that they fell to the floor in the doorway before having completely entered the house. Punctuating the shooting in the front hall, two shots from Morian's gun sounded from the kitchen, where Uwe had rushed in when he heard firing from the front hall.

"Let's get these inside," Lowell snapped at Lauersen. They quickly dragged the bodies into the hall and shut the front door. Lowell ran into the kitchen to check out the situation there; then he leaned against the wall and drew a deep breath before turning to Morian.

"Listen, Morian, we've got to get out of here, and fast. Check if these guys came in a car, and see if it has keys in it." He walked back into the living roon, where Lauersen was collecting the guns from the dead agents. "Lauersen, we have to get out of here right now. I think you should come with us, but do you know of a safe place where your wife can go and hide?"

Lauersen was prepared for just this kind of situation.

"Yes, she can go to my parents' house now, and then she can take the train to Randers and stay with her sister."

Lowell was relieved to realize that the Lauersens had given some thought to this kind of possible emergency. He pointed to the guns Lauersen was holding.

"The guns are fine, but be sure to get their wallets with their IDs and money."

Morian came back into the room.

"The car is out in front, and I found the keys in the pocket of the guy I plugged in the kitchen. He won't need them where he's going"

Lowell smiled at Morian's studied *sangfroid*.

"All right, we're going to be crowded, but let's go. Lauersen, what direction do you suggest we take?"

Lauersen had anticipated the question.

"My brother lives in Viborg. I know a forested area a few kilometers on this side of the town. We can dump the car there and walk the rest of the way. Do you know how to contact Lund?"

"Yes, if he's still at our contact in Copenhagen." Lowell thought for a moment. "But if not, the wife of the man we stayed with will probably know."

Lauersen dashed across his small yard to his workshop and extracted a Suomi machine pistol concealed under a floorboard. When Morian saw it, he grinned approvingly.

"So, we finally have some real firepower. Let's go."

Lauersen kissed his wife goodbye, as she left for her sister's house, while the six others crowded into the Opel. With Morian at the wheel, they drove out of town, heading for Viborg.

Mikkelsen

Retired ferry captain Ejnar Mikkelsen finished his breakfast and now turned on the radio to hear the morning news. More heavy fighting on the Eastern Front. A new German tank, the Panther, had taken the field and was far superior to the Russian T-34—or so the reports claimed––which was giving the Wehrmacht further superiority. With contempt, Mikkelsen grunted in the direction of the radio, "If you bastards are so far superior, how come your Eastern Front keeps moving farther and farther in *this* direction?"

He put the breakfast dishes in the sink, lit his pipe, and glanced through the window to see if any boats were entering or leaving Frederikshavn's harbor. No, no traffic today. The rays of the morning sun reflected brightly from the blue water of the Kattegat; the elm in his garden still had all its leaves, but they had turned yellow and flaming red. Beauty all around, but it offered him little pleasure. When his wife died, pleasure had suddenly drained from his life. He rarely saw his two daughters. Both lived in Copenhagen, had careers of their own, a good thing, of course, and he didn't really miss them much...just missed Marie, the loss nagging so...all the time. They say that life goes on, but it doesn't, really. He still went through the motions, a matter of form, without enthusiasm keeping up a daily routine...not for anybody's benefit in particular...just habit.

The telephone rang, actually a rare occurrence these days. He picked it up.

"Hallo...who?...Aage Jorgensen?...what brings you here...sure, I have time, in fact, lots of it...yes, come right over, you remember where I live...sure, bring your friends."

What could have brought Jorgensen here? And with two of his friends? Well, he'd soon find out. They knew each other well, ever since, years ago, they had both worked on one of the Belt Sea ferries, but hadn't seen each other now for some years. Better make another pot of coffee.

Almost an hour later, Jorgensen stubbed out his cigar and took a swig of coffee—Mikkelsen's second pot.

"So, Ejnar, there you have the whole story. I need your opinion and advice, and we sure could use your help, but I have to caution you that there is risk involved. As we saw in the Bodega bar, those Gestapo guys are killers."

Mikkelsen cocked his head at his old friend and broke into derisive laughter.

"Aage, for these young guys," he nodded toward Lund, Janiak and Lowell, "there is lots of risk, and for you at your age, there's still some risk as well, but for me? Hell, what have I got to lose? Since Marie died, my life, what's left of it, does not have much attraction, anyway. This is actually the first worthwhile project that has come my way." He paused to light his pipe, his hand shaking slightly with excitement. "Now as to laying our hands on a usable ferry, here is the situation. We have three of them laid up here as of right now. One is on land and has been reconditioned. Count that one out. One is undergoing engine repairs, not really needed, but the engine is in a hundred pieces, and that keeps it from being requisitioned by the Germans. So we can count that one out, too. The third one, *Prins Axel*, is moored at the north pier. It is the oldest, which is probably why the Germans have left it, so far. They prefer to steal our newest and best materials. I don't know if we could start it up, but I can sure as hell find out. Halvorsen would know, and he will keep his mouth shut. He sailed as chief engineer in the ferry service, but he was pushed into early retirement, just like me. I'll give him a call and get him over here."

21

Moving

With growing incredulity, Sigurd Lauersen was listening to the story his brother was telling. Bent's description of the downing of the pickup plane was dramatic enough to impress anyone, but the shootout in his own brother's actual home totally staggered his imagination.

"So the bodies are now lying there, waiting to be discovered?" Sigurd was trying to get his mind to accept the enormity of the event.

The passing of twenty-four hours had allowed Bent to come to grips with the happening and mentally put the matter behind him.

"Yes, or perhaps they have already been found, but the Danish police will probably move slowly in whatever moves they make. You see, we took away their IDs, so the police will have a good excuse not to inform the Germans right away, even if they guess their identity."

Morian interrupted their conversation.

"Look, we have to try to contact Lund and inform him of what happened. I have the phone number of the people in Copenhagen where he is now. I won't call from here, in case the Krauts are listening, but can you take me to a hotel or restaurant where I can make the call?"

Sigurd nodded, gathering his wits.

"Come with me, we'd better not waste any time."

Hotel Ansgar was quiet and its restaurant almost empty. The Lauersen brothers sat down and ordered a beer, while Morian went to the telephone at the desk and called Jorgensen in Copenhagen. Inger answered the phone. Aware that long distance calls were randomly monitored, Morian and Inger were both circumspect.

Hello, this is Morian, may I talk with your husband.

My husband left together with two friends for a visit to Frederikshavn.

Oh? That's rather a long trip. Who are they visiting?

Just an old friend and former colleague, his name is Lars Mikkelsen, perhaps you know him?

No, I don't think so. Well, if you talk with your husband, do tell him that we are a little group of six of his friends at loose ends on the road in Jutland.

Sure, I'll tell him, if he calls.

Morian returned to the table, took a swig of his beer, and reported the outcome of the telephone call. Bent Lauersen reacted with calm assurance.

"When the Germans identify the bodies, they are going to pull out all stops to catch us. I think it's necessary for us to move very quickly to stay ahead of them. I don't know what Lund is up to in Frederikshavn, but I think we'd better hurry and catch up with him. I don't want to try to telephone him up there. That might call unwanted attention to whatever he's working on."

Morian laughed.

"I have to agree with you. We can't afford to sit still for a moment at this point, but we'd better be careful. I suggest that we leave the car where it is now, but strip the license plates off it, to slow things down just a little. Sigurd, do you know if there is a night train we can take?"

"Northbound? I'm not sure, but let me check." Sigurd went to his desk and dug out a railroad schedule. "The first one is in the very early morning, ten past four, a slow run that gets to Frederikshavn at eleven thirty."

"Sounds good to me." Morian did not hesitate. "Let's take a walk to the car and get that taken care of. Then we can relax and enjoy your hospitality, maybe even catch a couple of hours sleep."

Frederikshavn

Soren Halvorsen was paying rapt attention to Mikkelsen's story as he was caressing a bottle of Tuborg in his right hand. Mikkelsen was close to finishing, having actually relished telling the story.

"And so, these young men have come up with the bright idea that the Danish state should lend them a ferry to take their whole party to Sweden."

At this punch line, Halvorsen broke into laughter even more uproarious and exuberant than Mikkelsen's had been an hour earlier.

"That's the best goddamn trick to play on the Krauts and our pussy-footing government that I've heard of yet!"

Mikkelsen was laughing too.

"Yes, Soren, I fully agree, but now the question is, can we start up the engine on the old tub? What do you think?"

Halvorsen drowned his laughter in a large swig of beer.

"Hmm...I don't see why not, but we had better check things out on the spot and maybe give it a try."

Mikkelsen agreed.

"Lund, to be less conspicuous, I think we'd better leave your friends here, while the four of us go and check it out."

Asking Hansen to explain the situation to Janiak, Lund left with Halvorsen and the two ferry captains. The little group went to the office of the harbor master, Ole Kuhlman, where Halvorsen picked up a ring with the keys for *Prins Axel*, explaining offhandedly that Lund was a writer working on a book about the Danish ferry system, and he wanted to show him the old *Prins Axel*. After a polite but brief conversation, they proceeded to the north pier.

The ferry *Prins Axel* had been built and launched early in the century, at a time that now seemed so utterly distant as to be in another era. The red plush upholstery in the main salon was dusty but still presentable. The original steam engine had been replaced with a Burmeister & Wain diesel, but the compressed air tank used for starting showed zero pressure.

Halvorsen was not discouraged.

"That's not surprising. It probably has a small leak, which goes unnoticed when it's in regular service, because the compressor keeps recharging when the engine is running. I think I can get hold of a bottle of compressed air which we can juryrig for short term, improvised use."

"Then you'd better go and find one," Mikkelsen said, "and you two," he gestured to Lund and Jorgensen, "come with me and let's do some planning."

They all climbed ashore and divided accordingly. Back in Mikkelsen's home, the five men gathered again around the kitchen table. After Lund had explained their findings briefly to Lowell and Janiak, he turned to the situation at hand.

"Mikkelsen, if you think we can count on Halvorsen getting the engine started, then I'd better get the rest of our group up here so we're ready to leave. What do you think?"

Mikkelsen nodded.

"Sure, but do you think it's safe to telephone them?"

Lund smiled.

"Yes, if I am careful about how I phrase my message."

He called the operator and placed the long distance call to Holstebro. After a few minutes, the operator came back on the line and told him there was no reply. Abruptly, Lund hung up the telephone and became dead serious.

"There is no answer."

The little group fell silent, as everyone considered the implications of this piece of information. Jorgensen was the first to speak.

"If I am correct, the only way they could contact us would be by calling my wife. Let me call her and check."

Lund was skeptical.

"I cannot imagine why they would not be in the house and answer the phone; neither can I imagine why they would call your wife. But time is precious, so go ahead. I think you'd better take a chance and call her."

Jorgensen's long distance call went right through, and he got his wife on the line.

Hello, dear, how are things at home?

Just fine, but I miss you. A couple of hours ago I had a call from Mr. Jensen. He was traveling with six friends. He asked about you and I told him you were visiting Mikkelsen in Frederikshavn.

Oh? Well then I'll probably see him shortly. Keep well, dear. I'll be home soon.

Jorgensen reported the outcome of the conversation, and his listeners cheered up.

"My guess is that Bent's home has somehow been compromised, forcing them to evacuate," Lund speculated, "but in any event, they are free and on their way to us. Let's concentrate on getting the ferry ready."

Expansion

Incredulous, Brigadefuhrer Werner Best stared at the teletype message. He started to get up but decided to stay, slumped back in his chair and finally called his Gestapo colleague, Heinrich Erhardt.

"Heinrich, you won't believe this. Could you please come to my office?"

"What? What is it Werner?"

"Please come, Heinrich, and I'll show you. I need to discuss this with you."

Brigadefuhrer Erhardt walked quickly down the long corridor to Best's office and entered without giving Miss Thoene time to announce him. Without speaking, Best handed him the teletype. Erhardt read it, sat down, and read it again.

"My God, Werner, how can this be? How many SOE agents can we be dealing with?"

Best was shaking his head.

"Heinrich...Heinrich...do you realize that my entire staff in Copenhagen has been very nearly wiped out? I have only one person left, plus a female secretary. And these were all seasoned agents. How can I possibly explain this to the Reichsfuhrer?"

Erhardt looked thoughtful. Normally, it was good news when other departments encountered difficulties, but this calamity tended to spill over and threaten his own turf. Joint planning was still in order.

"Werner, I think we have to take a new approach, more...uh... positive, perhaps even aggressive. This is all quite contrary to accepted behavior between intelligence agencies, even when they work on different sides in the war. I think we can make a case that SOE is breaking some unwritten rules with such unrestrained killings. We must try to make the point that we need to strengthen our exposed personnel in places like Denmark. We simply need more personnel. These events clearly call for expansion of our strength."

Best pursed his lips and rubbed his chin. Erhardt's take on a situation was always different from his own. In this case he liked the other's idea. With luck, it might make a discussion with the Reichsfuhrer into a sensible proposal for organizational expansion rather than a feeble lament, or a negative, whiny report.

"Yes, Heinrich, I think your analysis of the situation is clear and convincing. And I think we had better see the Reichs-fuehrer immediately, before Jantz has a chance to present a distorted picture of the happenings." He picked up the phone and called Frau Gruber, Himmler's secretary.

"Frau Gruber, Brigadefuhrer Best here. Brigdefuehrer Erhardt and I would like to see the Reichsfuhrer, if it is convenient."

His tone was just polite enough to please Frau Gruber. Moments later, she called back. The Reichsfuhrer would see them.

Departure

The night was moonless and a light rain was falling, reducing visibility to near zero, as the SOE agents with their three German wards, accompanied by Morian, Viggo Hansen, and Bent Lauersen, made their way on foot in groups of three to the north pier of Frederikshavn harbor. Concealed in the intense darkness, Lauersen was carrying his Suomi gun to give the group some clout in a possible encounter with a German patrol while under way. They all climbed aboard *Prins Axel*, where Halvorsen was still working on the engine, assisted by Mikkelsen and Jorgensen. Halvorsen greeted them cheerfully and reported his findings.

"I've gone over the engine quite thoroughly. It seems not to have suffered unduly from being out of both service and maintenance for three years. The starting tank is up to half pressure, which is the most I could produce. The B&W diesel is an excellent engine and will surely rise to the occasion by starting, and then taking all of you to Sweden."

He paused and smiled.

"We'll soon know if I'm right. After you've left, I'll tell Kuhlman, the harbor master, that we have sent the ferry to safekeeping in Sweden, so that he can concoct a suitable story for the police to tell the Germans."

He looked around the group.

"Now, who's going to be the skipper taking this here vessel across?"

Lund started to speak, but Mikkelsen quietly broke in. "I'll skipper this party to Sweden." They all looked at the old captain, and Lund said, "Mikkelsen, it will have to be a one-way trip. You will have to stay in Sweden beyond the foreseeable future. Once it is known that you have left, there is no return as long as the Germans are running things here. If you were to return, you'd certainly go to prison, or worse. Are you sure you want to spend the rest of the war on the other side of The Sound?"

Mikkelsen laughed.

"I'll be happy to take advantage of whatever hospitality the good Swedes offer these days. There's really nothing to keep me here."

Morian broke in.

"That's an ideal solution. I don't want to match my maritime skills against a real pro. Thanks, Mikkelsen. Then I'll handle the engine, if Halvorsen will give me a quick introduction."

Halvorsen and Morian went over the controls and the simple telegraph between bridge and engine room. Then Halvorsen pushed the starter valve. With an explosive release of compressed air the engine turned over once...twice...then caught with a low, harmonious rumble. After quick goodbyes Jorgensen and Halvorsen climbed ashore and cast off the moorings, letting *Prins Axel* slowly nose away from the north pier and out through the harbor entrance.

Jorgensen and Halvorsen watched in silence, as the old ferry vanished in the darkness.

Postscript

As a meeting place, The Star in Godalming had all the charm a venerable old English inn could hope to possess, but the two dinner guests hardly noticed their surroundings.

Esther was eagerly relating to Lowell, in a mélange of English and German, how she and Ilse had been taken to a vacant farm house in Surrey, where they were making an intense effort to become fluent in English under the tutelage of a local school teacher. Esther wanted to return to London and take up nursing as soon as her language proficiency was judged adequate.

In the meantime the two women were spending their free time working in the garden, and they had just been told that Hans Holzinger would be joining them shortly from London, where a battery of technical experts assigned by Minister Sandys had almost finished extracting all the useful information their prize informant was able to provide about the V-2, Hitler's new super weapon.

Listening entranced, Lowell watched in silence the lively play of emotions on her expressive face, as she told about their work in the garden, harvesting a few scurvy apples and some self-sown vegetables. He felt ever more strongly drawn to this woman whose

life had so nearly been snuffed out by the giant killing scheme the Nazis were implementing. He realized that he loved her and wanted to marry her and take her home to Boston with him.

Suddenly becoming aware that she was doing all the talking, Esther stopped abruptly and met his eyes across the table.

"You are not saying anything."

Her statement in English was perfectly phrased, but for some reason it made them both laugh.

"I enjoy just looking at you," Lowell said with perfect honesty, then added, "whether you are speaking or silent, and I hope you will soon qualify for a job in London so I can see you every day."

Esther blushed and lowered her eyes.

"I hope so, too."

Breaking through his armor of Boston propriety, Lowell started to blurt out a spontaneous marriage proposal, "I...you...." when another layer of his mind interposed his obligation to SOE. With an extreme effort to let reason take precedence over emotion, he stopped, his voice choked and tense, as he continued and lamely stammered, "I...I hope the war will be over soon."

Reading his mind with ease, Esther smiled happily, her eyes widening to become topaz jewels.

"I hope so, too."